Sleepless

Table of Contents

Remember. 9

Chapter 1: Fourteen day remaining 12

   May 8th 4:00 pm 12

   May 8th 6:45 pm 15

   May 8th, 10:15 pm 21

   May 8th, 11:45 pm 29

Chapter 2: Thirteen day remaining 37

   May 9th, 12:45am 37

   May 9th, 3:15am 38

   May 9th, 6:30am 40

   May 9th, 6:45am 46

   May 9th, 10:15am 49

   May 9th, 11:05 am 56

   May 9th, 2:45pm 58

   May 9th, 5:30 pm 63

   May 9th, 8:15pm 66

   May 9th, 9:05pm 69

   May 9th, 10:30pm 71

Chapter 3: Twelve day remaining 77

   May 10th, 1:30am 77

   May 10th, 5:15am 78

May 10th, 8:45 am 80

May 10th, 6:00pm 81

May 10th, 8:00 pm 84

May 10th, 10:15 pm 85

May 10th 11:25pm 87

Chapter 4: Eleven day remaining 90

May 11th, 5:05am 90

May 11th, 7:45 am 93

May 11th, 3:30 pm 96

May 11th, 5:45 pm 100

May 11th, 6:45 pm 109

May 11th, 9:10 pm 111

May 11th, 11:05pm 114

Chapter 5: Ten day remaining 120

May 12th, 1:10 am 120

May 12th, 4:20am 121

May 12th, 7:45am 129

May 12th, 9:00 am 131

May 12th, 9:10 am 136

May 12th, 12:45pm 138

May 12th, 1:30 pm 144

May 12th, 2:15 pm 147

May 12th, 4:00pm 152

May 12th, 6:30 pm 154

May 12th, 7:45pm 158

Chapter 6: Nine day remaining 161

May 13th, 6:15 am 161

May 13th, 6:30 am 163

May 13th, 10:00 am 165

May 13th, 10:05am 169

May 13th, 11:15 am 174

May 13th, 11:45am 177

May 13th, 4:45pm 179

May 13th, 7:00 pm 183

May 13th, 8:25 pm 185

May 13th, 8:40pm 191

May 13th, 10:22pm 193

Chapter 7: Eight days remaining 195

May 14th, 6:25 am 195

May 14th, 8:07am 197

May 14th, 8:25 am 199

May 14th, 9:50am 202

May 14th, 9:55 am 204

May 14th, 11:00am 209

May 14th, 12:17pm	211
May 14th, 1:45 pm	214
May 14th, 2:20 pm	220
May 14th, 3:30 pm	224
May 14th, 5:15 pm	228
May 14th, 6:45 pm	234
May 14th, 8:10 pm	240
May 14th 10:45 pm	243
Chapter 8: Seven Days Remaining	247
May 15th, 12:15 am	247
May 15th, 12:20 am	250
May 15th, 3:33 am	254
May 15th, 6:12 am	259
May 15th, 8:20 am	260
May 15th, 9:05 am	265
May 15th, 11:10 am	267
May 15th, 12:10 pm	274
May 15th, 12:20 pm	279
May 15th, 7:10 pm	283
May 15th: 10:24 pm	292
Chapter 9: Six Days Remaining	300
May 16th, 2:45 am	300

May 16th, 3:15 am 304

May 16th, 7:00 am 305

May 16th, 9:13 am 307

May 16th, 10:00 am 311

May 16th, 1:19 pm 317

May 16th, 5:45 pm 324

May 16th, 8:15 pm 326

May 16th, 9:30 pm 329

May 16th, 11:45 pm.....................................330

Chapter 10, Five Days Remaining 333

May 17th, 10:15 am 333

May 17th, 11:58 am 339

May 17th, 1:20 pm 340

May 17th, 3:25 pm 342

May 17th, 4:15 pm 349

May 17th, 7:00 pm 353

Chapter 11, Four Days Remaining................359

May 18th, 1:25 am 359

May 18th, 3:15 am 364

May 18th, 8:05 am 366

May 18th, 2:30 pm 369

May 18th, 5:45 pm 373

Chapter 12, Three Days Remaining 377
- May 19th, 9:00 am 377
- May 19th, 10:17 am 378
- May 19th, 10:45 am 386
- May 19th, 11:07 am 391
- May 19th, Noon 395
- May 19th, 4:23 pm 401
- May 19th, 4:38 pm 404
- May 19th, 5:30 pm 413
- May 19th, 10:45 pm 415
- May 19th, 11:06 pm 422

Chapter 13, Two Days Remaining 425
- **May 20th, 7:50 am** 425
- **May 20th, 8:16 am** 428
- **May 20th, 9:30 am** 430
- **May 20th, 12:15 pm** 434
- **May 20th, 3:25pm** 441
- **May 20th, 5:00pm** 443
- **May 20th, 10:50pm** 444

Chapter 14, The Last Day, The Heart of Brutality 446
- **The Way of the Spirit** 446

- The Way of the Butterfly 449
- The Way of the Samurai 454
- The Way of Mercy 462
- The Way of Vengeance 465
- The Way of Shadows 468

Epilog 470

[Mission Update.] 470
- February 6th. 470
- April 16th. 471
- May 3rd 472
- May 9th 474
- May 10th 475
- May 12th 476
- May 13th 477
- May 14th 478
- May 16th 480
- May 18th 480
- May 21st 480
- Also by Dustin Feyder: 487

Remember.

The value of (A) is equal to (A), this is the **law of Identity.**

The value of (A) is not (B), this is the **law of noncontradiction.**

(A) necessarily stands in opposition to (B) only in the absence of (C), this is the **Law of Inclusion**.

To remember these laws is to have a bassline understanding of the universe, and a foundation by which to understand it. I will not forget, that just because I could not imagine something that it is not unimaginable, this is the **Fallacy of Incredulity**

I will remember, that nothing will ever be true because I said it, even if I might say something that is true the truth remains true regardless of who is telling it. this is the **Argument for Fallacies Authority**

I will remember, that just because I am right that does not make you wrong this is a **False Dichotomy.**

and a violation of the **Law of Inclusion.**

I will remember, that no matter how alike two things may look they are not coequal this is a **False Equivalency**

and a violation of the **Law of Identity**

I will remember, that all **Beliefs** are **Tentative**

I reserve the right to change my mind at any time, I will remember that "that which can be asserted without evidence can be dismissed without evidence" (dr. Cristopher Hitchens) I will remember, to be intellectually honest. I will not allow myself to be confused by magical thinking. this is the creed of the **Free Thinker**

"I want to believe in as many true things and as few false things as I can" (professor Matt Delahanty of the Free Thought Library) and "Ignorance is not just what you don't know, it is what you won't know." (President Aron Ra of the A.C.A) I will remember that people have an obligation to protect the people around them. this is the cornerstone of **Humanism**

I will remember, respect is earned not given. I will remember, 'the **Blood of Battle** is thicker than the water of the womb' and that family is not whom you are related to but whom you relate with. I will remember that everything I am is in my mind and once that is gone so to am I. I must remember, that at the end of my life that my ideas will be **All That Remains.**

I will remember to write down **My Thoughts.**

So that **You** too **Can Remember**.

Chapter 1: Fourteen day remaining

May 8th 4:00 pm

Flies circle angerly. The smell of rotting meat runs thick in the air. A broken window cast burning sunlight on an aged face. Eyes are swollen shut; mouth sits open, giving the flies a place to nest. A photographer, Orochi Arnoldo, walks around the tiny shack with camera in hand, taking pictures of the humbled house.

Constable Kogatana, Jo. Slides open the door stepping in. He is a towering figure; his hair is short and speckled black and white. His eyes are cold and hard. He dresses in an old suit — gray with a hint of blue. Jo takes off his gloves as he approaches the dead body on the floor. Jo kneels, he wipes the sweat from his eyes. Today is the fourth day in a row that the temperature has failed to drop below 100°f.

Orochi kneels next to Jo. "so, who is this piece of beef jerky anyway?"

Jo slaps the photographer with one of his gloves then points at him with a disapproving gaze. "Boy," he protests. "you are from the city, so maybe you don't know how people in Chīsana-Mura talk, but around here, we don't speak ill of the dead." Jo stands up. He walks around the room, looking at the decor lying about "his name is Nobani." Jo takes a labored breath "that is four people this month. Dammed heat."

Arnoldo looks to Jo, "so; you think he died of natural … ?"

Jo doesn't let him finish his thought, "I will let Dr. Tsu make that call." He digs around in his pockets, pulling out his phone. "but I don't see anything here that would say otherwise." He shoots his gaze back to the photographer, "let's step outside."

It is hot out, maybe hotter than it has ever been. Flies plague the village. The river is high. In spite of the heat, it has been raining heavily almost every night. The town is divided by the river. On the east bank is the school, hospital, and most of the residential housing, Upon the hillside marking the gate that leads out into Shika woods, a Shinto temple. On the west end of the river is where the lumber mill once stood, but in recent years it has fallen into disrepair. Now the west end is mostly farmland. Chīsana Mura is a geographically isolated place. Mountains, rivers, and miles of forest have turned this village into a world of its own.

Outside Jin Kogotana has tracked down his father, A blanket in one hand being used to tie up a boxed lunch. Jo left house without pocking a meal. Jin is the tip of kid that would notice just that and go chasing his father down. Jin hold up the box to his father. Jo takes it and brings it out to his car.

Jo looks to the boy. "You didn't need to come all the way out here. I could have met you at Oso's if you had given me a call."

Jin smiles "I was already out and about. I am planning on meeting up with Sakura and Odette soon." He looks into the house "I know this place. Nobani-son, right? What happened."

As they wait for the hospital truck to show up and start cleaning up Jo explains "keep this between us." Jo request "because we are still looking into it."

Jin nods, "I understand."

"Takashi thinks the water is contaminated on this side of the river. It seems kids and old men are getting the worst of it."

Jin asks, "what are the symptoms?"
"inconsistent to say the least; dry skin, skin decolorization. But one thing seems clear, people that get sick don't get better."

Jin lowers his head in contemplation "how are we going to take care of this?"

Jo laughs hardy "don't worry, you will have disaster to handle later, I will handle this one. You should run off and play."

Jin stands firm, "I will do whatever I can to help you."

Jo grunts with a nod, "I trust you will."

May 8th 6:45 pm

Setkura Nekoba is the chaplain of the Shinto temple. He is charged with the public face of the church. Organizing rituals and services, offering tours of the sacred Shika forest and the temple. But on top of all of that, protecting the holy ground and the monks, that is also his duty. After all, someone needs to take care of the business end of things. Most monks have taken vows that prevent them from interacting with the public, Nekoba, on the other hand, he is not a monk. He is an employee of the church.

A parade of candles and incents are set up around the chapel. Nekoba and Kogotana work to dress a body, a giant of a man, elderly, and badly burned. This was meant to be a wake. But no one in town knows this stranger. He had outlived his friends and his family. For the last year of his life, Kogotana was the only person he had spoken with.

The door to the temple is pushed open as a child walks in. A girl not yet thirteen, dressed in a fluffy and flowery dress, vest, and a wide-brimmed cap that looks like it belongs on a madam in a Victorian-era painting. From one arm dangles a book bag, as both hands are dedicated to closing the umbrella she is holding.

Nekoba calls over "welcome if you are here to pay your respects to Mr. Sirosanto. Please sign in at the book on the podium to the right of the door."

The child walks over to the book and writes her name down, Eva Masumo. Eva walks over to the altar and looks down at the body. She folds her hands and lowers her eyes in a moment of prayer.

Kogotana speaks up, "are you acquainted with Sirosanto?"

Masumo shakes her head, "not so much. I am not acquainted with anyone. But, I have been reading over some old headlines. We have had a lot of wealthy and successful people pass through here, including Emperor Nobunaga. Sirosanto had been a horse breeder in his youth. The paper boasts that people came from all over the island to see his horses." She looks up to Kogotana "you are constable Jo Kogotana. Your sister Shojo Kogotana is a real-estate princess living in Hon Kong."

The constable straightens his stance, "it seems you know something of my family."

"There are lots of families with interesting past. Oso Hanzo, his father, was a spy working for the imperial house. Shazuki Tenzuma's great grandmother was a herbalist. To the Tenzuma, healing runs in their blood. Then there is Takashi Tsu; he was the only person in his family in 200 years to leave the village. Then Reko at the forge, he and the other Jet's say they have been keeping the fires burning for 20 generations…"

Jo cuts Eva off "I'm sorry, I think I missed your name, can you repeat it please?"

"Eva Masumo," Eva explains

Jo lowers his head, thinking. "I don't think I have had any dealings with Masumo family in some time." He looks to the girl, "where has your family been as of late?"

Eva explains, "we are living out in Shika woods, we are woodsmen. Doing what we have been doing forever. Making and selling charms."

Nekoba, after finishing dressing, the body steps around the other side of the altar. "Well, so long as you are here, young lady.

Perhaps you would like to help the constable and I?"

Eva looks up to the monk, "how can I help?"

The monk picks up a basket of flowers. He hands it off to the girl. "the constable and I are going to pick up that raft there." He points to the table that the body is now tide to "we are going to walk it out the front door, then across the bridge and down the steps to the riverbed. Walk in front of us and sprinkle flowers on the road."

The ritual is an old one. In modern days this funeral right is all but forgotten. With more than half of the families living on the island having adopted new religions, very few still remember when or why this custom had begun.

After death, a body is dressed in a cotton gown, bleached white. The skin is rubbed down with baking powder, then painted white. The dead, tied to a raft, then lowered into the river behind the temple to be washed out to sea. Four candles are set on the raft to see off the dead.

As the raft starts its trip downriver, Eva looks to Jo, "did you know him?"

Jo offers a soft reply, "I may have been the last person that did." He takes a deep breath, "it is sad. To watch the past get dragged down the river."

Eva rests a hand on Jo's back "would be less sad to see the young pass?"

Nekoba is the one to reply, "young, old, loss is loss irrespective."

Masumo looks up to Nekoba, "do you believe death is forever?"

Nekoba shuts his eyes and drops his head, thinking, "I don't know. Some of the monks think death is a doorway to another world. Others think it is like sleep, and you wake up in a new body…"

Masumo runs back up the path; she stands on the bridge; she raises a hand overhead and waves at the raft as it reaches the moth to the ocean. She shouts out, "Goodbye, Sirosanto-son; have a good trip. We will see you next time."

The raft vanishes out to sea. The setting sun pulls it from this world, it seems. Eva still waving and smiling as she watches the sunset. The hot wind whispers, her skirt flutters. The aging constable and the young monk join her in watching the skyline

May 8th, 10:15 pm

Well after dark, a half dozen kids have made their way into the wood. Reje Tenzuma walks with his younger sister Leta Tenzuma. At the meeting spot already waiting are Sakura Tomoji, Ri Hanzo, Jin Kogotana, and Odette Tsu.

As Reje approaches, Jin sets down the fire poker he was unsung to steer up the campfire, and walks over to Reje, offering him a hug. Jin looks to Leta "well; it looks like we have a new cutie."

Sakura, is digging around in a cooler looking for something to cook "good, I was getting bored of trying to look up Odette's skirt."

Odette laughs, "if you wanted to see my panties, you could just ask."

Sakura jokes, "that would take all the sport out of the game."

Reje barks, "play nice!"

Odette looks to the stars "Sakura, quick question, the school has your name listed as Tomoji in the year book, your dad calls you Hibiki, which one is right?"

Sakura explains "Neither, the name Tomoji was given to me by CPS and Habiki is my dad's name. my birth name was Takimaki."

Ri sits on a tree stump. "who's turn is it to start us off today?"

Jin walks back over to his set "well, now that we are all here. I think it is my turn to go first."

Odette pulls one leg into her chest hugging herself as she leans over slightly, she pushes down on her skirt to make sure she is covered "I hope you have something better than "Mr. Bighands this time."

Leta looks back and forth as her brother chooses a place for them to sit in the circle, "what is going on?"

Reje grins, "just a little club. We come here, eat hotdogs, tell ghost stories."

Jin looks around his friend, "Does anyone here know Akadama Azure?"

The group mumble and mummer in large. Odette is the only one whose voice is heard. "isn't that the old women hunter?"

Ri leans in to whisper with Odette, "that was Usagi Aki."

Jin starts to tell a story. "Moji, he used to go to our school. Spent his nights hanging out at the beach house, just like we sometimes do. He was even friends with Mr. Tomoji..."

Sakura cuts in "...I don't remember anyone named Moji going to school with us."

Jin continues, "back in September we had some great storms. Cold winds. Well, it was a good time to be a surfer. Moji liked to surf; he hit the waves at sunset. Then he spent some time laying in the sand. And after that, it was time to hit the showers and go home. Moji tied up his surfboard and went into the shower room. He washes himself off in the public shower. He is alone; it is dark; he then steps into the stall and locks the door..."

Odette cuts in, "I didn't know that they had stalls on the boy's side."

Reje looks to Odette, "why wouldn't we?"

Odette turns to Reje, "I thought you had the foot wash thing. And all stood shoulder to shoulder doing your thing."

Ri shakes his head, " Boys can't shit standing up."

Odette nods in understanding "ow."

Leta looks to her brother, "foot wash?"

Jin goes on, "Moji sits down and does his thing. He then reaches over to grab some TP… and freezes. He looks over, and the paper-towel dispenser is gone! The bathroom door opens as a new man walks in, a tall, pale man. Moji sits, his pants around his knees not sure what to do. The new man whispers 'Red and Blue.' He repeats 'Red and Blue.' Moji watches as the shadow of the man stands outside the stall. The pale man calls into the booth 'Red or Blue?' Moji whimpers, hand reach over the top of the stall holding the door. 'Red or Blue?' the voice calls in again. Moji pushes his hands to the walls backing away as far as he can from the door. Moji mumbles' Blue?'"

Jin jumps to his feet, shouting! "and with that, the door brakes open, reveling the blotted white-skinned beast, the monster picks up Moji in both of his giant hand, flips him upside down and shoves him into the toilet drowning him in brown water!"

An unfamiliar voice speaks out, "an Onryo that hangs out in bathrooms? I have never seen an Onryo in a bathroom." Everyone spins to face the new voice. A child is sitting amongst them, all-of-the-sudden. An umbrella laid across her lap, and her legs folded at the knee.

Ri speaks up, "hay, what a lucky day, another girl."

Eva kicks her feet back and forth, thinking, "but I think I could see how such a monster would come to be. I remember a story about a man from the second Victorian era. Dr. Johnathan Snow. A man that ran across all of the western-world, chasing a monster that drinks the water from the skin men. All the men around Snow feared a toxic gas called Miasma, but Snow thought the monster he hunted was a bug called Dysentery, I think. Or maybe it was Cholera or E-coli. I can't remember. But a doctor chasing a bug that makes people pee themselves to death. That would make for an interesting ghost story."

Ri speaks up, "I think our time is up Jin; it is my turn to tell a story."

Jin takes a bow waving his friend on "you have the floor."

Ri starts, "All of you know the story of our town, right? You all know how Nobunaga came to visit our town generations ago? Nobunaga had a regiment of ghost hunters that followed him around. Nobunaga was hunted by monsters all his life. One day he encountered a fox named Tamamo-No-Mia, the fox witch tried to drink his soul as he slept by the mighty Nobunaga knew at once the threat he had encountered. He covered his temple in magic scrolls to frighten the fox and forced her to take her true shape. He chased the fox, 100,000 samurai chased the monster from the capital all the way here. Tamamo-No-Mia is the child of Amaterasu-ōmikami, the most powerful of the elder gods. O-kami would not let her beloved die in battle, so she came to earth in the shape of the white dog."

"O-kami sets up a game. The fox and the emperor must do battle here in our township. But Nobunaga is no foul; he knows that the fox will cheat no matter the nature of the game. So he has his wizards gather around him and cast a spell on the village. One hundred families, chosen as a sacrifice. One hundred men must stay in the town forever. Nobunaga must do something to keep the fox distracted, keep her attention on him and not on his wizards. "

"Nobunaga tells the fox to sit. And he too will sit. The fox and the emperor lock eyes. The game ends when one of them can sit no longer. Tamamo hates sitting still, but she hates losing even more. So, the fox sits as does Nobunaga. They lie, and they watch each other for 36 hours before Nobunaga faints. "

"The wizards and Wiseman pick up the emperor and pull him away from the fox before she can attack the holy king. Tamamo jumps to her feet, and she runs at the wizards. The demon fox shows her fangs. But then, a wall of fire erupts from the ground."

"A cage had been erected, A cage of 100 doors. Each door sealed with a soul ward. So long as the children of those that died to seal to door remain in the village, the door remains locked. To this day, Tamamo sleeps at the center of the monument of the hundred seals."

Odette explains, "I have seen the monument. It is a thing of beauty. The statue of Tamamo-No-Mia is amazing."

Eva adds on. "there are lots of spirit cages around Chīsana-Mura. There are a dozen lining the beach shaped like Tanuki; there is one outside Oso's shop that looks like a Neko...."

Jin points at Odette, "do you have a story for today?"

Odette looks over to Reje "isn't Tenzuma next?"

Reje shakes his head. "I closed out last week; you can go next."

Odette nods "ten-feet-tall." She starts as she leans forward, encouraging everyone to get in closer. "I was out in the garden behind my house, and I saw a woman kneeling in the bushes, I asked her, 'who are you?' "

"and she whispers back to me 'people call me Ten-feet-tall'…"

May 8th, 11:45 pm

The kids sit around the fire most of the night; everyone gets to tell a story, Eva, revealing the last story of the night. As Masumo tells her tall, the sound of foxes yelping in the trees grows slowly louder, "People like to look at the world as if there is good and there is evil. But things are never that easy. There has never been just good and evil. These are ideas that humans had concocted to try to make things easier to understand. There are things in the world, strange things, old things, things we can't hope to understand. Forces so great and mighty that the wisdom of men because like bloodstained rags. Let me assure you the forces of the unknown are powerful and unpredictable in ways that are disturbing to mortals."

"maybe one of you had been friends with Toboai? He was a kid, not so unlike you all are. He lived in a two-story house. He worked nights at the fish market. One day he came home from work to find his bedroom window open. He walked to it and looked out, noticing the window adjacent to his was open also. There is a gate between there yards and a walkway on both sides of the fence. He shuts his window."

"the next day comes around, and when Toboai walks up, he sees his window is open again. He stands up and shuts his window. Again, the window in the house across the street is open also. There is no one in the other house. There hasn't been in months. why is that window open?"

"day after day, the window is open time and time again. After a week, Toboai looks down and sees that the fence that divides his yard from the other house has fallen over. Then a week after that, the walkway had been torn up. Toboai asks around; no one knows why."

"Toboia nails his window shut, but nothing changes, he wakes up in the morning to find his window open anyway. How strange, he looks across the yard. He can see things in the house across the way he couldn't before. The room across from his is a bedroom, girl's room. There is a table and a mirror that can be seen just barely in the darkness of the other house. Has someone moved in?"

"Next, Toboia nails a blanket to the wall to cover his window. But it seems that the universe itself would not allow that to be. The blanket would not stick. No matter how many nails he used, the blanket kept falling from the wall."

"Toboai awakens in the morning and looks out his window. The house on the other side of the way feels ominous. Toboai picks up a broom and reaches it out the window. He can touch the window of the other house with it. The house itself has moved four feet closer to him, at least."

"For days to come, Toboai refuses to look out the window. He tries to tell the people around him about what he saw, but he can't find the worlds. The next time he looks out the window, he can touch the window of the other house with a bare hand. It has moved another three feet. The time after that, it is less than two feet between him and the next house. But no one but him can see it."

"Toboia sits huddled in the corner of his room looking at his window. He can no longer see outside. His window is laid flush with the window to the other house. How can this be, once the houses were divided by a fence and two walkways. Now the two houses are as one. A thin layer of glass is all that separates the two of them. what will Toboia discover tomorrow when he awakens?"

The crowd has fallen silent. The fire blows out as it has found its way to nothing more than dyeing ashes. Sakura Tomoji takes a deep breath, something in Eva's voice has her shaking. she laughs to try to calm herself. "I want you to come out here with us more often. There is just something about you I like." Sakura stands up. "I will be back." she walks off into the trees vanishing from sight.

The barking of foxes grows louder, Eva looks back and forth "maybe we should relite the fire?"

Ri nods and starts to set up the fire pit again. Leta speaks up, "Gays; it is almost midnight, shouldn't we call it a day?"

There are a few moments of mumbling before a begrudging nod finds the crowed. Although the kids had each arrived in the forest alone, they walk together in a group as they leave. All the kids live within a mile of each other.

Jin lives only a block away from the school, making his house the first stop, then Ri and Sakura, Odette house is near the heart of the township, the hospital being the nearest landmark. She ends up walking alone end.

When Odette finds her way home, her uncle Dr. Takashi Tsu is awake. He stands over the kitchen sink, a toothbrush in his mouth, he is a straggly man, long arms and legs, a narrow body, his hair long and undisciplined, a three-day growth on his face. He is dressed in tank top and slacks that are losing their color from days of wash and wear. Takashi is in his forties and leaving like a twenty-year-old. He looks like a man that his to much on his mind to keep it all straight.

Odette runs up to her uncle; she grips him from behind, squeezing him. "Takashi!" she squeals, "on your way to work?"

Takashi washes his face in the sink then grabs a box of dry noodles, eating a fist full of them dry "Back from your latest sexual exhibition?"

Odette chuckles, "no sex this time, just ghost stories."

Takashi shrugs as he picks up his coat "well, if things ever get worse, then that let me know. I can take care of things for you."

Odette shakes her head "I have no idea what you mean. So, why are you leaving for work at midnight?"

Takashi expresses, "another small intestine infection it sounds like. I need to start mapping the path of infection; see if I can't work out where ground zero is."

Odette makes her way to the back room to change into her housecoat, "how would one know if they had an infection of the small intestine?"

"skin around the lips and areolas turn black, and the skin around one's joints turns red and inflamed, cracks and peels away from the body, fingernails become brittle, eyes grow a film over them. The body stops holding salt; liquids pass through the body without being absorbed into the bloodstream. Your symptoms may vary." Takashi reads off a list of possibilities slow and dry.

Odette comes back now in a pink robe "are you describing an infection or zombification?"

"if you like that, you should read the paper I just saw on 'Deer Rotting Flesh Syndrome.' It may be the most horrible thing the world has seen in 75 years. Acts like rabies and spreads like influenzas" Takashi looks for his keys.

"I wish you would cook your food before you eat it." Odette finds his keys for him lost in the folds of the couch

"It is fine; I was eating like this all through my 20's."

"Takashi, you're not 20 anymore, you are going to get sick doing stuff like that."

"after being exposed to a thousand exotic parasites, hundreds of unnamed viruses, and every carcinogen known to man, I would be very disappointed if uncooked noodles were what killed me." He tips his head up and calls out, "oh, I also got a call from my sister, your folks just reached London. Everything went fine; they will be home in 16 days."

And with that, Takashi walks outside and unties his bicycle from the tree in the yard.

Chapter 2: Thirteen day remaining

May 9th, 12:45am

Oso sits on the ruff of his house, a bottle of wine in one hand, a bandana tied around his head. He is still dressed in his coat and apron. Oso walks hunched over, he is a small man, he is slim with long hair, his beard is cut into handlebars.

A bell rings on the first floor of the house. Oso yells down the steps, "Boy! Is that you?"

Ri calls out, "yeah."

"Come up here."

Ri crawls up onto the roof with his father; once there, the two of them sit and watch the stars. "Dad, have you ever been to the Tamamo-No-Mia shrine?"

Oso takes a drink of his wine "I have been there. My name is one of the ones on the gate."

Ri looks to him with wide eyes, "then is there really a fox demon?"

"Jo his been to New York. That doesn't mean there is a Spiderman." Oso hands Ri the wine offering him a drink.

"How old is the shrine?" Ri takes a sip then lays back

Oso shrugs, thinking about it "not that old. I think it was built around 1950 or 1960. It was built by the school by some hotshot artists. Everyone in the town was asked to put a 100 something yen on the table. Grandma loved the idea, she handed over 250,000 yen for the job, most of what our family had." Ri rolls over and offers his father a hug.

May 9th, 3:15am

Ri has gone back to his room, his room is on the second floor, facing the forest. Ri can't seem to sleep, something in his room keeps calling to him. Every time his eyes shut, there it is, the whispering. Ri sits up in bed and looks around. It is dark, light creeps in from under the door, and from out the window, the night is clean. The sky is clear. But wasn't it starting to rain as he was walking home? Did it pass?

A clicking sound, something is tapping at the window. Ri stands up and walks over to look outside. There is a light in the trees, half a mile away, a shimmering in the dark. The sounds of animals somehow can still be heard. Scratching at the wall. A bark. Ri jumps around, looking to the door.

Anxiety sets in. Ri can feel eyes watching him. He walks out of his room, searching for the sounds in the dark. Around the corner, down the steps. Oso is asleep in the front room, sitting up at a desk. He was balancing his checkbook when he fell asleep.

A bell rings, the front door is open. Ri walks over to the door and slowly pushes it shut. The barking of wild dogs seems ever closer. The light in the kitchen flicks on. The sound of dishes breaking on the floor echoes all across the house. A shadow walks across the kitchen. A woman, tall and trim. Large hands, a long nose. A palm slaps the wall, a large furry hand.

Ri cries. "Dad! Dad! Dad?" but Oso is drunk, he can't wake himself.

The shadow whispers, "Ri Hanzo." A light voice, an airy sound. Longs black hair is blown in the wind, the shadow moves slowly out of the kitchen. Still bathed in darkness. Its face cannot be seen. Its legs are long and digitigrade, ending in sharp claws, four-toed feet.

The women makes a beast-like yelping sound. Ri yells again, "Dad!" he turns and runs, he falls out the front door and onto the street. The boy runs down the streets, vanishing into the night.

May 9th, 6:30am

Setsuka Tenzuma stands before a map in Takashi Tsu's office, Takashi has his head down, a cup of tea gripped in one hand, one arm folded under his head covering his eyes. It has been over a month since Takashi has taken a day off work, and it is starting to show. The man acts tireless, but no one can work 28, 16 hours days in a row without it beginning to take a toll on their health.

Setsuka is dressed in a lavender coat, she has brown-red hair tied up in a bun, she has on gold eyeliner and a hazelnut lip gloss, she is the same age as Takashi, the two had gone to school together, still in spite of having two kids and a stay-at-home husband ,Setsuka looks much younger and stronger. Many people mistake her and her daughter for being siblings.

"and where is patient number 4's home?" Setsuka asks

From under his arm, Takashi mumbles, he doesn't need to look at his notes, he has them all memorized "A-6."

"and where do they work?" she asks next

"C-9" he adds

Setsuka takes a step back, looking at the map, "that means that three of the people that came in yesterday with this infection worked within four blocks of well #7."

Takashi grunts "1/3 of the district work less than a mile from that well. I feel as if, If that well was contaminated; we would have a much bigger problem on our hands aright now. And besides, well, #7 is right outside the glassworks. Why haven't we seen anyone from there come in yet?"

Setsuka nods as she draws on the map, "I think I should call the glassworks, ask them if their water is being pumped in from elsewhere."

Takashi sits up "we have less than 3000 working-age adults living in the village. Everyone here eats at the same restaurants, shops at the same stores, drink at the same tea house. The behaviors of this infection don't seem to be adding up for me."

Setsuka asks, "what are you seeing, that I am not?"

Takashi stands up, he pulls a piece of rice paper form his desk "what bothers me is what I am not seeing." He lays the rice paper over the map "four years ago, when we had the Nora outbreak, we saw a flower of infections. Once we got the call from Tokyo about the man they found at the trainyard, we found everything. We were able to walk backward and find that what ended at the high school started at the hibachi. There was a line that could be drawn showing where everyone that got sick crossed paths. Patients 6 and 7 both eat at the steak house on Saturdays, 9, and 12 were sharing a room at the B&B. 11 worked as an engineer and had been fixing the drains under the school… and so on, and so on." Takashi shows off the sketch he had done of the town as they had investigated the last pandemic. "do you see anything that looks that here?"

Setsuka folds her arms as she stares at the map "what I see looks more like raindrops than a flower. A splash that hits one or two people then disappears."

Takashi asks, "only to come back a mile away the next day? What is the mechanism."

"Hopefully, when we treat our next patient, we will be able to find out."

There is a knock on the door, Jo Kogotana stands at the door, Jo coughs to get the attention of the two doctors. Setsuka looks between the men. She turns to face Takashi. "Take a break, Takashi, go get something to eat. I will wait for you here."

Jo and Takashi walk quietly to the across the hospital and up the stairwell to the rooftop. Jo hands Takashi a lunch box, and only then do the two men speak to one another. "What time did you get to work today?" his voice is low and crackling, it is early, and Jo is already sore from arguing with his subordinates.

The sun is low in the sky, the day has hardly broken. The humidity is mild, the sun has yet to start baking the countryside "I think it was close to 12:45 when I clocked in."

Jo huffs as he opens his lunchbox, inside there is cold fried fish and leftover potato wedges. Takashi, on the other hand, has cold soup and sliced fruits. "you have been on the clock for five and a half hours already? You work harder than me, and I have the whole town to take care of."

Takashi tips his head back, drinking the soup in one long gulp. "you protect the town's property; I protect the people. The way I see it, I can't afford to be any less vigilant then you are."

Jo eats slow. His eyes wander his mind hard at work. Still thinking about the events of the past days, always looking for links between people and places. Trying to dream up how things have come to be where they are. "I dread to think about what may happen if you or I ever get sick."

Takashi rests his back to the wall and slowly slouches over "it isn't hard to imagine what would happen. Jo, I was just taking a headcount. If my numbers are right, 53% of the village will be over 60 before new years day. And 20% of the town is under 16."

Jo rolls his eyes side to side to try to understand where Takashi is going with all of this "So?" is the only thing he can seem to mutter.

"So,… after you and I die-off, this town is going to have one hell of a labor shortage." Takashi jokes.

Jo grunts, "I proffer not to think about my mortality."

With a sigh, Takashi responds, "Death denial is not a cure for death. If it were, I would have a lot less work to do."

Jo looks up, remembering last night, "Takashi, have you seen Masumo lately?"

"Masumo? No, he hasn't been in here. Not so far as I can remember." Takashi explains

Jo asks, "what about his daughter or wife?"

"From what I heard, Ms. Masumo moved to Hiragana. I assume that the rest of the family did as well. Why?"

Jo reaches a hand back, rubbing his neck "I saw Eva Masumo yesterday, at the temple."

May 9th, 6:45am

Oso woke up early, he fell asleep after sitting up much of the night drinking. He walked around his house, looking for Ri. Not finding him, Oso called Jet and Tenzuma to see if his boy was with them. Getting no reply from Tenzuma, Oso makes his way to the school to see if he can trace down his son there.

Several hundred students walk in a block to the school. The school itself is wrapped in a tall gate. Oso waits at the entrance. He watches as kids file into the building. He looks about frantically looking for anyone that he knows Ri spends time with, anyone from his class.

Oso spots Odette, she walks near the rear of the group. She keeps her distance from people, Odette suffers from a level of anxiety, she needs to keep at arm's length form anyone to feel comfortable.

Oso shouts, "Tsu!"

But Oso doesn't get the chance to talk as he is interrupted by a tall, powerful-looking woman. One of the teaches, dressed in a black university coat and checkered dress. Everyone that knows her calls her Ms. Machohero; she had planes to become a pro-surfer, but do to trouble finding sponsorship, she had to fall back on her secondary interest, a masters of communication.

The athletic women pushes one of Oso shoulders then grips him by the other to spin him around. Oso looks up at her, a look of surprise on his face from having been snuck up on so laconically. Oso stutters "Machohero-son?"

Machohero slaps Oso then shoves him backward. "Hanzo!" she stomps forth, "you smell like cheep whiskey!"

Oso holds up both hands comically "what, I want to talk."

Machohero grunts as she steps forward, shoving Oso across the street "I know all about you and how much you like to talk!" Oso quickly finds his back to the wall. "Students only on campus. now get out of here before I call constable Kogotana!"

A number of the students have gathered around hearing overheard Machohero's shouting. Machohero pulls a hand back, throwing a haymaker punch in hopes of knocking out Oso. Oso drops his weight onto his back foot and lowers his body slightly, Oso hooks one arm out into a pushing block and lifts his other hand to his side getting into a modified cobra stance interrupting the attack.

The two stare each other down in a power struggle. Everyone knows Oso is an alcoholic; everyone knows that he abandoned his job as an imperial intelligence operative after the death of his wife and became a chef using his military pension to buy his shop. Oso wanted to be close to his son.

What people seem to not remember is Oso had served 5 tours of service as an infantryman and has training as a rifleman, swordsmen, and has tactical hand-to-hand training all paid for by the emperor. Oso didn't need to let himself get hit. He chose to get hit, but with his back pressed to the wall, he isn't going to get hit again.

Machohero brings up her other hand to tack another swing; Oso grips her by the wrist and pulls down on her radial bone, forcing her to kneel by jarring her forward. With Machohero on her knees, Oso explains, "Ri, he wasn't at home when I woke up. Have Mr. Gogiro call me if Ri isn't in class." Oso pushes Machohero over. He then walks away briskly.

May 9th, 10:15am

Oso returns to his shop. He equips his kimono and obi, he needs to work; it is the only thing that is going to keep his mind clear. After all, what fear is greater than the fear of loss? He gets a bucket of water from the backroom and pulls open the gates so that the open-air patio is visible from the street. Oso washes every table, then goes back to the first starting again. He focuses on his work with the utmost intent.

Reko Jet is his first customer of the day. Reko is a mammoth of a man, he stands about a foot taller than anyone else in the village, and he is stacked like a 'Man of Iron' contestant, 2% body fat weighing in at 375lbs. Reko can bench-press 800lbs, and he looks the part. Reko has gone bald, but only on the head, he has long hair on his arms and back, making him look like a silver-backed gorilla. Reko walks around shirtless; he has on leather pants and an apron, long leather gloves, and a tool belt hands from his hip.

Oso sniffs at the air then walks behind his desk, "one bowl of Meso."

Reko takes a seat, "and a plate of egg noodles, stack them high."

Oso scoops of some noodles and fish, he pulls a knife from the magnetic hanger overhead to sidestep and chop up some veggies. Oso works diligently. He keeps his head down, looking like a man with places to be.

Reko leans over the table, watching the chef, "you look like the walking dead." His voice is deep and grumbling.

Oso places a pot of water on the burner "are you drinking red or white tea today?" Oso is in no mood to talk.

"do you have any of that grapefruit tea left?" Reko asks

Oso shakes his head "Sokayura came in here, she took my whole stock with her."

Reko nods, "then I will take the white tea." The giant leans back in his chair, folding his arms as he waits for his food to be cooked.

Oso looks up from his work for a moment, "Reko, how old is your daughter?"

Reko responds, "she will be 10 in July."

Oso nods, "do you think our community is safe?"

"safe enough that I don't have locks on my door." Reko expresses, "is there something on your mind Hanzo?"

Oso places the plate of noodles and a cup of soup on the table, "I am concerned. I am not sure of Ri came home last night. I hope he is out with Tsu or Tenzuma or some other girl, he is the right age for that sort of thing. But I can't help but think. What if he isn't? Could something have happened? Is there someone in this town that may try to hurt a young boy?"

Jet expresses, "Have you called Kogotana?"

"Should I?"

"I would."

Oso nods. "I need to make a phone call." Oso slips off into the back room.

After Oso vanishes into the back room a young girl steps in, she pushes the bead door off to one side and takes a set at the bar. Them ten-year-old looking child turns in her seat, listening to Reko. "what is that you have there?" she requests

"Meso with egg noodles," Reko explains

"I think I will try the same thing. It smells good." The girl giggles. Eva, after a minute of kicking her feet and fidgeting in her chair, stands up on the chair, trying to see into the backroom.

Reko notices the girls is uneasy; he speaks in a slow, deliberate voice, "Take it easy on Hanzo, he is having a hard day."

Eva looks over, "yeah? What is going on?"

Reko tips his head back to drink the last of his soup "Ri didn't go home last night."

Eva nods "yes he did, I walked him home. Jin and Odette were with us also."

Reko rubs his chin, "I am almost sad to hear that." Reko pulls some money out if his pocket, he sets it on the table then walks out of the bar. "Make sure you let Oso know that when he comes back up front."

Oso comes up form the back room a short time later, he is toweling off his hands as he calls out thinking Reko was still in the bar "Jo is on his way here he should be…" Oso freezes, looking at the little girl.

Eva reports, "Reko had to leave, he told me to let you know that Ri had gone home last night."

Oso leans onto the table, looking at the girl, "Are you a friend of his?"

"Not really, we just met yesterday." Eva retorts.

"How old are you? You look a little younger than my boy."

Eva laughs, "older than I look."

With a shrug, Oso pushes himself upright, "is there anything I can get for you, little lady?"

"Two things, I want to try a plate of Meso and…" she digs around in her pockets, pulling out an egg-shaped coin "I found this as I was walking through the park, do you know what it is?"

Oso leans over, looking at the coin, it is a faded yellow and orange color with raised writing on it and a hammer impression on one edge "this is a Nibu-kin galleon coin; this is from the Meiji era. This has been out of print since… since 1870 I think."

Eva turns the coin in her hands, looking at it, "is it worth anything?"

Oso nods "about 200,000 yen I would say. if I were you, I would keep that out of sight."

"Thank you, Hanzo-son." Eva takes a bow, "you are very smart."

Oso gives Eva a bowl of soup "If I were as smart as I thought I was, I wouldn't be in this bar."

Eva looks to him with wide eyes "it is a nice bar."

"I wanted to move to Akita years ago, get out of this town. but I never did." Oso reminisces,

"why?" Eva asks,

"This town has bad memories in it," Oso explains.

"if you left, wouldn't the memories follow you?" Eva eats her soup happily

"I guess so," Oso starts cleaning his cutting board. "It is hard to outrun the past, isn't it?"

With a strange calm, Eva replies, "there is no outrunning the past. It is always behind you… I guess unless it isn't." Eva places a pocket full of coins on the table to pay for her lunch. "I will see you later, Hanzo-son!" she jumps up to her feet then runs off.

May 9th, 11:05 am

Jo Kogotana slaps the table between him and Oso Hanzo, Jo shouts "What is the matter with you!?!" there is a deep gloss of anger to his voice as Jo slaps the table emphasizing every word he speaks "Why Didn't, you, call, me, first?" Oso opens his mouth to talk, but Jo won't let him, Jo points at the chef, "How long have we know each other Oso?" his voice suddenly turning soft.

Finally, able to talk, Oso replies, "30 years, I think."

Kogotana nods, "I thought so." Jo sits down at the bar, "bring me a coffee."

Oso does as he is asked; he brings Jo a cup of coffee.

Jo loments for a moment, "and it isn't just you. Everyone around here is all smiles and laughs when strolling down the road, but so few of us know each other, trust each other. Ms. Moha, she and I have shared a fence for fifteen years, and not once has she offered me a drink, nor has she sat down with me for a meal. You would imagine in a place like this everyone would treat each other like family, but no one does."

Oso tries to make light of things "I do treat me neighbors like family, I avoid them."

Jo drinks his coffee in one long drag then flips the cup over, setting it down like a shot glass. "I will have the deputies do a sweep of the village. They should be able to finish a matrix scan before 6pm, I will have Nekoba go with the monks Tomi, Tami, Tobi, they will run the mountain trail, look for signs that anyone has been up there. Nekoba and the Moji brothers shouldn't have any problem with that. Maybe I can get Machohero to grab some volunteers to scan the woods. People that get lost out there tend to not come back, but it is worth a look."

Oso is stunned, the thought of the woods makes him unsettled, and the thought of Ri out there even more so. "sounds like you are going to mobilize the whole town."

Kogotana nods. "if I am lucky."

May 9th, 2:45pm

Under orders from Kogotana, Nekoba starts on his way up the mountain trail, a dozen monks walking with him. The trail going up the path is lined with ropes showing the intended route, eons ago the mountain had a village atop it, time has claimed the old town. Snow that never melts and trees have grown through the ancient monuments, the top of the mountain is a world forgotten. A place where the shadows of the old gods can still be seen burned onto the face of the earth.

Scars of war hidden by time and memorial. Sacred land viewed by only a chosen few. This place was once called Bancho, now it has no name. Only haunted dreams. Nekoba at the had of the group walks with a lantern, a thin red thread tied to the wrist of each man leading them back to the last. The last generation of monks had a crippling fear of this place. The elders passed edict about how men were to act as they ascended the path.

"I have never seen the northeast summit, have any of you?"

Tomi is the one to reply, "no one goes to the northeast summit. Not since Egaru ordered the road closed."

Tami, the second of the triplets, continues, "not even the records from the old town are still in our temple. The elder wanted them burned…"

From atop one of the effigies cut into the stone, a childish voice speaks out, "one of many failings of the temple I feel. One can not outrun their past." A childlike demon sits on the head of the monument, her legs folded, her umbrella tipped slightly forward to hide her eyes from view. The shadow cast by the umbral sends down an unearthly blue light; within the mantel darkness, not only is the light dampened, it is cast in night. To look at the world through the parasol is to see into the past.

The older of the monks seem to at once recognize the face of the Shinigami. Tomi, Tami, Tobi as well as Nekoba stand their ground. Maybe they don't see the demon, perhaps they don't recognize it, or maybe they are too proud and bold to show fear.

Nekoba orders, "who are you!"

The god of death giggles "promise not to tell?" she waits for a moment "I am the grim reaper. Or sometime Efrafra, Cheron, Chronos, Death. In your tongue, I am called Shinigami."

The three monks raise their hands into an aggressive stance. They are ready to protect themselves from the monster that stands before them. Nature itself opposes this action. Deer, rabbits, giant cats, wolves, and monkeys living in the woods step out of the darkness creating a wall around the four men and the spirit.

Shinigami speaks in a kiddy voice, "Nekoba, you are not like the people around you. You do not fear death."

Nekoba explains, "I don't believe I have anything to fear. Once I am dead, I am dead. I will not be aware anymore; therefore, whatever is left behind is no longer me."

The phantom looks confused, "and me sitting here is not enough to change your mind?"

"you say you are Shinigami, and my friends seem to have taken you at your word. But I see nothing that I find convincing of that claim." Nekoba stands firm.

The ghost twirls the umbrella in its hands, playfully, "And what would it take to convince you of who I am?"

"I do not know, but I have no doubt that anyone worthy of the name Shinigami would know."

The ghost smiles; she excepts what has been said, "you are at peace. That is why when you die, you will sleep soundly. Those three, on the other hand, their rest will not be so claiming."

Tobi explains, "she is controlling the animals with her thoughts, I can see the ghost in their eyes."

"Nekoba, do you want to know about this place?" the phantom asks.

"What happened to this village?" Nekoba asks.

"I did." She explains, "once, many years ago. This place was a place just like your home. A town that sprung from the ground around a church. A rich man came to town, he brought gold wine. And all the town loved him for it. He also brought with him slaves and a slave's marketplace. The church turned a blind eye. Then the rich man took a wife for himself, and this made his daughter angry because the wife he chose was a slave girl. The daughter stabbed her mother-in-law and pushes her down the well. Then came a great sickness. The slave haunted the town from inside the well. In her anger, the dead called on me to take vengeance for them. And so, I raptured the village. Your village is built on the graves of those that came before you." There is a moment of silence, then the spirit goes on, "but that is not the real question, is it? You want to know about the boy, Ri Hanzo, is he alive? Am I right?"

Nekoba nods, "yes."

The spirit continues, "he is not dead yet, but it is up to you to decide when he will die."

Nekoba shouts with impunity, "not today!"

The ghost asks, "but if you believe that death is the end of life, then why not today? Why should it matter when someone dies?"

"because I do believe in agency, and there is no infringement on one's freedoms more sever then death," Nekoba explains.

"then the boy will not die tonight. Continue on the path, take the fork that goes down the south side of the hill and follow the falls down, walk along the river until you see a tree with a dreamcatcher nailed to it. The boy is there. But he won't be if you do not make haste…"

May 9th, 5:30 pm

Nekoba makes his way down the other side of the mountain. As he is doing so, dozens of kids from the school and several teachers have fanned out in a search line. Reje and Leta Tenzuma find themselves walking the path parallel to Nekoba.

Leta waves as she calls out, "Nekoba-son!"

The chaplain stagers a few steps as he walks across the shallows of the river. Reje runs up to catch him, and Leta grabs

one of Nekoba's arms to stabilize him.
Nekoba acknowledges them "the Tenzuma's.
thank you."

    Leta ask, "are you part of the search party also?"

    Setkura nods, "I was walking the path around the mountain."

    Reje points out, "I think you overshot, the path ends about three miles back that way. Doesn't it?"

    Nekoba is torn; he doesn't know how much he should say about what he has seen. He chooses cation "I had picked up a trail some time ago, I think young Hanzo came this way."

    Leta asks, "why would someone come out here? What is this direction?"

    "nothing for about 20 more miles, the closest thing to us that way is Yanaka." Reje explains, "at least to the best of my knowledge." Movement up ahead catches Reje's eye, just around the river bend, a hand is waving, half-covered by long grass. Nekoba and Reje run off ahead.

Leta calls for help as she thinks she knows already what they have stumbled on, "Okāsama!"

The fear of others proves merited. Ri is there, laying in the wet sand, his clothes missing, his body covered in hundreds of tiny scratches, water from the river running over his lower half. His eyes are rolled backward, he is chatting incoherently. Setsuka Tenzuma is the next on the scene as she comes out form a nearby tree. She is shouting over her radio as she runs.

Reje and Nekoba pull Ri up onto dry land. Setsuka places her bag down on the ground she starts to pull out bandages and peroxide as she looks over the boy. She recites the condition to herself as she does. "eyes are swollen, blue rings around lips, multiple lacerations to the abdominal section, puncher wound below the floating rib. He has lost some blood. We are going to need to get him back to Takashi…"

Reje asks, "are these the type of injuries you would expect after one day on wood?"

Satsuka explains, "no, these are the type of injuries I would expect after an animal attack."

Hastily Tenzuma preforms first aid to dress the wounds and ready the boy to moved back to town. Tenzuma looks to her son "I know you and your sister have been sneaking out at night, playing in the woods. I should like to ask you to not do so anymore, but if you must. Stay together."

May 9th, 8:15pm

Takashi steps out of the operating room. He digs around in his pockets, looking for his cigarettes.

Oso is waiting at the vending machines alongside Nekoba.

Jo Kogotana approaches from the other end of the hallway.

Takashi doesn't say a word. He waves for Oso and Kogotana to follow him as he walks to his office. Oso hastily asks, "Is Ri ok?"

Takashi remains silent as he hands Kogotana a cigarette and lights it for him then lights his own. Only after taking a drag from his cigarette does he respond "he needed a transfusion; he was suffering from internal bleeding. He was exposed to a drug also that I don't recognize. Toxicology is working on breaking it down." He takes another hit "I have done all I can do. If the boy is still alive at 6am, he should be fine."

Takashi puts out his cigarette softly, saving the other half for later. "but there is something on my mind, as I was sealing the cuts on the boy's body, I spotted something that bothered me. A burn mark on his neck, and a matching one on his wrist. Looked something like a rope burn to me…"

Hanzo becomes agitated. "Takashi! What are you trying to say?" he stomps a foot and bites his lip to try to keep calm, his fingers scraping his thumb, betray his anger.

Jo steps forward, placing a hand on Oso's chest to hold him still "let us go to my place and talk Oso, you are tired and hurt. You need to rest."

Oso circles one hand to the outside and brings up his other arm to wresting a hand on Jo's chest, pushing him back "what are you doing Homes, keep your hands off of me."

Jo reaches for his gun, Oso, for the knife he keeps hidden in the sleeve of his coat. Takashi reaches for a cup of coffee "Gentlemen, it has been five years since the last time I had to treat a gunshot wound. I am not feeling confident at the moment. So, please don't kill each other in my office." The voice is calm, collected. Takashi is a man that has seen it all. He has no fear of blood, no fear of death. Or if he does, he doesn't show it.

Takashi takes a drink the rolls his head back, stretching "now, I haven't accused anyone of anything. There are a lot of ways a boy that likes to play outside may get hurt. Lots of poisonous flowers grow around here, there are more than a hand full of old things in the woods that may have any number of yet undiscovered funguses on them… I haven't called CPS or anything. I just want you and Jo to talk. If Jo tells me that everything is on the up and up, so be it. I would rather this matter be handled between the three of us than anything."

May 9th, 9:05pm

Oso is sent to the drunk tank for his own protection, Jo fears that Oso is emotional and may do something irresponsible if left alone. On his way home, Jo stops at the temple.

As Jo pushes to door open, Nekoba calls out to him "welcome back Kogotana-son, if I am not mistaking, you have spent more time here with me this week than you have with your wife. Tell me, how long has it been since you have been home?"

Jo explains, "two days. I haven't been home in two days."

Nekoba is putting out the candles around the chappal "how do you do it?"

"insomnia helps, training, drugs." Jo thinks, "At my best, I worked 5 days without a break."

Nekoba nods, "that must be hard on you and your family."

"they know I am an honorable man, and my work requires diligence…"

Nekoba cuts him off "...I think your work requires about a dozen more capable hands."

Kogotana changes the subject, "There is something I need to ask." Nekoba looks up, waiting to hear what Jo has to say "you found Ri at the riverbed. But you weren't at the riverbed, you were on the hillside path. What brought you to the river?"

Nekoba freezes for a moment, the vision of the childlike ghost and it's spinning umbrella etched into his mind "I saw something, something I don't know how to describe."

Jo narrows his eyes, drinking in Nekoba's words, looking for hidden details "try."

Nekoba shuts his eyes with a nod, "do you know about Shinigami?"

Jo explains, "I know the local ghost stories as well as anyone. My nephew was very interested in them before he went mad and got himself arrested, Ichi would go on for hours about ghost kids and winged skeletons standing at his window. what of it?"

"in the old village, a number of my colleges saw something that they are convinced was Shinigami," Nekoba reports

"and what do you think?" Jo request.

"I think that mass hallucinations often show us what we are conditioned to see." Nekoba returns his douter to the mount on the wall "we all used to share stores, or we heard our parents or grandparents spin fish stories of one sort or the other. So, we see what we expect to see. Now, if we saw what we lacked the words to describe, that would be something."

May 9th, 10:30pm

Jin, Odette, and Sakura stand around the campfire. Jin looks around "is this it? Is no one else coming? Didn't we all say we would be here at 10?"

Masumo shouts out as she stumbles over some tree branches, "I am here also!"

Jin throws his arms out to the sides, "Where are Reje, Leta, and Ri?"

Odette sits on a log with her legs folded leaning forward as if to hug herself for warmth "Ri was hurt, didn't you here?"

Jin shakes his head, "no, no one told me."

Masumo sits down with Odette, "are we still going to have our storytime without him?"

Odette opens the icebox she had dragged up to the campsite and pulls out a bottle of flavored water "Jin, your dad is the constable, how did you not hear about Ri."

Jin explains "I haven't seen my dad."

Odette nods in understanding, "I haven't seen my folks in days, they are in London on business."

Masumo looks up and kicks her feet back and forth, "I like London."

Sakura holds her hand out for a drink also, "you have been to London?"

Masumo nods, "I have also been to Brazil, Mexico, Canada, France, and Russia."

Sakura smiles, "It sounds like you traveled a lot."

"Egypt is the next place I want to go to." She smiles and giggles

Odette looks to her, "what is in Egypt?"

Masumo shakes her head "I don't know, I haven't been there."

Jin points to Odette, "do you want to tell the first story of the night?"

Odette nods, she leans in close to the flames "over the last serval night we have remembered all the old ghost stories, all the screamers all the tails of undying things. But there is a monster we have forgotten, I fear. I recall a story about a man from Shinjuku. A man who loved computers. His name is lost, but his story still lives on."

Odette sits back, her feet drift apart, one hand tocks between her thighs to push her skirt down, holding it still as she turns her eyes to the clouded sky. Storm clouds are gathering off the coast, a thick wind is stirring "The Shinjuku man was forgetful, sometimes he forgot to shower, sometimes he forgot to throw away spoiled food. But he was a man that loved his work. Sometime he remembers having gotten married at a young age, sometimes he remembers he had a baby with this love. But then he remembers his work. He works long nights; he is awake early in the morning to continue his frantic typing."

A soft rain falls on the forest. Masumo throughs some more wood on the fire to keep it burning through the mist. "the man from Shinjuku was working on writing an important piece of software. A new security sweeper that would stop one's camera from being turned on remotely. He was almost finished with his work when a storm started. The Shinjuku man's house was struck by lightning. The power goes out."

"for the first time in maybe days, Shinjuku man stands up from his desk. He looks around his apartment. The dishes haven't been washed in over a week, boxes of Chinese food are stacked high on the floor. The trash can is rancid. His hands shake as he walks over to the phone he has on the wall. He stops as he sees the receiver is missing. The Shinjuku man often forgets things; maybe he dropped the phone in his room. When was the last time he had been to his bedroom? Did he sleep in his room last night? Or the night before? He can't remember."

"he looks to the walls, he has many photos like so many others do, pictures of kids, a young woman, a baby. The baby is his, he can remember that, and The woman he is married, He remembers. His wedding ring sits on his computer desk. Why did he take it off? That he can't seem to remember. The Shinjuku man walks around his apartment. His bedroom door is pinned shut by the boxes his new computer came in months ago."

"The Shinjuku man wonders, did his wife leave him because he works too much? Did his wife understand that he works so hard because he wants to give her things? So many things come rushing to his mind, maybe, just maybe he is neglectful. Maybe he is forgetful, but that doesn't mean he is unloving."

"Shinjuku man starts to dig through the boxes, he throughs them over his shoulder one by one until he can reach his bedroom. The door opens, a dry, burning smell fills the room. In the flickering lights from the street, there is a crib and a queen-sized bed, an armchair. In the chair sits two mummified bodies. A woman and a baby, a phone in the woman's hand. The Shinjuku man's wife never left him. He killed her with his negligence."

Chapter 3: Twelve day remaining

May 10th, 1:30am

      Ri awakens, he lays in his hospital bed. The room is dark, lighting flickers in the window. There is a tapping at the window. Ri sits up, he looks to the window. There is another tap. Ri stands, he limps to the window looking out. He is on the third floor, he looks down into the garden.

      A woman stands amongst the flowers, she is in a white gown, her dress seems to emanate light, the girl waves a hand calling to Ri. "come down here, boy." She holds her arms off to the sides, inviting a hug.

      Ri is entranced, he turns and walks out the door to his room. No one takes notices of the child walking. His arms held to his sides loosely, he sways like a drunken man. Down the steps, he walks to the front door and around to the garden. The phantom waits, her skin a fading blue, her hair black and flowing.

"Take off your clothes." The ghost request.

Ri unties his robe the drops it to the ground showing off his chest.

The ghost holds out her arms invitingly. Ri walks into the arms of the phantom. She slides her arms around his back, pressing her head to his chest. Slowly she kneels in front of him. She opens her mouth, licking up his stomach. Ri tips his head back, he takes a hard breath.

May 10th, 5:15am

Takashi is asleep face down on the love seat in his sister's house when his phone rings Takashi picks up his cellphone weakly, he mumbles barely aware of his surroundings "Dr. Tsu."

"Takashi," an excited voice calls over the phone, "Muro Handa, at the toxicology lab. I just finished running the test on the samples you sent me last night."

Takashi asks, "did you email me the data?"

Handa explains, "this was a bizarre one. I thought it was some sort of toxin at first, but I called up my friend Lichi Lin at Watory to get a second set of eyes on the job, she had another idea, Trypanosoma-cruzi."

Takashi asks for clarification, "Kissing bug?"

Handa agrees, "That is what Lichi thinks. She did mention that there was something alien-looking about it, though. The sample was large, like, it would have taken a thousand or more bugs, large. And there were trace amounts of Salvia divinorum, galantamine, succinylcholine, and Gamma-aminobutyric acid."

Tsu rolls of the couch then jumps up to his feet "that is a hell of a tonic. Dulled nerves, tactile hallucination, paralytic…"

Handa cuts him off, "assuming it doesn't kill you. It would be a hell of a trip. Any idea where this stuff came from?"

Takashi lowers his head as he struggles to think "no." the other line starts to beep, "can you hold on for just a moment, Handa?" Takashi changes lines, "Dr. Tsu."

The voice on the other line is that of one of the overnight nurses "Doctor, we need you right away..."

May 10th, 8:45 am

Jo Kogotana arrives at work late. He had been awakened by a call from the hospital, something unthinkable had happened, and it is now Jo's job to deliver the news to Oso. Jo unlocks the drunk tank letting light into the room. Oso is asleep on a cot with his arms pulled across his face "Hanzo!" Jo shouts.

Oso groans as he sits up. "Jo?" Oso looks side to side as if he can't remember where he is.

"There has been an accident. Ri was declared dead at 4:55am" Jo explains

Oso shoots his gaze to Jo awaiting more information

Jo lowers his head, rubbing his eyes tiredly, "multiple simultaneous organ failure. There was nothing that could be done."

Oso orders, "I want to see the body for myself."

Jo nods, "of course you do. The body was released to the temple for dressing after the autopsy, we can go at once. I would imagen they will have everything prepared by noon. They have been getting a good deal of practice lately."

Oso's head drops, he rests his hands on his legs as he silently weeps for a moment before he whispers his discontent "what fouls corruption has come to our home? I have outlived both my wife and my son, Jo."

Jo stands with his hands folded in front of his body. There is nothing he can say. So, he waits.

May 10th, 6:00pm

The main hall of the temple is dressed, Oso has spent much of the day gathering photos of his son and bringing them to the temple to decorate the room. Calls have been made. Everyone that Oso knows it seems has gathered to witness the ceremony. But once the viewing has officially started, Oso makes himself scarce.

He hides in the baptismal room, not wanting to be seen. There is nothing he wants to say; there is nothing that can be said that would ease his suffering.

Oso can't stop himself from thinking, what had happened? What could have been done? If he hadn't been drinking two nights ago, could he have protected his family from this? Oso is not sad, he is angry.

Someone has to pay for this. Someone needs to be put to blame. Maybe there is someone that Oso can talk to. Reko Jet! Hanzo has a sword, a seven-body sword he had inherited from his grandmother, a blade so sharp it could rend the flesh of a god should he need it to. But the edge has not been cleaned in a decade or more. Reko will clean Oso's family sword for him, then Oso will administer justice the way a samurai dolls out justice. He is a warrior, and warriors have a way of fighting evil. They run in through with a blade!

As the sun starts to fall low in the sky, A parade lines up to carry Ri to the riverbed. Nekoba is the last hand to touch the raft as it is lowered into the water. There is a cold silence as the raft rolls.

A bad omen comes to pass. As the raft Ri is tide to slides under the bridge, it is caught on a rock. When it emerges on the other side, the raft has rolled over, so Ri is now on the underside of the raft, and it is an empty looking one that makes the last leg of the trip to the mouth of the river.

In Chīsana-Mura, many people are subject to superstitions. An empty raft floating downstream is a warning, disaster is coming, the spirits want everyone to witness this to keep their eyes open and their wits about them.

A gasp of surprise fills the air at the grim sight. Eva Masumo slides in alongside Nekoba as whispers start in like thunder shattering the reverence. Masumo looks up at the chaplain, "why is everyone so …"

Nekoba finishes Masumo's thought, "distressed?" Masumo nods "the kami have just sent us a message. The dead are meant to be looking up at all times after their body is dressed. If they are facing any other direction, then the dead may be led astray by Haru, or Baku, or any number of other mischievous spirits or worse yet, they may unwittingly summon an Onryo to lay a curse on the land."

Masumo watches the young monk with wide eyes "you don't believe in such things, Nekoba-son."

Nekoba shakes his head "I don't, but Hanzo does, so too does Reko, Machohero, Gogiro, and most of the town's elders. I wonder what effect it has on the universe when so many people start to worry all at once? Fear can't be made flesh, can it?"

May 10th, 8:00 pm

The festivities are over, the crowd has thinned. Oso stands alone on the bridge. Storm clouds grow thick. A wall of water can be viewed off in the ocean sneaking slowly to the shore. As the rain sets foot on the land and cascade of fog is pushed across the town, shadows stretch, vision blurs. How can it be that the day is so hot and the night so cold, so dependably? It is as if heaven itself is angry.

The monk Tomi rests his hands on the banister of the bridge, leaning over it alongside Oso. "It is 10 days until the Festival of Drums. Last year you and Ri took the stage with my brothers and I during the first dance. You are not a monk, but you know that part. You are welcome to dance with us again."

Oso shrugs, then nods, then shakes his head. Oso can't find the energy to talk. Instead, he reaches over and sets a hand on Tomi's back, Oso then falls over and cries. Tomi grabs Oso helping him to his feet. The monk can think of little to do but lead Oso back into the temple to rest.

May 10th, 10:15 pm

Leta and Odette walk home side by side. They had stopped to buy Mochi on the way Leta had a relationship with Ri dating back years, at one point in time she was talking about the possibility of mirage in some distant future, but Ri wasn't ready for a talk about such things. Ri was more interested in sneaking around the school and kissing in hidden corners.

Ice-cream is a bandage for an open wound, friendship, an anesthetic, but it will take time for the healing to begin. Odette walks Leta home and into the arms of her brother. Dr. Tenzuma is just getting home from work as Odette is walking away from the house. The two lock eyes, but there is nothing to be said.

From there, Odette walks the rest of the way alone. She stops for a moment at a park halfway between their homes. There are three statues of tanuki; each is holding a basket. Odette kneels down, tucking her skirt between her thighs as she places a yen in each of the baskets.

The tanuki is part of some older faith, some forgotten ritual. Throughout the town, there are many statues and tiny structures that act as spirit huts. Places that people leave gifts for the dead that in some way appease them.

After that, it is a short walk the rest of the way. There is no meeting with her friends, no ghost stories today. Takashi pulls up on his bike alongside Odette; he has a stack of books in the basket on the back of his bike. Odette looks her uncle up and down, "doing some light reading?"

Takashi jokes, "I have the sudden urge to take up entomology."

Odette helps Takashi carry the books inside "why?"

"I have a friend in Wales that recommended it." He explains

May 10th 11:25pm

Leta goes to bathe. She soaks herself in hot water, letting the sounds of silence quite her mind. Steam fills the room. A whisper calls out to her from the fog hissing her name. She closes her eyes and lowers her body. She picks up her knees so she can lower her chest under the surface.

The voice whispers again. Leta fails to take notice. She pulls an arm across her face hiding from the pain she is feeling. Reje taps on the door shouting out the time. Leta gets up. As she towels off. The shadows in the bathroom dance. The reflection in the mirror seems unstable, showing Leta two echoes of herself. Strange things a tortured mind can do.

Leta walks back to her room, two towels tied around her body. Leta is just reaching the age where she finds skin something worth showing off. The body is something to be admired. Posters hang off her wall of actors and performers, images to remind herself of what she wants to look like. Her room has a parapet that leads onto the roof. As she turns on the lights to her room, a fantasy manifest.

Ri sits on the window seal, looking into the room. One hand holds the banister overhead; the other sits on the rim of the window, one foot in the place the other outside. He is dressed in his funeral robe, but he seems very much alive.

Leta sits on her bed an lets her towel fall off. Ri jokes, "undressing for me? I didn't think you wanted to do things so quickly."

Leta lays down, "Don't tease me."

Ri jumps into the room, he climbs up on the bed and crawls forward over Leta provocatively "I will tease you however much you like."

Leta can feel the room growing cold; she looks up at Ri, Leta may be a daydreamer, but something about this dream feels wrong. The hands of Ri grip Leta by the arms holding her still, two extra hands find her chest. Leta lowers her head, looking down as Ri licks up her chest.

Where Ri had been now laid atop her a white-haired monster with six arms, three-fingered hands, and giant eyes. It opens its mouth, showing a spearing tongue, Leta takes a shocked breath and screams!

Chapter 4: Eleven day remaining

May 11th, 5:05am

It isn't until Reje is getting ready for school that Leta is discovered. Reje calls for his mother, this is the second time in two days that Reje has had to do this. Leta is rushed to the hospital Dr. Tsu, Dr. Tenzuma, and four others work swiftly to revive the child. Tenzuma explains quickly as they work, "she seems to be suffering from TTS."

Dr. Tsu calls out, "has she been given Symjepi?"

Dr. Tenzuma explains, "yes."

One of the other doctors asks as they enter the emergency room, "what was the cause of the reaction?"

Dr. Tenzuma replies, "As of yet. Unknown."

Reje stands in the waiting room as his mother treats his sister. Jin Kogotana had witnessed the commotion and had laid chased to see what is going on.

Jin is dressed in his school uniform; Reje, on the other hand, is a mess, having fallowed his sister and mother dressed in nothing more than his flannel pajamas and tank top. Jin stands shoulder to shoulder with his classmate "what is going on?"

It takes Reje a few seconds to collect his thoughts, ultimately he fails to keep his calm Reje grabs Jin and starts to weep, "something is not right man. People are sick, my sister is sick, Ri is dead. How does a fourteen-year-old die of multiple organ failure?"

Jin is ice cold, "stand up straight." He commands

Reje takes a breath and tries to quite himself. He nods with a week, whimper, "yeah, keep cool."

Jin places a hand on the back of Reje's head, pulling him in close to whisper "I heard Hanzo-son talking at the temple, Ri didn't die, Ri was killed. Maybe the person that killcd Ri knows how your sister got sick."

Reje shakes his head, not understanding at first "what do you mean?"

Jin plays the detective for a moment. "Wednesday Ri goes missing, Thursday he dies, Friday Leta is sick. I think there is a connection. Don't you?"

"What is the connection?" Reje is calm; Jin is lost in fantasy, and Reje is getting sucked in.

"First place, I think we should look is the lumber yard." Jin smiles "after school, you, me, and Odette will go talk to mister Masumo."

Reje asks for clarification, "Mr. Masumo?"

"Ri went missing right after we met Eva, right?" Jin looks determined

Reje nods along "yeah. We can meet up at Oso's place…"

Jin cuts Reje off "after school, we meet at the park near the temple." Jin explains, "I don't want my father or Hanzo-son involved until we know more."

May 11th, 7:45 am

Oso walks into Reko's house down on the beach. Oso has his chest bound; his back is garbed in a flowing robe adorned with a Kitsune-Oni print. Oso has tided his hair up and back and shaved the top of his head, leaving only his ponytail intact. Oso has three swords strapped to his obi. Oso has become a strange sight to behold. Even in this village, a day's walk from the next nearest town, Oso has stepped backward in time, he has become, Ronin.

Reko slides open his bedroom door, hardly awake enough to understand his surroundings. At first, all that registers is the shadow of a swordsman in his doorway. Reko picks up a hammer from the nearest table and flips it about demonstrating his competent.

Oso draws his sword and drops to his knees; he spins the blade laying it to rest across the sleeves of his garment as he bows his head. "Jet-son, I ask you, give me your honor and blessing, clean my blade. Make it ready for war. So that should meet with man or beast on the road that lay ahead, my steel may bend, and my enemies may break."

Reko's eyes become clear, he lowers his hammer to his side "I will clean your sword. It will be so sharp that it will cut even a kami should you need it to. But I have no idea what war you are talking about." Reko takes Oso's sword. He flips it around, looking at the insignia on the blade. "the Hanzo stamp. This blade was forged back when my family and yours were one." He then spins it the other way looking at the reverse of the blade "the Shogun Seal. This sword was blessed by land-masters. With one swing, it killed three pigs. When this blade was new, it would have been one of the most beautiful blades anyone had ever set eyes on. But now the edge is warped, the glisten has faded. I will see to it that this blade shines again."

Reko throws coals onto the flame, he tends to the bellows. The furnace is stoked. Red light brings illumination onto the darkness.

Oso sits and stares with all his might. His anger is infused with the heating metals. The booze was gone from his veins; all that remains is an emphatical purpose. What evil brews in the heart of this man?

Hours pass, the hammering of steel becomes like the beating of drums. Sweat, stem, burning iron. Strength, power. The grinding of a wheel, painting of oil. This is how a blade is forged, this is how a life is taken.

When the blade is restored, Reko places it back in the care of Oso. "if I hear about you doing anything stupid with that, you and I never talk again."

Oso bows, he returns the sword to its home on his hip "my honor has been solid. It must be restored by the blood of monsters."

Reko looks concerned, "I am sure I don't know what you mean."

"Haven't you seen it?" Oso stands tall, "the ground under our feet is sick. The corruption spreads to us in our sleep. The Kami told us yesterday at Ri's ceremony," Oso hides a hand in a fist "Buddha, give me vengeance or give me glory. I care not which."

Reko punches the wall alongside himself as Oso turns to leave "you are scaring me old man. Talk about Budha and Kami. Last time you talked like that, I found you swinging from a tree. I don't want to be the one that needs to cut you down again."

Oso offers his friend a glance. "then grab your sword and gather your courage. I am going to climb the mountain. Look for the animal that hurt my boy."

Reko wipes his hands clean as he shakes his head angerly "you are foolish. But, if you insist on running into the woods, sword-in-hand, you are going to need someone by your side."

Oso lowers his eyes in gratitude, "thank you, Jet-son."

May 11th, 3:30 pm

Reje waits outside the school, he crosses the street to the park and kneels down in front of the three Tanuki statues. He rubs his hands together and digs around in his pockets. He finds a pack of gum and opens it. he gives a piece to each of the raccoon statues then takes one for himself "Offer me safe travels Baku." He bows to the effigy.

Jin looks down the road behind him then back to Reje as he approaches. "how did you get here so fast? Classes got out less than five minutes ago."

"that is easy, I didn't go to my eighth class today," Reje explains.

Odette comes running after them; she slaps Jin across the back in greeting. She then freezes, looking between the two of them "why do the two of you look so sour? Minstrel cramps or something?"

Jin places his hands in the pockets of his blazer then nudges off in the direction of the church "we need to keep moving, we have miles to travel and not so much daylight left."

"Leta is sick," Reje explains.

"so… where are we going?" Odette asks

Jin explains, "Masumo mil."

As they start to walk, Reje asks, "hay Jin, how do I get a green coat like the one have?"

Jin expresses, "get your GPA up to 3.88 then join the honors club."

The road leading up to the mil is old and crumbling. The heavy rain over the last several weeks has cussed clay under the road to erode, the pavement slants, and is cracked. It will take some time to clean up the messes left by the storms.

The old-growth forest around the mil has been leveled. The grounds have not been adequately worked. Even with the trees gone, the land is baron. The mil stands a lonely structure, a graying tower of wood and stone in desperate need of care.

Reje comments, "is this the right place? Does this look lived in, to you?"

Odette looks back at Reje as he is standing at the end of the group, "I don't see any other lumberyards around."

Reje questions, "Honestly, when was the last time anyone saw the train stop here or a truck drive down this road?"

Jin shakes his head, "I don't know."

The kids approach the structure. They push open the door to reveal a room filled with rusted tools. Flies swarm violently. Cracks in the wood leave stripped shadows on the walls. A log sits in the belt half cut. A spider's nest tied tightly around the sawblade as if to jam the blade.

Jin whispers with his friends, "so, this is where Masumo lives?"

Odette walks around the rusty room. She points, "there is a latter over here." She looks up to a small box of a room hidden off to one side of the interments, "any idea what would be up there?"

Reje comments, "observation deck, maybe?" Reje grips the latter and shakes it, "want me to go take a look?"

Odette nods and waves him forward "after you."

Jin walks around to the window that lumber is lowered from after getting cut. He freezes, looking down at a broken section of the floorboard. He kneels down as he pulls a flashlight from his belt. He looks into the hole struggling to make out what is under the floor. A coppery scent accosts him as the light off his flashlight is being reflected back at him. "what is that?" he whispers.

Reje gets to the top of the latter. There is a tiny bedroom, a large toy chest with the lid open showing off a collection of puppets. Another corner of the room has a net of stuffed animals mounted on it, lovingly organized. But the bed itself has something far more unearthly to share.

A cocoon, three feet long, two feet wide, split open as if it had recently birthed a butterfly, embryonic fluid still clings to the mouth of the nest, having yet to evaporate thanks to the shadows of the room.

Reje stars, frozen in fear as he tries to understand the thing he is looking at. Reje loses his grip, he falls off the ladder, he lands with a terrible crash. Odette picks him up. "Reje, are you ok."

Reje is shaken, his points at the door. "it is time to leave, it is time to leave." When he fell, he suffered several deep cuts from splintering wood, and no doubt, he is bruised awfully, but physical pain means little to him at the moment as the sight of the human-sized cocoon is solely too horrifying to be ignored.

May 11th, 5:45 pm

Odette, Jin, and Reje make their way to Jin's house. Only once there does Reje notice that he is hurt, Reje explains what he had seen, his friends believe him. Nothing about what they had seen seems right. Jin calls his father, explains to Jo what they had done. It takes some convincing, but Jin talks Jo into picking him up so the two of them can go back and investigate deeper. Masumo is a monster, Jin knows it.

As the two drive, Jin gives directions, but quickly things start to look out of place. Heavy construction equipment fills the clear-cut fields. The tower that is the sawmill is painted a deep red with a white outline. A half dozen trucks are parked waiting to be loaded up. It is not the most lively of places, but it is many times more alive then it was 2 hours earlier.

Father and son step out of the car side by side. Jo offers Jin a disapproving gaze, Jin responds with wide-eyed confusion. The two approach the front door of the mil. Jo knocks on the door. Quickly the door is pulled open by a straggly looking old man.

Jo steps back with a look of shock, "Mr. Sirosanto?" Jo exclaims.

The old man cleans his hands off on his coat. "Sirosanto lives on the other side of the river. I am Masumo."

Jo collects himself, "of course." Jo bows, "I am constable Kogotana."

Mr. Masumo looks back and forth between Jo and Jin, "May I be of assistance to you, Constable?"

Jo questions, "are you the father of Eva Masumo?"

Mr. Masumo shakes his head "no, my son Hegaru is her father, I am her grandfather."

Eva comes running to the door to see what is going on. "Jin!" she shouts. Jin is shaking his head in disbelief, nothing is the way it should be right now. "Papa-son, can we invite them inside?" Eva asks.

Mr. Masumo nods, "we just had a major equipment failure. I sent everyone home, so I see no harm in it." Mr. Masumo sidesteps to let the two of them in. The mil is not modern. But it is well maintained, the saw itself looks like it must be close to a hundred years old. The walls are adorned with dozens of woodworking tools. The place is freshly painted and smells of motor oil.

Jo questions, "is it just the two of you here?"

Mr. Masumo confirms, "has been for years. Ever since my good-for-nothing boy turned away from buddha…"

Jo cuts in, "go on."

"Hegaru was once a devotee, just like all of us. But then he had this crackpot idea about how Buddha and Moses were brothers. He wrote a book about it, and the next thing we know here comes Templeton institute gifting him 100,000,000 yen and paying him to do a twelve-year tour of all the biggest archeological sites around the world. He had brought Yuri and Eva with him, but Eva wanted to come home to her old man." He grins

Eva grabs Jin by one arm and runs over to the ladder that goes up to the next floor. "come on, let me show you my room." Jin is pulled by the surprisingly strong little girl. At the top of the ladder is a pristine small room. Stuffed animals line the bed, the toy chest overflows with puppets. A tiny stage has been assembled to do marionette shows within. There is no dresser and no clothes visible lying around.

Jin examines the room with the utmost interest. Eva picks up a few of her puppets she hides under the stage to do a demonstration for Jin. Jin has little choice but to sit and watch. Eva starts to tell a story with her toys.

"in a faraway place once there were many butterflies. But the garden was large and wasp and misquotes and spiders invaded the garden. The garden got sick, and a beautiful matriarch amongst the butterflies grow afraid. Shi came up with a plan to protect the other butterflies. Shi found a rock, and She laced it with seeds, seeds that had been dipped in the blood of the Queen. But the king of mosquitos saw what Shi was doing. The king went to the oldest of all things. The Millipede. The king of Mosquito's was clever. He found the seeds of the butterflies, and he hid with them his seeds."

"this the Queen of butterflies knew nothing of this as Shi sends the rock off into the Never. Through the great mist and across the void. Then the Queen slept, sure now that her children would never know the pain and fear that She lived with. The blood of the mosquitoes mixed with the blood of the butterflies. Through the magic of the Never, they became as one. A new beast. Tall and proud, fine and beautiful like nothing else ever had been. And now a new matriarch has grown from the ground. Shi brings with her a new power. The power to take others in her embrace and fill them with the love that is her."

"but the land that they live in, it is young and lonely. So, the Queen must sleep. Wait for the world to mature, ready itself for her love. After all, mice and horses make poor subjects. The Queen in her slumber dreams. What sort of people will she meet when she wakes up? Will they love her as much as Shi loves them?"

"as the queen slumbers, a new garden grows around her. Then a boy comes to her garden. She shows her favors to the boy, Shi takes him in her embrace. Grate and powerful, the matriarch of the butterflies, tells the boy, 'I need and want you to love me.'

"The boy then tells her 'you have asked for this, so I will do it for you.'"

"and Shi says onto the boy 'Because you have done this, for you, I shall give you a gift.' The Queen from beyond the stars has power, power Shi is willing to give. When the Queen grows sick, or old, Shi can discard her skin and underneath reveal a younger self, one from before she became old or ill. She takes the boy and gives him her tongue. The says onto the boy 'you now have my power, should you have become unwell take of your skin and you will be well.'"

"but butterfly magic it seems the boy cannot mimic, and he grows old, and his body turns to dust. This brings pain to the Queen, and Shi cries for the boy, and then it rains. The rain washes away the dust of the past and reviles the seed of rebirth hidden in the clay. Then Shi bites her hand and lets her blood drip onto the seed of rebirth, and then the boy comes back, now he too is a butterfly… and all in the world is right again."

"except, the boy is confused when he awakens, in his confusion, he hurts the Queen. The Queen falls to the ground, her wings broken. And the boy cries, he does not understand. The way of the butterflies is not like the ways of the boy. He does not understand that the Queen can not die. Shi only sleeps, and when shi awakens, Shi will discard this old body and have a young one again."

"the boy runs into the trees, vanishing into the blackness of the garden. The Queen wakes up, and Shi cannot find the boy. But the Queen has special sight, her eyes can see fair, her ears can hear well. She spreads her wings, and She takes to the sky, her wings turn day into night. And now all things can be seen by her. The Queen flies into the garden now knowing everything that happened as She slept…"

The voice of Jo Kogatana shatters the air, "Boy. Come here!"

Jin holds up his hand to Eva asking her to wait, Jin slides down the ladder to his father. Jo grabs Jin by the arm and pulls him outside.

Mr. Masumo questions, "Is everything alright constable?"

Jo explains, "we will need to continue our conversation later." Jo freezes for a moment looking at the inside of the door noticing the smoothness of the wood, the latch from the inside is missing, there is no bolt to hold the door shut, the only thing that could have kept the door is if a board had been lied across it to pin it closed. "I recommend that you start locking your doors at night. There may be a killer on the loose."

Mr. Masumo nods, "won't you stay for a drink? I have sake."

"I will give you a call." Jo pushes Jin outside; Masumo pushes the door shut, locking it with an audible click.

Jo and Jin approach the car. Before they get in, Jo looks up and down the street, he is sweating, he wipes his face on the sleeve of this coat. "Stop." He orders. Jin freezes in place. "Look around you, do you see a phone line or a radio tower from where you are standing?" Jin shakes his head. "do you hear a generator running?" Jin shakes his head again. "is there any evidence of a powerline going into that shack?" Jo points at the mil. Jin shakes his head again. "That is what I thought." Jo opens the door to his car, "Get in, now.

May 11th, 6:45 pm

Jo, as they drive, picks up his phone, making several calls in quick succession; first, he calls home, he orders Jin's mother to stay home and to keep Reje and Odette with her. Then he calls his office, he tells Deputy Useto to stand guard at his house. Then Jo calls Tenzuma at the hospital, he orders her to meet him at the door, exclaiming he is on the way.

Jin is trying desperately to catch up, he doesn't understand what is going on, he is still confused about the very appearance of the mil then alone anything that happened in it "Dad, what is going on?" Jin is just short of shouting.

"you told me that the mil was dilapidated when you went there, right?" Jo asks

"Yes," Jin replies.

"but it wasn't when we arrived together?" Jo inquires.

"apparently not." Jin shakes his head in frustration.

"where their lights in the mil?" Jo sputters.

"I think so?" Jin is unsure.

"and where was the light coming from?"

"…" Jin has no answer, the place was illuminated, but he can't recall seeing any lamps or lights of any kind. Was he not paying attention? Or were there merely none to be seen?

Jo notices the hesitation, "then you saw the same thing I did." Jo goes on, "do you know what I think?" the question is rhetorical, "I think we have both been drugged, and one or both of use are hallucinating right now."

"Which one of us?" Jin asks

Jo replies, "can you solve the problem of hard-solipsism?"

Jin shakes his head as he thinks, "all reality must be run through the filter of experience. If the brain is articulate matter, then thoughts, feelings, and memories are chemical reactions that can be manipulated with sufficiently advanced technology. With this problem in existence, it becomes impossible to rule out the possibility of reality itself being altered artificially. This hypothetical stretched out to its logical most extreme would mean that all of reality could be a fails memory. This being understood, for evidence to be considered evident, we must assume that we are in a shared experience, and the world we are in, even if it is a simulated word, must have rules that are a constant."

Jo nods approvingly, "you and I are going to go see Dr. Tenzuma. I need to know if what I just saw was real or not."

Jin looks to his father, "what did you see?"

Jo fails to reply.

May 11th, 9:10 pm

Takashi walks up and down the length of his office, a fist full of papers in hand. He reads over a medical chart, then shuffles backward several pages comparing it to another. After staring blankly at the page for some time, he nods to himself.

Takashi reaches into his coat pocket, pulling out a cigarette.

The doctor falls into his chair then picks up the phone calling down to the records office. The call is short and to the point "Moto," he questions as the other line gets picked up "can you run a scan of the town records, I need to know when the last time anyone in Chīsana-Mura was treated for Kato disease."

With that call out of the way, he changes over lines to call another department. He postponed this action when there is a knock at his office door. Shazuki Tenzuma walks in, she sets a folder on the desk. Takashi picks it up; he opens the folder examining it "Dr. Tenzuma. I want a blood test done on everyone that passes through that door starting tomorrow."

Tenzuma tips her head questioningly, "that is somewhat untraditional. Does that include our staff?"

Takashi nods, "everyone." He starts to roll up the sleeve of his coat. "you can start with me."

"and what is it that we are testing for?" Shazuki asks

"Trypanosoma."

Shazuki repeats, "Trypanosoma?"

Tsu leans back in his chair and waves one hand dynamically "think about it like a contagion, a residual left behind by bug bites."

Tenzuma clarifies, "we are looking for saliva?"

Takashi nods "with a potentially very dangers combination of enzymes in it."

"As you wish, doctor." Tenzuma expresses, "but this could be costly to us in the long term."

"we will let someone working in the office deal with that." Tsu jokes.

The radio on the desk clicks on "Dr. Tsu, Dr. Lin is on line six."

Tenzuma dismisses herself to gather her tools.

Takashi picks up the phone, "Chīsana Mura first Medical, Dr. Tsu speaking…"

Lichi Lin does not let Takashi finish introducing himself before she starts to talk, "Dr. Tsu, the sample that you had sent to Watory was contaminated with an irradiated macro-viral substance that is self-replicating and mutagenic. I advise that you contain or destroy any remaining samples at once."

"Say again." Takashi request

"you have an uncontained super-virus in your lab. Contain it!"

Takashi drops the phone, he runs out of his office, tripping over a table on the way and bouncing off a wall as he dashes through the hospital hallways. Of all the things at can be in a lab, a contaminated specimen is one of the things you lest want laying around.

May 11th, 11:05pm

For the first night in many nights, the sky is clear, the air is crisp. Nekoba walks through the garden of the temple atop the hill. He turns his eyes to the sea, only to witness the unforeseeable. A cargo tanker as veered off course.

The massive steel ship is on fire as it barrels across the sea and into the mouth of the river. The 40-foot-tall goliath of a ship smashes through the three bridges that connect the east and west banks of the town. As it is partly pushed up onto land, it knocks over Reko Jet's house then inches its way ever so slowly upstream until it has fully beached and lodged itself within the wall that rests at the foot of the monastery.

Nekoba stares in disbelief for some time as he is looking down at the burning ship. People from all over town leave there houses to come and observe the disaster. Fireteams and EMT gather to search for the injured and to extinguish the flames spewing from the vessel.

The ship is the 'Chang-Shi'; this boat has been lost at sea for 70 years. No one is looking for it. The hall is melted from salt, the crew is long since dead. This can only be described as a ghost ship. What can possibly have pulled it up for the depths? How can it have run ashore, in this tiny town, up such a narrow river? A Scott or an Irishmen would call it devilry. The Buddhist can only call it the machinations of the Kami.

Stalwart men work through the night to contain the fire. Once the flames are vanquished, Nekoba gathers the monks to mount the ship in search of injured, a hopeless mission, but brave men will do what brave men must.

The remains of the crew of the Chan-Shi are found deep in the bowels of the ship. Gathered around the furnace, havening been brought low with blades and pistol in hand. Warriors, all of them, doing battle under the captions command. A horrifying evil having descended onto them. The water sucked from their vain, reduced to salt bathed skeletons.

A chattering fills the air. The buzzing of flies echoes definingly for only a split second before a voice from the shadow calls the darkness back into hiding. "Not that one. That one belongs to me." The ageless, sexless voice commands.

Tobi kneels alongside Nekoba, looking at one of the fallen men, "who are they?"

Nekoba studies the markings on one of the men's coats to the best of his abilities "China men. Mercenaries, if the pins on this man's coat are to be believed. The crew of the Chang-Shi had been slain by pirates. Then someone else slew the pirates."

Tomi takes a sword from one of the dead, playing with it, "who, or what do you think did this?"

Nekoba pushes up his glasses as he stands, "we will know soon enough, I fear." He looks to the three brothers, Tomi, Tami, and Tobi, "Run to fetch the constable. This will require much explaining." He looks down, "and we will need to dress the dead." As the monks leave Shinigami fades into this reality, she sits with her legs folded, her umbrella pulled in front of her face, "I think 'thanks' are in order."

Nekoba looks up at the phantom, "and what am I thanking you for?"

"I have chosen not to let you die today." The monster explains,

"instead you have killed these men?" Nekoba question "and leveled a mile worth of our village?" Nekoba holds out his arms, questioningly, "what has happened that has called this wraith onto us?"

"my children have been misbehaving, nothing more." The ghost explains, "Nekoba, you assume that evil actions serve an evil propose. It doesn't. It is nothing more than the nature of the universe, the nature of god. All things crumble to ashes, all things burn. Until such time that there is simply nothing left. At which point, even the mightiest reach their arms into the heavens and wait to be reaped. Then I will harvest them too."

Nekoba squints, "and still you feel the need to play games? How strange that a beast with no need for space or time still has a need to entertain itself. I would have imagined that a thing like you seem to be would be above such triviality."

"Nekoba," the spirit calls "once again, you stand at the crevasse. A choice soon, you will be asked to make. Are you sure you feel no fear?"

"if you wished to claim my soul, then there is nothing I can do to stop you. I could try to outrun you with tonics and herbs, but in the end, I will still be wallowing on the floor, clenching my chest, struggling to take my last breath. There is no need to fear the reaper. I only hope that when I die, the prosses is expeditious."

The phantom kicks its legs and leans forward hugging its stomach as if it thought it was a girl leaning in awaiting the ending of a bedtime story "Setkura, what if I told you it doesn't need to end that way?"

"I would ask, what other options are there?" the monk replies

"what if you could discard that weak, sickly skin and go back in time instead?"

There is a long pause as Nekoba thinks "… I would be interested, I would also want to know what is the price?"

The skeleton laughs a soft laugh.

Chapter 5: Ten day remaining

May 12th, 1:10 am

Jo and Jin sit in the lab, hours have passed, the clock ticks slowly. Jin has fallen asleep, Jo has his arms crossed watching the time roll by. A scream fills the air, a siren howl. The sound of metal clatters. Jo jumps to his feet. Jin shakes himself awake. Jo runs off, chasing the sound.

Leta has awoken, she has pulled the sensors off of her body and torn off her clothes. As Jo comes into sight, Leta has punched out a nurse. The young girl barks and snarls like a wild animal. Dr. Tenzuma and two other lab assistants have gathered around to try to subdue the mad girl.

One of the lab aid grabs Leta to try to pull her to the ground, Leta finds the pin in his pocket, pulls it out and stabs at him. The assistance takes the shot to the collar bone and staggers away. Leta howls as she looks at her mother. Arms outstretched, mouth open Leta, runs at her mother bellowing.

Dr. Tenzuma tries to talk to her girl, pleads with her to calm down. Leta tackles Shazuki. As Leta brings her head down to bite at her mother, Shazuki pulls an arm across her face defensively. The two roll around on the ground, struggling. Leta wraps her jaws around Shazuki's arm, biting into it savagely.

Jin chases after his father arriving just in time to witness Jo grabbing the nude, lunatic Leta. Jo grabs Leta from behind wrapping his for arm under one arm, and across her neck, he braces with his other arm in a sleeper hold.

For only a few more seconds, Leta fights. Her eyes turn red, her head falls back. Leta collapses in Jo's arm. Other Doctors and nurses swarm into the hallway to care for those that had been assaulted. Jin and his father share a discomforted gaze.

May 12th, 4:20am

Oso and Reko have been walking through the night. Around midnight they had set up a small fire and lead out sleeping bags. The two had walk most of the way around the mountain and found a deep gorge that a river runs into and seems to be emptying into an underground waterway. It is there that the men stopped to rest.

The two look over their map, it is only a few more miles to the old town, if they were to follow the path up the mountain. From this side, it is a much shorter walk then it would have been leaving from the church to get there. The main road is only a half dozen miles the other way. But if they keep going the direction they were facing, they are halfway to the city right now.

But their rest is far from restful. The sounds of shouting in the forest wake them, quickly they spot the glow of flames. Off-road vehicles have driven past here, several dozen men dressed in hazard gear are stomping around in the forest armed with napalm throwers. Oso and Reko sneak in close.

Jet asks, "Any idea who these guys are?"

Oso nods as he whispers, "NDF troopers."

"The National Defense Force?" Jet clarifies.

"The Emperor's own." Oso starts to sneak back to camp.

"what are they doing?" Jet asks

"I don't want to know." Oso explains, "it is none of our concern, let's just give them space."

But Oso has hardly had time to turn around before a voice shouts out to them. The NDF troops must have spotted them before Oso and Jet had. A rifleman stands behind Oso, his gun high and ready. "YOU HAVE ENTERED A RESTRICTED AREA!" the footman commands, "IDENTIFY!"

Reko comments, "you don't look like one of the Ichishin-Magami monks to me. This is still part of Shika woods, the monks own this land." Reko moves a hand onto his belt, laying it to rest on his tool pouch. Several more men in hazard gear start to make their way over to see what is transpiring.

Oso puts his hands up "Major Oso Hanzo, NDF, homeland division, 119th regiment, 1971-1994. Retired with honors! Reserves office 1994-1999, Statis, inactive."

The soldier lowers his weapon, "Sir. Tell the baboon to keep his hands where we can see them and come with me. Sir."

Reko looks to Hanzo, "Sir?"

Hanzo comments, "you know that I served in the NDF."

Reko comments, "I didn't know that you were a major."

Reko and Hanzo are led down the hill and up the road to a temporary encampment. They are pushed into the command tent. A man in a decorated army uniform sits and waits for them. Hanzo knows this man on sight. "Captain Izu"

Izu pulls a bottle of wine out of his backpack and sets it on the table in front of him "It has been some time since we have seen each other major. Lieutenant Colonel now. When you left. They gave me your job."

Oso nods along. "I see."

Izu grabs a cup from his knapsack "care of a cup, Major?"

Oso shakes his head, "I don't drink."

Izu looks up, confused. "Well, that is a change. I seem to recall you were a fan of imports when you and I were stationed together."

Reko clears his throat, "Izu-son, have you seen anyone else out this way?"

Izu takes a drink then leans back in his chair, looking up. "what do you mean?"

Oso cuts in, "Ri is dead."

Izu squints as he leans forward, staring as Oso. "the baby?"

Oso nods. He then turns his back to bite onto one of his hands, overtaken by sadness and anger. Reko elaborates, "poison. Hanzo thinks the killer is hiding in the woods. That is why we came out here."

Izu expresses, "I am sorry to hear that. I never got married, never had any kids that I know of… but I can imagen…"

Hanzo steels his nerves, "Izu, what are you doing out here?"

Izu takes a labored breath, "I am not permitted to say."

Hanzo adds, "we are on privet property, are we not?"

Izu nods "this is still part of Shika, yes. But it is unavoidable that we are here."

"And why is that?" Oso asks.

Izu adds, "I am not permitted to say. Come on, Major, you remember how this game is played."

Oso shakes his head "you are going to make me do this?"

Izu repeats, "I am not permitted to say."

Oso lets out an annoyed hiss. "If I were to ask, what could bring someone like you. Out to a location similar to this one, what might you tell me?"

Izu leans onto his desk and folds his hands "under that hypothetical. I may explain to you how a piece of cargo that could have some value might have been lost in transport. If that were to happen, someone like me could be asked to go to a place like this to attempt to locate the supposed lost item."

Hanzo asks for more information, "and why might someone like you bring men with napalm guns with you to recover lost cargo?"

Izu evades. "if, somehow, the information would have been made available to our hypothetical person. to the effect of, that the lost cargo could somehow become active. In some way, and may attempt to resist containment. Maybe it would become required that the destruction of the lost object would be preferable to the lost object being allowed to leave the island. Under that impression, I may feel it wise to bring such weapons."

Reko steps forth, "Active? What does active mean?"

Izu shakes his head "What are you saying? I didn't say anything to the alike."

Oso cuts in, "And what sort of contained object might you be describing, hypothetically?"

"What sort of object would I fear escaping the island?" Izu explains, "I biological, chemical, or radioactive weapon. One that may, per se, have the ability to influence people in an undetectable way. One that could possibly be reprogramed to convince someone to bring harm to themselves."

Izu points over to Reko, "Major, I am sorry about what has happened. I want to offer you my condolences. But I need to ask you to go home. Leave things in the hands of the NDF. And if he has family living in town. Tell them to go to Tokyo at once. Things could start getting complicated very quickly."

"and what about me?" Oso asks.

"Keep your eyes on the sky, things are going to get interesting." Izu leans back in his chair, finishing his drink "I will have one of my men bring you back to the county road. You will need to walk the rest of the way."

May 12th, 7:45am

Jo is sent back to work. Takashi had been acting strange when he arrived at the office. Still, given what Jo learned once reading the morning reports, it is understandable. Jo Kogotana falls back into his chair at his office. He is tired, he is starting to shake, he needs to eat something soon, or he is going to get sick. He picks up the phone off of his desk, calling the operator.

Once the phone is picked up, Jo talks fast, wanting to get this over with as soon as he can "Patch me through to the 'Maritime Office of Busan' please."

The voice on the other side of the line replies, "this service has been suspended."

"then put me through to the secretary of the navy in Beijing," Jo request.

The voice repeats, "this service has been suspended."

Jo looks confused as he looks out the window of his office, "can you give me Yokosuka, Kanto?"

Once more, "This service has been suspended."

"wait, do you mean my service has been suspended?" Jo whispers, "do you know who I am!" Jo shouts, "I am the constable of Chīsana-Mura!"

"This service has been…"

Jo shouts over the voice, "I want to talk to the secretary of the emperor!"

The phone goes dead. Jo growls in anger, he picks the phone up and brings it overhead, threating to smash the worthless thing to pieces on the corner of his desk before he is interrupted by the phone starting to ring.

Jo takes a breath then picks up calmly. "Constable Kogotana speaking, how may I be of service."

The voice on the line this time is a deep, sexual, woman's voice. "Constable, you are in danger. But I want you to know that Watory still stands with you. We will do everything in our power to protect you and Chisana-Mura."

"What? Who are you?" Jo orders.

"Call me 'L.'" the woman request.

"what do you mean by danger?" Jo asks

"The National Defense Force is currently in Shika woods, they are preforming a slash-and-burn mission. But my sources tell me that they will not stop there."

"Slash-and-burn? Why? What are they looking for?" Jo calls out gruffly.

'L' explains, "I intend to find out. In the meantime, keep people safe, keep them alive. I will do what I can to help you from this side..."

The phone gets cut off again. Jo shouts, "Hello? 'L'? can you still hear me?"

May 12th, 9:00 am

Shazuki Tenzuma lays on a lab table. Her arm newly stitched and bandaged. Takashi Tsu lights a cigarette as he sits with her. He places a tray from the cafeteria on the end table for her. Takashi explains, "I have been looking over the lab test as they have been coming in."

Shazuki sits up and uncovers her breakfast, it is a grilled fish served with a side of noodles and chopped greens "anything interesting?"

Takashi lays down across Shazuki's legs and folds his arms behind his head as he looks to the ceiling fan watching it spin. "Everyone in town has been exposed to our mystery drug. Most of us in scant amounts. Leta, on the other hand, is at the same level as Ri was when he died…"

Shazuki grunts, "how has everyone tested been exposed?"

Takashi stretches, he takes a long drag off his smoke then drops his arms over the sides of the bed. "I would start with, 'how was anyone'?"

Shazuki changes the topic, "how is Leta?"

Takashi explains, "I have moved her up to the fourth floor. I am dedicating the south wing to the treatment of this 'kissing disease.'"

"Is that what we are going to call it when we make our report to the world health organization?" Tenzuma tries to act calm.

"I thought maybe we could call it Hanzo's disease." There is a momentary pause "Saliva seems to be the link. The kissing disease seems to nest in the oral glands. Mouth to mouth contact will, of course, allow the bacteria to spread. But, so will any other contact with saliva, even indirect. There is a threshold in place, it looks like. You don't get sick right away." Takashi sits up to look at Tenzuma. "Leta, she is past that threshold. She is at risk of suffering MOF at any time. You aren't far behind."

"Treatment options?" Tenzuma asks.

"A blood transfusion bought Ri a day. The bloodstream itself is polluted, maybe the marrow even. Which would prevent the blood from recycling naturally. The liver doesn't seem to recognize the contaminant, nor do white blood cells. This thing, it can hide from the body's innate defenses…" Takashi melts forward, resting his arms on his legs as he is thinking. He takes another hit off of his cigarette.

"how much clean blood do we have in stalk?" Tenzuma asks.

"Not enough," Tsu explains.

Tenzuma asks. "radiation?"

"We could try." Takashi shrugs, "the worst thing that could happen is…"

Tenzuma adds, "I am aware of the risks. I want Leta to be treated immediately."

Takashi stands up "I was expecting a shipment today, it is late. I am going to call the dispatch…" Takashi walks out of the room, his head down. He is in pain, but he is a man that knows how to hide his feelings well. Tenzuma's calm demeanor making it all the easier.

As Takashi walks down the hall, he turns on one of the overheads speakers. "Ready radiology lab seven. Repeat, ready radiology lab seven." Takashi stops at his office on his way down to the labs to make a phone call. The life of a doctor is never one of relaxation. Every moment of every day almost is consumed with: meetings, phone calls, letters, charts, and operations.

Takashi picks up the phone and calls the delivery company that works for him... no diel tone, no signal at all. The doctor reaches into his pocket, pulling out his personal phone, no signal. "that is concerning... "he mumbles. Tsu sticks his head out the door looking side to side. he points and waves at one of the nurses, "Arnaldo." He calls over.

A taller, skinny looking boy runs over "Yes, Tsu-son," he bows.

"do you have your phone with you?" Takashi asks.

"Sir, we are not supposed to have our phones with us when we are on this floor," Arnaldo explains.

Takashi repeats. "Arnaldo, do you have your phone with you?"

He ducks his head in shame, "yes."

Takashi holds out a hand, "give."

Arnaldo hands his phone over, Takashi looks at it and nods "you don't have a signal…" Takashi hands his phone back. "take a moment if you can, see if any of the phones on the rest of the floor work."

Arnaldo looks down at his phone as he takes it back "when did I…" he trails off into babble.

May 12th, 9:10 am

Nekoba takes a hammer form the tool room on the far side of the garden. He walks briskly to the shed that was the last elder monk's room. He looks side to side to see to it he is alone than with a swing of the knocks the doorknob off the door.

Nekoba whispers to himself, "the elder order the records from the old town burned. Why? What did he know?"

The room of the elder has been preserved. Nothing touched, nothing moved for fifteen years. The room looks strange for the office of a monk. A star map on one wall, a telescope, a dozen books lay open. A display case filled with bug dipped in wax to protect them from the passage of time.

A lurid sense lingers in the room, old and evil power. An unsettling smell. As Nekoba shuts the door, he spots a statue hidden from view. Six-and-a-half feet tall, moth wings that stretch eight feet filling most of the room. The face and body of a woman, but with four extra arms. And the eyes of the statue, dead and hallow. The eyes eat up half the surface area of the head. Sexual and deadly, the figure is carved with stunningly smooth features.

Nekoba jumps and gasps as he sees the hauntingly horrible statue. Once he has caught his breath after the shock of the almost human beast. Nekoba walks around the room, searching the chest and the cupboards. A stack of papers sits in a cabinet, eldritch drawings, a human head with a frog-like tongue hanging out of it, and teeth growing from a mass of flesh.

Madding writings, talk of a 'thing from the stars.' Waking dreams. A hungry demon. A phrase repeated time and time again, "Baptize She with fire." Nekoba reads the sentence aloud. "She?" he questions.

Nekoba turns the page frantically, looking form meaning behind the words. "At 8pm She crawled from the well..." he whispers as he finds another scribbled phrase. "She kissed my heart." And "Sleep will never come." Then "I wash my hair in wine, with a strike of a match..."

The door of the room is kicked in, Tomi stands in the doorway, a kali stick in hand. Nekoba looks up and starts to asks. "what is this?"

But Tomi does not let him finish the inquiry. The muscular young man grunts in zealous anger, he stomps forward and pulls back the hand with the stick and strikes Nekoba in deviant anger. Nekoba falls onto his side, bleeding. A single strike knocking him out.

May 12th, 12:45pm

Odette, Reje, and Jin meet at the park to have lunch, Jin looks between his friends "so, anyone want to talk about yesterday?"

Odette shakes her head, "not so much."

Reje nods, "same."

Jin grunts, "well, I do."

Odette speaks up, "where did you go last night?"

Jin explains, "my dad and I spent the night at the hospital."

Reje speaks up, "did you happen to see "Leta, or my mom?"

Jin nods, "you can say that." The three pass around a box of fish fries. "Leta flipped out and went on a rampage in the middle of the night. Took four men to hold her down."

Reje can do nothing but nod, "I had no idea my sister had that sort of…"

Odette cuts Reje off "she can't possibly, that is some otherworldly shit. What does she weigh in at? About 88lbs?"

Reje nods, "something like that."

Odette looks to Jin, "did you happen to take a head-count in homeroom?"

Jin nods "yep. Only seventeen people in my class made it today."

Odette calls out "twenty-two."

Reje adds, "nine."

"if those numbers area constant across all classes, that would mean that more then half the school is out sick." Jin extrapolates

"or dead," Reje adds

Jin places a hand on Reje's back "sorry. I know you and Ri…"

Reje shakes his head, "I wasn't the one that wanted to marry him."

Odette looks between her friends, "so, are we still all for Masumo is a monster?" Jin and Reje nods. "so, then what do we do about it?"

Reje pulls back his coat showing off the wakizashi hidden therein. "maybe violence would work?"

Jin looks down, "you aren't supposed to have that on school property."

Odette leans in, "you have a katana?"

Reje shakes his head "it is only a wakizashi. Ri gave it to me on my birthday."

Odette reaches over to slap Jin on the arm. Odette points across the way. "what is going on over there?"

The three kids all turn to look to the school.

Jo approaches the school in his car, a dozen other officers on bicycles close behind as well as a half dozen on foot are approaching from the park.

The kids stand up and run down to the school. The cops have been stopped by the school's locked gate. Apparently, someone saw them coming and tripped the security alarm.

As the cops wait at the gate, Ms. Machohero and Dean Gogiro come to the entrance to meet the police. Jo pulls out his badge and holds it up for the Dean to see as he walks over to them. "Is there something I can do for you officers?" he looks back and forth intimidated by the nearly two dozen armed men.

Jo explains, "I would like to barrow your satellite array."

Gogiro explains, "that will be difficult, officer."

Jo puts away his badge. "why would that be?"

Gogiro explains, "the satellite array we have was assembled in 1970. It is not quite as compact as the ones they have in the city. Now may I ask why you felt the need to come here in person?" he coughs, "and armed I might add?"

Jo places a hand on the gate to lean on it. Machohero steps between the Dean and the constable. "you may or may not have taken notice of this, but our town has been placed under quarantine. I have a friend on the outside that is trying to get us some more information. But communication has been restricted. Tell me Dean, does the name Watory mean anything to you?"

Machohero shakes her head, "no, now I think it is time for you to take a walk, Kogotana-son." She sneers

Gogiro holds up a hand calling Machohero back, "did you say Watory?" Gogiro pushes Machohero aside to get up to the gate, "where did you hear that name?"

Jo reaches into his coat pockets searching for something hidden therein "two places, first, my nephew Ichi worked for them before his accident." He finds an envelope. He holds it out in front of himself "Secondly, they sent me a letter telling me to come here if the phones went dead and to talk to you about the satellite array."

Shaking Gogiro request, "please open the letter, let me see the lower right-hand corner."

Jo unfolds the page and turns it to face Gogiro. Gogiro places his hands on his head, his eyes bulging out as he reads, he is on the edge of panic. "Machohero, unlock the gate, then go to the kitchen, get me a bottle of lemon concentrate, and a lighter."

Matchohero looks to the Dean, "say again, sir…"

Gogiro shouts, "do it now, then meet us at the astrology lab!"

Odette whispers with her friends, "is our principle experiencing a psychotic episode?"

Reje whispers back, "it sure looks that way."

Jin whispers as well, "what is on that paper that is upsetting him so much?"

May 12th, 1:30 pm

Gogiro, Machohero, Jo, and the kids: Jin, Odette, and Reje are all lead into the astrometric lab. A station is set up for them to work at. The police fan out around the school, watching and waiting for the boss to come back.

Gogiro sets up a large bowl and fills it with lemon juice. He takes the letter from Jo and sets it into the tub to soak. Odette leans into her friends to whisper with them. "what is going on, what are they doing?"

Jin folds his arms as he is watching in amusement "did you notice the paper, the odd color of it?" Odette shakes her head, Jin explains, "this is some old-world cop stuff, I saw it in one of my dad's books. That paper was woven, not a pressed one."

"This was used by government officials around 1800. This paper would be written with two types of ink. One an alkali ink the other an acrylic. You would write with the alkali first then write over it with the acrylic. This would hide the message. The page would be marked with an assortment of markers to tell the person receiving the note of what to look for. The paper would need to be dipped in acid then heated in a kiln. This would burn off the fake message leaving behind the real one if you did it right."

Reje asks, "so, why isn't this done anymore?"

"the precaution was to protect messengers from bandits. With radios now being cheap and easy to make, subterfuge like this is considered anachronistic." Jin smiles; he loves the strangeness of this all.

Gogiro takes a lighter to the underside of the page. Images start to appear on the page as the flames heat the paper.

Gogiro speaks up "three symbols: phonomancy, linguistics, arithmetic. The message is going to be coded, three parts."

A paint stripper is plugged in, the page is heated slowly. Words start to burn into the page. Gogiro gasps as he looks at the page. "what is this, what language is this written in?"

Jo stands over Gogiro, he looks at the page then back up "English."

Gogiro turns to face the constable with a shocked look "I can't read English? Can you read English?"

Jo looks to Jin, Reje raises one hand, "I can read English."

Jin looks to his friend, "you can?"

Reje nods as he approaches, "I had to learn English; all the best basketball games are played by American teams." Reje picks up the paper to see what he can. As he looks at it, he reads aloud. "Tsu, when you go to see the Queen, leave the tea. Once you are there, we can divide the pie. Go there if you need to talk around the hour. In the mirror,

you will see what you need. Signed "L.""
Reje shrugs, "that is it."

Jo picks up a pin to start to write down what Reje said: "it is a puzzle."

"it is a child's game as far as Watory is concerned." Gogiro explains, he looks at the note "Tsu without the tea... T is Su. Su divided by Pie, Pi... 3.141592653589793. The numerical; value of the word Su is 40. So, 40 divided by Pi is 12.73. Tune the satellite reservoir to 37.21Hurtz." Gogiro calls over to Machohero.

May 12th, 2:15 pm

It takes some time to get the satellite realigned. The room is large but tightly packed. Computer equipment that is archaic in nature stretches around the room. One-click at a time Jo and Gogiro search from the frequency in question. Only once the diel is perfectly in place does a voice come over the wire.

It is the voice of L that comes over the line "Allow me to apologies for making this complicated. You must understand that I am being followed, and this is the safest avenue that was left available to me." There is a moment of hesitation, "Mr. Kogotana, I trust that Dean Gogiro is with you?"

Jo picks up the microphone, "He is."

"and who else is in the room at the moment?"

Jo explains, "Usagi Mochohero is here as are a hand full of students, Odette Tsu, Reje Tenzuma and my son Jin Kogotana."

"are your enforcers in place protecting the school?" L asks next.

"They are," Jo explains.

Gogiro cuts in, "are you L, from Watory?"

L confirms, "you may call me L."

Gogiro takes the microphone from Jo. "can you confirm this?"

"Fine, asks Mochohero if she lost 5000Y playing POCHINKO last week Friday." Jo and Gogiro turn to look at Machohero; Machohero nods with a shocked look on her face. "or you can ask

Odette Tsu if she has the game 'Gems of War' installed on her phone. Or Gogiro, check your pockets and tell me, do you have three one-hundred-yen bills and fifty-yen coins in your vest pocket? If I am right about all of these things, that should demonstrate that I am from Watory."

Jo takes the microphone back, "L, how do you know these things?"

L explains, "when you have friends like mine, you would be surprised how much you can learn."

Jo orders, "what do you know about our situation?"

"My channels are being restricted; I am having some trouble procuring reliable data. But I am happy to help you as much as I can..." L begins

Gogiro interrupts, "why?"

L addresses, "Why help you?" she clarifies, "simple enough because I want to see the bad guys in jail, not dead. a corrupt man in prison today, and he may not want to talk, but give it time, and soon, they will tell you about anything you ask."

Jo whispers, "Please continue, L."

"the Hajoji company owns some amount of land near you. They were excavating the land. According to the information I have uncovered. A mineral was found of a yet undiscovered nature. It seemed to be conductive. Pulsating with energy not so unlike 235-U. It burned slowly, had a high energy yield. According to one report, a handful of men exposed to this radiation experienced sudden cell disfigurement. These men turned aggrieve, disorderly. It required the efforts of five men to subdue them. it seems that the NDF thinks that this radiation is present in the ground around you, and they are hoping to remove all traces of it."

"And what is it that you require from us?" Jo asks.

"first and foremost, maintain order. Things are going to get frightening, and when they do, you, Kogotana-son, will be the person everyone looks to for advice. Tell me, do you and your men have short-wave radios?" L inquires.

Jo explains, "I upgraded to satellite radios a year or two ago. I think I still have the short-bands in my storage locker."

"Get them, have your men use them. Work in shifts. Keep on the move. Keep your radios on a rotating frequency for your own protection. You are going to need to do a public address. Let people know that the road out of town is blockaded and that there will be no contact coming in from the outside for an undisclosed amount of time. You are the law. So long as people follow you, most of you will still be alive at years end." L explains.

"This will be challenging..." Jo whispers.

L hears him, "If it were simple, I would have put my trust in someone else." L continues, "do you know where Takashi Tsu is?"

"Not at the moment. But most days around this time, he is at home." Jo retorts.

"stay close to Tsu. He is stronger than you think when the chip hit the table, he will fight for you."

Gogiro asks, "if anyone in town become sick from this radiation, will Takashi be able to treat them?"

"That is unclear," L explains

May 12th, 4:00pm

Oso and Reko are brought home after being taken to a military facility to be debriefed. They are each issued a gag order. A mile from town, the two are pushed out of the truck they were in. As they round the bend, it is clear something odd had transpired in the time that they were away. Several bridges are missing, Reko's house has been leveled, one wall of the temple yard has been knocked down. What looks like a cargo ship is blocking the river rerouting it thought the farm district.

Reko whispers to Oso, "where is my house?"

Oso points to the temple, "what happened at the church?" Oso slaps his friend on the back. "Let's go see Nekoba; he tends to be a man that knows things."

A look of crushing defeat on his face, Reko nods and follows Oso as he runs to the church.

A Pa-kua is drawn on the temple gate, and the door is barred. There is a wagon out front, the bodies of a dozen dead are packed inside awaiting the monks to bring in the dead to be dressed for their last rights. Reko looks disturbed as he walks around the temple taking in the strangeness of it all.

Reko runs a hand up the door feeling around the seal drawn on the door. "what is this?"

Oso looks it over "It is a Taoist magic seal. An anti-evil talisman that is meant to bind the dead to the ground. "Oso shakes the door and shouts, "Nekoba!" he calls a second-time "Nekoba, let us in!" but no one comes to the door.

Reko asks, "do you remember the last time the monks locked the gates?" Oso shakes his head "because I don't remember. Ichishin-Magami never locks the doors."

May 12th, 6:30 pm

Nekoba is pulled from the river, he is dragged onto the sands, his rob has been taken from him. His glasses are broken, as is his nose. The monks were not content to sham him; they wanted to embarrass him. It would seem the monks of Ichishin-Magami have little tolerance for people braking their taboos. After stripping and beating the young parish, they throw him from the walls of the church into the river below without ever saying a word.

"Mr. Nekoba, Mr. Nekoba!" Masumo shakes the monk, "please tell me you are alive!"

Nekoba coughs and whispers, "I am not dead yet."

Masumo leans over Nekoba "what did you say?"

He repeats, "I am not dead yet."

Masumo hugs Nekoba. "what happened? How did you get down here?" Masumo helps Nekoba to his feet, the tiny girl leads the priest back to the mil.

"It would seem that I offended my host," Nekoba explains. "I have a feeling I may have lost my job."

"boy, when you make a mistake, you make a big one, don't you?" the girl jokes. "My dad has some clothes that might fit you. Nothing as nice as that cloak you had on the other day, but it is better than walking around naked."

When they arrive at the mil, an alien light seems to shine from the windows of the structure. The door opens to reveal a greenhouse inside. Rose vines cover all the load barring supports. Shrubberies and bushes of an exotic nature fill every corner. Blue-black tulips draw lines leading around the greenhouse and call attention to the most magnificent of the vegetation.

Mr. Masumo is trimming the hedges as Eva walks in. Eva calls over, "Dad, Nekoba-son is hurt!"

The old man walks over "ok, go take a set over there," he points for Nekoba to take a set "let us see how bad you look."

Eva skips away, calling, "I am going to go get some clothes for him."

Mr. Mosumo grabs Nekoba by the cheeks and turns his head side to side, looking at him hard "you are a lucky kid if whoever hit you hit an inch higher, you would have lost an eye." He reaches over to pluck a leaf from one of the nearby flowers, "suck on his, it will make you numb, won't stop your bleeding, but at least you won't notice."

Nekoba leans backward as he looks at Mr. Masumo, "it would appear that some times the dead do come back."

"what are you talking about?" the grizzled man asks.

"you are Sirosanto," Nekoba explains.

"that is what the chief thought also." Mr. Masumo laughs, "maybe I do look like him after all."

"are you a Shinigami?" Nekoba asks.

"and here I thought I heard someone say you are an atheist." Mr. Masumo forces

Nekoba to open his mouth "you have good teeth, don't see any bleeding or swelling around in here. Take a bath and drink some tea, and I would bet you will still be alive come sun up."

Nekoba elaborates, "I wouldn't use the word atheist to describe myself; I think apistevist would be more conclusive. Or misotheist."

Mr. Masumo grunts, "I am afraid my Greek isn't so good anymore, you are going to need to elaborate."

Nekoba nods, "an Apistevist is someone that rejects 'faith' as a resin for belief, belief is a matter of conviction and conviction is a continuance of being convinced. Knowledge is a subset of belief. Therefore if one wishes to believe something, they should first be able to demonstrate the truth of their claims. A misotheist is someone that believes powers is a corrupting force and that absolute power would corrupt absolutely. So, by extinction, any creature that would declare itself a god would almost beyond doubt be evil. Anyone wishing for worship evidently isn't worthy of it. as anyone worthy of worship would not want it."

Mr. Masumo hums, "I bet you were a philosopher in your last life." He sits down himself, "you know, She likes you…"

Eva comes running across the room, holding up a suit, it is simple, black with a gray undergown. "I found one."

Mr. Masumo looks back. "I haven't seen that suit in 60 something years. Where did you dig that out of?"

"It was in the same box as this." Eva shows off a small glass box with a dueling pistol in it.

Mr. Masumo hands over the suit for Nekoba, "you can have this. I bet it would look good on an old soul like you, take the gun too, it completes the look."

Once dressed, Nekoba bows, "you are too kind."

May 12th, 7:45pm

Dr. Tenzuma has been sitting in a hospital bed all day, she has been sedated and ordered off of work. She stands up and walks across the room to take her med-chart off the wall. She whispers to herself as she looks over it. "Acidity 3.64?" she turns her eyes up thinking. "is Takashi writing in code?"

Tenzuma returns to bed. She lays down and taps the call button on the side of the bed. Quickly she is answered by one of the nurses. Tenzuma knows most of the staff, this nurse is no exception "Iwata." Tenzuma greats her.

"do you need help, Doctor?" the older women ask.

"Have you seen Leta in the last few hours?" Tenzuma inquires.

"yes." Iwata nods.

"How would you describe her condition?" Tenzuma pushes.

"radiation seldom show results after only one treatment," Iwata explains.

"Nurse, I would like you to write me a prescription for 500mg of D-38." Tenzuma orders.

"I can't..." Iwata starts

Tenzuma cuts her off "...Then I require a work 'release' form."

"no, you are not healthy enough to return to work," Iwata explains.

"Nurse, we have all field 'quality of life' releases," Tenzuma explains

"you suffered a concoction and laceration; you are not actively dying of osteogenesis-imperfecta. I am not going to falsify medical records." Iwata protest.

"then find me someone that will!"

Chapter 6: Nine day remaining

May 13th, 6:15 am

Odette was off to an early start. She was showered and shaved by 5:30, with her parents out of town and her uncle working unpredictable hours she has become exceptionally self-reliant. Today is a half-day of school, she thought this would be the best time this week to walk down to the market and restock her supply of noodles and broth.

But why walk alone if you don't have to? She walks across the park stopping at Reje's house. Their car is nowhere to be seen, but that is hardly a surprise. Dr. Tenzuma is no less dedicated to her work then Takashi. Odette bends down to pick up the mail that had been haphazardly thrown on the front step.

From there, Odette knocks on the door and calls in "Mr. Tenzuma! Are you up?" Reje's dad is an Otaku, a stay-at-home dad that fancies himself as a visionary artist. Yes, he has worked on some comic books over the years, and was invited to consult on a movie once upon a time, but 'Big and

Important' would be being a little generous.

After a minute of waiting, Odette yells again, "Mr. Tenzuma! I am heading to the store; do you need anything?" she remains another few seconds, "well, what the hell." She mumbles. She walks around the back of the house to Reje's bedroom.

The window is open, the blinds are missing. "well that typically isn't a good thing." Odette whispers to herself. "I swear, Reje, if I climb in this window and find you dead, I am going to kick your ass." Odette jumps through the window. The room is in tatters, but that is not unexpected.

What is unexpected, on the other hand, is Reje's sword snapped in half lying on his bed. Odette freezes as she spots the blade on the bed. "ok, how does that happen?"

Odette arms herself with the flashlight she keeps hidden in the back of her dress. She calls out, "Reje! Mr. Tenzuma!" she starts to walk around the house. She searches Leta's room, the bathroom, then makes her way down the steps to the master bedroom and the kitchen.

Overturned chairs and a tipped over refrigerator are telltale signs that something has gone wrong

Odette sneaks out of the house. Whatever has happened is beyond her. It is time to bring in the constable to look around. At the door, she bumps into Masumo, her umbrella draped over one shoulder to hold the rising sun at bay. The tiny girl tips her head with a smile, "Odette, I thought you lived on the other side of the street. I was looking for Tenzuma." Eva leans off to the side, trying to look around Odette.

Odette hides her flashlight; she looks around confused. "Reje isn't here."

Eva asks, "Then why are you here?"

Odette explains, "I was going to go shopping for them."

May 13th, 6:30 am

Jin approaches Oso's tea house. A stack of papers in hand, his father has asked Jin to assist him in delivering a notice to all the shop keeps of the new protocol for contacting the emergency services. In lack of any other leadership, Jo Kogotana has become the makeshift Shogun.

Starting May 14th, 6:pm will be lights out. Anyone seen on the streets will be arrested. The festival of drums being exempt. As Jin is approaching Oso's place, a monk is standing outside the shop, a bottle of paint in hand, seemingly drawing on the door.

Jin calls out, "Hey, what is all of this now?"

The monk looks to the boy, he doesn't say a word, he continues his work.

Jin approaches, "This isn't the temple." Jin places a hand on the monk's shoulder spinning the monk to face him. The monk grunts and pulls open his robe, brandishing the mace he has tied to his belt.

The door to Oso's shop opens; Reko Jet stands in the doorway. "something on your mind, gentlemen?"

The monk turns to look at Jet as he growls and places a hand on his weapon. Reko groans in return and places one hand on his hammer. The monk looks up, calculating his odds in hand to hand combat with the blacksmith. The monk does not press the point anymore, he instead takes a bow and walks away.

Jin looks up at Reko, "out and about early today?"

Reko moans, "I lost my house. Oso offered to let me stay with him until I can rebuild."

Jin pulls out one of the flyers "By orders of the chief constable, you are required to place this notice on display in your shop." Jin freezes for a moment, "Oso,... Hanzo-son is required to display this notice."

May 13th, 10:00 am

Dr. Tenzuma sits in the lab on the first floor, the window she has blinded, the door locked. She sweats profusely. Her head is down as she studies a blood sample, one arm bandaged and tied to her chest with a sling. Her hear only barely held back by a set of sticks she has woven into.

Tenzuma whispers to herself, "I was right, The bug is a sleeper. But, can be teased awake. It hides inside red blood cells. But what is the trigger?" Tenzuma leans back in her chair. "this is a job for a chemist, not a GP." She takes a deep breath and nearly screams in frustration before the door unlocks, she quickly sits up and composes herself.

Takashi opens the door and turns on the lights, a cigarette hanging from his lip "aren't you still on medical leave? I don't recall clearing you to clock back in."

Tenzuma explains, "I don't report to you, I report to CDCI, all the heads of staff do."

Takashi smiles, "yeah, have they been answering your calls?"

"No," Tenzuma explains.

"then that makes me the sitting director," Takashi adds.

"Can you please turn the light back off and put out that fig?" Tenzuma complains, "it is making me feel light-headed.

Takashi turns Tenzuma to face him. Takashi squints as he leans in, "your eyes are dilated in an unusual way…" Takashi leans side to side, looking at Tenzuma from different angles, "you know, people tell me all the time that doctors make bad house guests… or something like that." Takashi reaches into his pocket, pulling out his lighter, he plays with it as they talk, "How are you feeling?"

Tenzuma rubs her eyes, "I am feeling a burning sensation between my eyes." She takes a breath, trying to relax "I had a thought earlier. Do you think that a psychosomatic disorder can lead to physical dysfunction?"

Takashi spins his lighter in his hand as he leans over Tenzuma looking at her notes, "I wouldn't expect it to. Not unless the condition you are referring to is a symptom not…"

Tenzuma's vision becomes disoriented. She suffers from audio-exclusion for a few seconds. "Takashi…" she whispers.

Takashi looks over to Tenzuma. One of Shazuki's eyes bleeds; her eyelids pull back strangely, and her face twists into a smile. A voice speaks that only Tenzuma can perceive "Bring us Takashi." Tenzuma jumps from her chair, she growls like an angry tiger as she grabs Takashi pushing him back and dragging him into a wall.

Takashi lowers his head, protecting his neck, he presses his hands to Tenzuma's shoulders to hold her at bay. Her mouth drops open, and a tongue lined with teeth peeks out, like some form of evil fish the teeth wiggle as fins, a deep purple gel collects at the tip of her tongue.

Takashi is bent over backward, forced to lay on the lab table. In a desperate struggle, as a distraction, he flicks the flint on his lighter, this works to force Tenzuma to look away. When she does, Takashi grips one of the microscopes on the table and swings it like a hammer.

Tenzuma falls to the ground. She looks calm and relaxed as she lies on the ground, stunned. Takashi drips the microscope then pulls out his pack of cigarettes, he lights himself a fresh one and looks around the room. he picks up the phone and turns on the P.A. system "Service

Blue to microbiology, service blue to microbiology."

May 13th, 10:05am

Sakura Tomoji, who has been missing from school for the last two days, has returned. She was the first person to show up for homeroom. Having little else to do, she pulls out an art pad and a box of panicles. Sakura has an interest in surrealism style art. A few years ago, there was a revival of surrealism in the west. because of the interconnectivity of the world today, she had opportunities to view the newest and strangest of this.

Sakura, even though she is a girl, is uncomfortable with her femininity. If not for the school dress code, she would never wear skirts or modern bathing suits. They are to tight and reviling for her taste. Instead of dressing in the blue coat and white blouse that most of the girls her age dress in, she has gotten permission from the school to wear a white sweater over her uniform. It was custom made for her with the school emblem on the back.

She dyes her hair blue and wears it short. She cares around a Walkman and likes to wear earbuds. She is viewed by most of the people around her as a troublemaker with weird and macab taste. They are not wrong. But given her unique home life, this is understandable. At least by those in the know. Sakura's mother was weak, her father wicked.

Sakura suffered some abuse; she will not talk about it to anyone. About seven years ago, this led to an altercation, a murder, and a suicide by cop. Sakura is the only kid in Chīsana-Mura living in foster care.

Quickly Jin and Odette arrive. Typically the three of them do not share a homeroom, but with so many students and teachers alike out sick, the school has consolidated. Sometime putting students form three or four classes together with a single instructor.

It would seem today Reje is missing. Jin, as he takes his seat, looks over to Sakura. "where have you been all week?"

"Mom is sick. I have been looking after her." Sakura explains

Odette sits at Sakura's other side, she reaches over and takes Sakura by the sides of the face making the girl look at her. "your eyes are bloodshot, and lips are discolored, haven't been sleeping have you?"

Sakura nods, "good guess."

Jin looks around, "Has anyone seen Reje?"

Odette shakes her head "I went by his house. The place was thrashed."

Sakura turns in her chair, "why, who? There have been no crimes like that in this town in a decade, right Jin?"

Jin shakes his head, "well…"

The P.A. system turns on "Attention," the voice of Gogiro comes over the wire. "By instructions of the Chief Constables office, I am instructed to read the following message aloud." There is a moment's hesitation. "All classes scheduled to start at 7:am are to be concealed. All classes starting after 5pm are concealed as well. By orders of the chief, all shops are to be closed at 7pm, and no one will be allowed on the streets after 8pm without accompaniment by a depute of the chief. The blade restriction as been temporarily ratified. Under the conditional law, anyone of the age of 14 or more may care with them a retractable blade up to 16" or fixed blade up to 20"."

Gogiro turns the page, "As some of you may already be aware. A disaster of unknown nature has occurred somewhere in Japan, and the NDF has been mobilized. To facilitate this, several government services have been suspended. The post office is closed, the national bank is shut down, all telecommunication has been suspended. The brave man and woman of the Chīsana-Mura police department have agreed to stay on without pay until this situation has been resolved. As has the fire brigade."

The page is turned again. "anyone and everyone in town that is adept in the trades is asked to behave honorably during this time. Gas and electricity are still available as of this time. Should anyone have the desire and ability to assist in keeping these services functioning, please do so. Anyone working in produce or grocery, please see to it that your friends and neighbors do not need to do without. Be responsible, but also be charitable. There is no need for anarchy or suffering. We will endure."

"the chief will be in radio contact as often as is possible. The deputies will walk the town in shifts guaranteeing excitability. That is all."

Sakura looks to Jin with a disapproving gaze. "so, your dad is the Emperor now?"

Jin shakes his head slowly he pulls his phone from his pocket, he flips it open then shuts and hides it again "you missed the razor's edge of the statement. There is a philosophy that states, 'the world is never more than three days from anarchy.' We are about to find out if that is true."

Odette joins the conversation, "I remember something about that. Some sorts of invisible truths that lead to the collapse of civilization once they are broken."

Jin nods "our culture, it is a house sitting on the sand. There are things we have all talked ourselves into believing, 'the home is sacred,' 'the water is clean,' 'money has value,' 'someone is looking out for us.', 'the law guarantees us safety.' This foundation is eroding away quickly. My father has moved into a position to try to slow the coming storm."

Sakura watches Jin "elaborate."

Jin continues, "the bank is closed, that means that our money is useless. The internet, radio, and television are offline, and the post office is closed, which means that the lines of communication we count on are gone. My father cant contact the 'Office of the Majesty'; we are cut off from the government. So my dad has chosen to act as the interim government. We follow his lead or ..."

Sakura finishes his thought, "these so-called civilized people all around us start eating each other."

Odette nods, "that sounds like the short and skinny to me."

"you got to love universal entropy," Sakura whispers under her breath

May 13th, 11:15 am

Jo approaches the hospital. A monk is standing out front, drawing graffiti on the door of the structure. Jo waves the monk off, then marches into the hospital. A sneer of entitlement burned into his eyes.

Jo punches the secretaries' desk demanding to see Takashi. A confused nurse slowly points Jo around the corner to the laboratories. The door Jo is lead to has the windows blinded, the door locked, a blinking light overhead informs the staff that the lab is in use.

Jo knocks.

The door is half-opened by Takashi, a cigarette hanging from his lip, he leans out the door "Did we have an appointment today?" he speaks in a drugging voice.

"Give me that." Jo takes Takashi's cigarette; he throws it at the ground "I am not here on a social call today. I had questions to ask."

"and what would that be?" Takashi pulls out his pack of smokes to pick out another one to replace that which Jo took.

Jo takes the cigarettes and proclaims, "this isn't good for you!" he throws the pack of cigarettes across the hall.

Takashi comments, "you look worse than usual."

"Takashi," Jo asks, "Are you affiliated with a woman calling herself L?"

Takashi shuts the door behind himself and locks the lab "I don't recall knowing anyone by that name."

"How about Watory?" Jo asks.

"I only know the name in passing." Takashi expresses, "one of my coworkers put me in touch with a specialist working for them. I think they are an oversees academics organization. Something like Mensa."

"do you trust them?" Jo orders

"I don't know them." Takashi explains, "but knowledge is useless if you don't use it. so anyone that wants to share their insights with the academic community is sure to find open arms and scrutinizing eyes."

"Do you know anything about the Hijoji company?" Jo asks

"yeah, I buy most of my drugs form them." Takashi nods.

"are you aware of any experiments they are performing? Anything dealing with radiation?" Jo inquires.

"that isn't their typical mode of operations." At that, Takashi stops Jo, "Now, can you tell me where this is all going?"

Jo reaches around Takashi, pulling him in close, he whispers, "let's take a walk."

The radio on Jo's hip beeps. "Constable, we need you at the corner of Temple and River street…"

Jo looks to Takashi, "I will be back."

May 13th, 11:45am

Outside Ichishin-Magami, six cops are in an argument with four monks. The hospital truck that had been there to deliver a hand full of dead to be blessed has been rolled over, one monk stands over the truck with a wine barrel, another dawns a touch.

Jo arrives on the scene in his car. He stands up and approaches boldly

One of the cops' demands, "Set down the touch."

The monk holds his ground, two others move into place to stand between the cops and the truck. The police are armed he clubs, the monks with half-staves. The monks walk forward, ready to fight with the police.

Jo walks between them, he reaches onto his hip and pulls his gun "That is enough of that!" he orders. Jo cocks his gun and aims downrange. "you will put out that touch at once." The monks don't pay any heed. Jo fires a warning shot into the air to demonstrate that his gun is loaded. This creates one of the most terrifying sounds that one is likely to hear.

The monks have never seen a gun fired. It has been illegal for anyone other than military personal to have a gun in the village since 1966. Jo has one of the only guns in town. The monks drop their weapons. Kogotana points to the monks, "Detain them." the four monks are chained up and dragged off.

May 13th, 4:45pm

Odette arrives at home, she calls out "Takashi! Are you home?" she walks around the house, finding she is alone again. "well, it is easier to cook when you are cooking for one." Odette grabs some cheese and some milk from the fridge, then some rice, butter, and broccoli from the pantry. She boils herself a rice and vegetable hotdish.

After that, Odette spends some time reading, then it is time to do some stretching and time for a bath. At school, one of Odette's friends slipped her a naughty magazine. She flips through a few pages but finds it to be of little interest. Especially after the government-mandated 'black-boxing' that adult magazines have. "What is the point of a skin magazine if all of the skin is blurred out? I am more likely to see a naked body in a kids show thin in this adult publication."

Odette walks back to her room nude, there is no one home, and it is nice to fan out and relax sometimes. She looks through her dresser picking out an outfit for tomorrow. All classes for Saturday are canceled. Odette looks at a few pairs of tights, a few pairs of jeans, and over her collection of shorts and skirts debating which one would fit her best.

"the pink jeans and the cat shirt. That is a fun outfit." She then looks at one of her skirts, "I like the green one, but I don't know if green is in season right now."

There is a tapping at her window. Odette looks over to it, her blinds are shut, a shadow is looming beyond. Odette picks up her housecoat and ties it on, she picks up a tea tumbler from the nightstand in her room and grips it by the base.

The tapping comes again, a whisper is shouted through the glass "Odette?" there is a pause, "Odette, let me in."

Odette approaches, she pulls open the blinds, the shadow is gone. One more tap, this time from off to one side of the window. The voice is that or Reje "Odette. I want to talk."

Odette opens the window, Reje appears from one side and slips into the room dressed in a long camo coat and a jungle hat he must have taken form his father. Odette is shocked by the odd look and behavior, she swings the teacup slapping Reje across the face with it forcing him to look away, she then uses the cup as a hook to grip him by the back of the head and grabs his shoulder with the other hand. She pulls the boy forward, delivering a crushing knee strike to his chest, then a second, then cat steps past him to throw him at the ground.

Odette stands over Reje startled; she pulls back the cup, threating to swing it like a hammer into her friend. Reje curls into a ball on the ground, "Odette!" he shouts.

Odette drops onto her friend with a falling knee strike kneeling atop him. "Reje!" she shouts "why are you sneaking around like a creeper?" she pins him to the ground.

"Odette, please let me up." Reje request.

Odette steps away. Reje stands up. His eyes are wide, his skin jaundice, his teeth are peeking over his lips. Odette looks him up and down, "what happened to you?"

Reje explains, "Ri came to my house last night, he was looking for Leta."

Odette expresses, "Ri is very dead."

"Maybe it wasn't him, it was something wearing his skin. When he, it, couldn't find Leta, it took my dad, dragged him off into the woods. It then came back for me. It chased me to the park. I hide in and amongst the tanuki…" Reje explains, "I think L is wrong, this isn't some sort of government conspiracy, there really is something living in the woods, something, evil."

"so, why do you look like you are sitting on Death's door?" Odette asks.

Reje comments, "the flies." He walks to the window looking out to the church. A bright light is burning within its depths, "all the insects in and around the forest are tainted." He looks down at his hands, his fingernails are craked and ready to fall off. "I was stung, he undoes his shirt and looks to Odette, he pulls open his shirt to show off a fissure in his chest that is pulsating with yellow-green ooze.

Odette shakes her head, "we need to get you to Takashi, that looks bad."

Reje shakes his head, "it won't help. Once stung, the monster in the woods are attracted to you. During the day, they are slow, sluggish, tired. But come sunset they will be on the hunt again. They will find me and once they do…"

Odette backhands Reje. "shut up! Your sick; you're not dead."

Reje explains, "you don't understand, they are in my head, I can feel them thinking. They will come. I came here to let you know, I am going to go into the woods looking for where they nest, I am going to burn them." he pulls out a lighter and some grill gas, "burn them all."

Odette frowns and nods, she turns her body stepping into a circle kick, she hits Reje in the chin with her heel, he spins around a half dozen time then falls over, killed over…

May 13th, 7:00 pm

Reje can hear voices, his vision has gone dark.

"Why did you tie him up?" it is the voice of Jin.

"he was acting crazy, more so than usual." It is Odette this time.

"the pipe that goes to the city gas line." Sakura Tomoji explains, "galvanized brass going to six feet of concrete."

Reje shakes his head and forces himself awake. He is in the basement of Odette's house; he is lying forward onto what looks like a radiator, his arms are chained together. "Hay, hay, hay!" Reje protest.

Sakura leans on the wall looking to Jin and Odette, "so, am I invited to spend the night?"

Jin speaks up, "I think it would be for the best that the four of us never leave each other's sight."

Reje yells, "come on, on tie me!"

The conversation continues as if they couldn't hear Reje, "I have some cheese and rice if you guy would like some."

Sakura explains, "I want to go by Oso's in the morning, I need a new knife.

May 13th, 8:25 pm

Nekoba walks through the woods, a strange smell draws him ever more rooted, in a trance he climbs up the hillside and makes his way to the forgotten village. In short order, he has pushed some overgrowth out of the way to discover a door marked with the emblem of some old and forgotten faith. He pushes the door open and walks into the desecrated church.

With a few moments to look at the drawings on the walls, Nekoba has worked it out. "This is a Krishna temple. But, what would a Krishna church be doing so far out east?"

Masumo sits on the rafters twenty feet overhead. She calls down "the same thing anyone does when they run away from home. The Krishna came here looking for safety. 500 C.E. was not the best time to be a Hindu." Masumo pushes herself off the rafter and falls into Nekoba's arms, pushing him over. She smiles and giggles as the small girl sits upon the young priest, she then stands up and walks over to the front of the church "Empress Theodora had a distaste for people of faith, non-roman Christians more so than most. If you were going to have a god, it better be hers. Between the Byzantines and the Persian empires, that was a few decades of discomfort for everyone."

Nekoba sits up; he rubs his head and turns to look at Masumo; strange light comes in from the window over her head, casting a shadow of monarch wings growing from her back. "you sound like you were there."

Masumo turns on her heels, spinning to look at the priest, "I was."

For only a moment, the magic that hides Masumo's real face fades, her eyes turn gigantic, she grows four arms, her skin becomes white, and she has wings made of silver, she is the statue he had seen hidden in the elder's house. Nekoba craws away a few steps. "you, are, a monster?"

"From your perspective, I can see why you would come to that conclusion." Masumo comments. "but I don't think it is all that simple." She steps into that shadows retaking her human shape. "I am Shi, the butterfly."

It takes some time for Nekoba to collect himself. Masumo tips her head with a smile, "follow me! I want to show you something." She runs off to one side of the room and pushes open a door in a hidden corner of the church.

Nekoba feels compelled to follow; he considers his feelings and comments, "can you control people's thoughts?"

As they climb down a spiraling stairwell, Masumo explains, "sort of. I can send people... and animals, ideas. If I do it right, you cant tell the difference between my thoughts and yours. It takes a strong mind to work that one out."

"how?"

"Smells." She explains. "the nose plugs into the cerebellum, or whatever it is, and that lets me sidestep the other senses. Now, if I were to make a mistake and use too much of the drug that allows me to do this, it would cause all sorts of trouble."

As they move down the steps, they arrive in a vault-like room, bookcases, dozens of them, treasure chest stacked high, oil lamps light the way. Nekoba admires the room, "what is this?"

Masumo explains, "this is Chīsana-Mura. At least as much of it as my family could protect." She walks over to one of the chests, opening it. She reaches into her pocket and pulls out the gold coin she had shown Oso, she drops it into the chest along with a stack of rings and necklaces. "A strange thing happened a few decades ago. People started to grow a sense of nostalgia and justifying there lives with trinkets and charms. I have been collecting these lost tokens for years and bringing them here to hide after people die."

"are you unique? Are there others like you?" Nekoba request

"I am the only one called Shi the Butterfly. But there are others of my race here, Sirosanto, Muha… a few dozen others. We have been in this town just as long as you have. You just never notice us. We call ourselves Chromon." Masumo explains.

"Why do you look, human?" He asks

"a few drops of human blood added to one of our cocoons allows us to mimic your shape and behaviors."

"Do you know what killed the Hanzo boy?" Nekoba inquires

"another animal, it looks like my people, but they are not us. We call them Sanguine."

"How old are you, Shi of the Butterflies?" Nekoba wonders

Mosumo leads Nekoba to a reading room "If you mean this body, only about 32 months old. But, that would only be a half-truth. My people, when in a genetic bottleneck, can lay an egg that houses a clone or ourselves, our memories mostly intact. Do to limited partners, most of us have had to rebirth ourselves hundreds of times. I think this is my 17,000th time being reincarnated."

Nekoba sits down, he is fascinated by the story "how much time passes between regenerations?"

Masumo looks up to the ceiling of the room "depends on the weather, if it gets to cold, we will hibernate for several hundred years, but with how warm as it is right now, we could shed our skin and be back in a week. There was one point in time when a lake formed around me in my sleep, I was asleep of over a thousand years."

"and these Sanguine? What of them?"

"they nest inside living things, infect the brain, kill the host, then metamorphose the body into a usable shape. I can't remember my first life anymore, but I think they were a predator of ours."

Only now does it occur to Nekoba that he should ask, "why show yourself to me?"

"that is easy enough. Every generation, we look for people that have a mutation that will let us bring them into our folds. Nekoba, you may be able to breed with us. If you have the desire and ability, we could make it most worth your time."

Nekoba lowers his head and rubs his eye. "I… I think I need some time."

May 13th, 8:40pm

Jet stands over the flooded remains of his house. He looks down into the rubble, and he stares, he has been watching the ground for several hours. As if the force of will could turn back time, he suffers in silence.

Sirosanto walks up alongside Reko, he holds out in front of himself a plastic horse, blue with a red main. "I found this down there in the sand," Sirosanto explains. "I think it is yours."

Jet looks at the toy. "That is Ahiru's, I gave it to her on her birthday."

Sirosanto inquires, "Has the body been unearthed?"

Jet shakes his head "no, Ahiru and Kuma are both still missing. Them and more than a hundred others." Jet looks over, "I am sorry old-timer, are you and I related?"

Sirosanto ducks his head "Kuma never did like to talk about her family did she. She was my niece. That would make you my nephew, I think. It is to bad that. It is too bad it takes strife like this to set the pains of the past to one side so often."

"Kuma, she was like an angel of mercy to me. I am a lonely man, a man that likes to work hard, hammer out my own troubles. One day I am sitting and drinking tea with Oso when…" Jet lowers his head and covers his eyes. The thought that he is alone starting to erode away his defenses.

Sirosanto looks down the road, "it is well past sunset, if you have a place to stay, you should make your way there." Sirosanto sets the toy on the ground at Jet's feet then walks off.

A flashlight shines down on Jet from somewhere up the beach, a voice calls out "hay you! It is past curfew, get inside…"

Reko speaks up, "are you trying to tell me what to do."

A cop walks up to Reko, "why aren't you at home."

Reko points out into the water, "I am."

Reko is walked back to Oso's house.

May 13th, 10:22pm

Takashi steps onto the ruff of the hospital, hidden up one sleeve of his coat is a hypodermic needle. Work these last few days has been hard, hard enough that Takashi has felt the need to self-medicate. Even more so than before. Coffee and cigarettes aren't doing the job at this point. A little shot of amphetamine should help him keep his focus.

Takashi rolls up his sleeve and injects himself. He takes a deep breath and watches the sky waiting for the drugs to kick in. Evil eyes start to spawn around the ruff, just deep enough in the dark to hide their faces but not far enough to make them invisible. A half dozen voices speak in stereo.

"Tenzuma,"

"Bring us Tenzuma."

"the girls, give them to us."

"the mother and the child."

"They belong to us."

Takashi digs his feet into the ground "this is my town, my hospital, you can't intimidate me here!"

The voice whisper, "Bring us the mother, you can keep the child. She Is worth, less."

"the mother we want."

"she is good and strong."

"and virile."

Takashi pulls his arms into his chest and lowers his torso like a wrestler reading himself to body a charge "come and take her if you can!"

The monster taunt, "we can wait."

"Can you."

"you are human."

"We are not."

The eyes sink into darkness. Takashi has stood his ground. His spirit powerful enough to push away the evil. For now.

Chapter 7: Eight days remaining

May 14th, 6:25 am

Reje shakes himself awake; he had passed out at some point in time, still chained up screaming in the basement of Odette's house. Sakura Tomoji pours herself a cup of water from the wash sink she takes a sip then viciously throws the water at Reje. "wake up!" she orders.

Reje opens his eyes, he looks around drunkenly. The voices that had been calling to him in his sleep have silenced. "Sakura?" he looks up, dripping wet. "tell me this is water and not pee again."

"Come on, I haven't done that since we were eight." Sakura comment. "Odette tells me that you can hear the voice of the forest calling to you also."

Reje nods then freezes, "what do you mean also?"

Sakura asks, "when were you stung?"

Reje shakes his head "I don't know, everything is all messed up in my head "maybe it was two nights ago, maybe it was yesterday."

"I was stung on May ninth, at 12:33." Sakura explains, "and I am still alive."

Reje looks up at her, "that makes you stronger than me, no doubt about that. Why haven't the voices driven you mad?"

"Because I know how to quiet my mind." She explains, "if you tune them out, they hurt a lot less. I can try to show you how I am doing it."

As the two of them wait for the others to wake up Sakura give Geje her headphones, she turns on the tape that she had playing. A slow load clicking sound comes over the wire. Rhythmic, consistent, Sakura explains, "that is the sound of a pendulum swinging. It will continue for fourteen minutes and eight seconds, then a bell will ring. Hear no other sound. Let the swinging pendulum become your heartbeat." Sakura takes a slow breath; she folds her legs and rests her hands on her knees.

"you are a conductor. You are at a concert hall. The ceiling is forty feet high. You set a metronome on the desk before you, you pull back the hammer, the first tick, 9/10th of a second pass, the second tick. You look to the left, there is a sixty-piece band standing and awaiting your instructions. You look to the right, there is a ninety-nine-man choir. Lift one hand. A drum beats, the drum shadows the metronome. Every instrument strikes a harmonic chord. Every sound you know is attached to one of those instruments. Remember this image. Keep it in the back of your mind. You are the conductor; you have a gifted ear. You can choose to hear or not hear any sound you want. Now. Focus. What sound do you want to hear?"

May 14th, 8:07am

Takashi sits on the floor of one of the labs in the basement, he has brought Setsuka with him. This room was once part of a bomb shelter, but when the building was refurbished became an operating room. But most of the time, this part of the hospital remains locked. The embalming room is just across the way.

Tenzuma is tied to a gurney, Takashi has set up an EEG and a dozen other scanning devices to her body. All of which show her flatlined, except the EEG. Takashi has a digital camera with him. He sets it on the table nearest him angled down with a hand full of books. He looks at his phone, then looks for his smokes. Seeing he is out, he throws the pack off to one side and turns on the camera with the remote on his smartphone.

"It is 8:09 AM, May 14th. Setsuka Tenzuma was declared dead at 10:10pm, May 13th. The official cause of death, cranial trauma. Dr. Tenzuma has left in my care a collection of observations from her last case. As per her last wishes, I will be attempting to care out her final experiment in her absence." Takashi pauses the recording and turns the camera to face the lab table.

The body has begun to excrete a blue film. A plastic-like quality to it. "patient skin temperature is at 68.8°f, heart rate is 0 b/pm, brain activity is 2.5zH and sustaining." Takashi explains. "the room has been scanned for background EM. Interments are expected to function within 1.4 deviation. 0 detectable raspatory activity.

Skin and muscle are showing no signs of rigamortis. It would appear the vascular systems are functioning without the need for the heart to be beating."

Takashi walks around the room for a short time talking to himself "clinically, Tenzuma is dead. There is no doubt about that. But her body is not all dead, only mostly dead. At this time, I have yet to come to understand what this can mean. The body is covered in a protean jell. It seems to originate from the porous glands. Sings of swelling around salvific glands can be detected. Cancerous growth around the esophagus has been noted."

May 14th, 8:25 am

Oso's bar had a line waiting outside since sun up. Half of whom it seems to want to talk to Reko Jet. One of the men in town was even so nice as to go diving into the hollowed-out remanence of Reko's house and dig up his anvil and a hand full of other tools. With the blade ban lifted, everyone wants to have their family swords cleaned and polished by the most talented craftsmen in town.

Reko complains that he doesn't have a coal pit or an outdoor furnace. But the kinder men of Chīsana-Mura are more than happy to gather their skills, and construction of an open-air blacksmith shop is underway before 9am. There is no getting out of it. By noon today, the furnace will be lit, and it will be time for Jet to do what his family has always done.

Jo Kogotana is in the crowed also, accompanied by deputy Useto and a half dozen other cops. Jo, on the other hand, isn't looking to have his sword cleaned, he is looking for Oso. Hanzo runs from table to table, readying cups of tea and bowls of soup.

When Oso reaches Jo's table, Jo grips him by one arm to slow him down, "Hanzo, I need your help."

Oso stops, "what is going on?"

"These men, they have been working without a break for 18 hours. I need an extra set of hands." Jo explains.

Oso knows what Jo is getting at. "no, I don't do that sort of work anymore."

Jo holds up the orange scarf that has been being used to signify someone as an interim deputy. "I am on my way to Ichishen-Megami. I need you." He pushes the scarf at Hanzo.

Oso shakes his head, "I don't want it."

Jo insists, "yes, you do."

Oso pushes it away, "no, I don't."

Jo tries again, "Yes, you do."

Oso insists, "no, I don't."

Jo pulls the scarf into his own chest, "no, you don't."

Oso grabs the scarf and pulls on it, "yes, I do."

Jo comments, "If you insist," he gives the scarf to Oso, "then welcome to the police force. Ready your blade and follow me."

Oso looks shocked as he looks at the scarf then up at Jo, Jo slaps Oso playfully with a wide grin and walks off. Oso looks over to Jet, his mouth open, his eyes wide with confusion "what just happened?"

May 14th, 9:50am

Useto uses a shape charger to blow the lock of the temple gate. Then the police charge up the steps to the temple. Going through the temple, and around the back, the army arrives at the monk's hidden township. The center of the town is the statue of Tamamo-No-Mia, a bronze koi at her sides, a hundred shrine gates holding the mighty fox in place. Tamamo-no-mia is laid forward on her hands and knees, her tail up showing her fangs, she is a beast, but she is wrapped in a shrine maiden's outfit to mask her monstrousness.

Several dozen monks are dragging men from their homes and walking them to a funeral pyre. Stacked high on the ground are piles of burnt bodies. A witch hunt is underway. Jo Kogotana lifts a megaphone and calls out, "By orders of the Chief Constable, you are all to stop what you are doing and follow us at once!"

There is no debate, no collaboration. The monk's take up arms. Farming equipment, clubs, whatever happens, to be in arm's reach. This intrusion will not be tolerated. The police are not welcome in the township.

A monk charges Kogotana, Oso interrupts. Oso Hanzo is a superb athlete; he has the focus and the training to meet 8 men in hand to hand combat at once. The monk swings a sickle; Oso draws his family sword, slicing the head off the reaper as he slides in front of the constable.

By the rules of a Ronin, there is a continuum of violence:
When fighting a single man, the Ronin lets the challenger choose weapons.

When fighting two men at a time, the Ronin aims for crippling strikes.

Only when fighting three or more men, or an opponent with paralleled training, does one strive to kill.
Today Oso has no choice. Today he fights for his life.

Kogotana orders "subdue everyone!" a mass brawl breaks out. A hundred monks armed with staves and sickles vs. a few dozen cops armed with tactical armor and titanium rods. The fight is fast; the conflict is bloody. Jo Kogotana watches the battle from within. It is madness, and he is at the center. For decades the monks have been allowed to police themselves, today he brings order to them, forcibly!

May 14th, 9:55 am

Jin walks up and down the length of Odette's room, the two girls watching him with interest. Jin bites the palm of his hand as he struggles to piece things together in his mind before, at last, he calls out, "How does one beat an illusion?"

Odette calls out, "you can't lie to a camera."

Sakura lowers her eyes in irritation "that is objectively untrue."

Jin produces his phone from his pocket. "I have a 720I camera on my phone, do you think that would work to break this illusion?"

Odette leans back, looking up. "we need to first agree on something that we think is an illusion then use the camera to photograph it. that way, we know if the camera works to fillet out illusions."

Jin recommends, "let's do a test. We will start with Reje. Take a pic of him, then each of us, and see if we all agree with who each other are." Jin takes the girls to the basement.

Reje is still tied up. Jin takes the photo then turns to look at the others. He shares the photo "does anything in the picture, not agree with what we see sitting before us?"

Odette leans in close "what is that purple glow?"

Jin nods, "then you see it also. Reje isn't glowing when we look at him with the naked eye, but he is when we snap a photo. I assume that is what the monsters do to hide themselves." Jin takes a pic of Odette, he looks down at it then turns it to the others "everything looks normal." Odette nods, as does Sakura.

Next Jin points the phone at Sakura, Sakura pulls his arm down "I haven't had my picture taken in 10 years. And I am not in the mood to have it taken today."

Jin explains, "Reje and Odette have had theirs taken already."

Sakura snarls, "If you take my picture, I will drop you like an MC drops the mic."

Reje's head drops back as if to look at his friends upside-down. "she doesn't want her picture taken because she is a monster, she is infected just like me."

Odette and Jin wait to see what Sakura has to say for herself. Sakura rubs her eyes with one hand then nods, "he is telling the truth." She unbuttons her blouse to open it. she shows off her chest and the festering yellow and black scar under her floating rib. "I was attacked by a white beast the same night as Ri went missing."

Sakura goes on, "I was stronger than it expected. I wasn't confused by its illusions, I fought it off. It stabbed me with its beak. Then jumped into the river to get away."

Jin asks for clarification, "you fought it off with your bare hands?"

Sakura denies, "no, I found a section of rebar barred in the mud, some lost material from when the bridge went up, I would guess."

Jin presses, "what was the White Beast?"

"I don't know. It had a beak, antenna, four arms, two sets of wings, and stood about 5'9". It wasn't human, I can tell you that much. It had some sort of biological armor. Boney scales that covered the backs of its arms and legs and barbs around its joints. Like a dragonfly, I guess." Sakura recalls.

"and you fought it off?" Odette asks

Sakura confirms, "didn't seem any stronger than you or me. When I hit it, it cowered away..."

Jin interrupts, "why didn't you say any of this before?"

Sakura folds her arms, "would you have taken me at my word?"

Odette shakes her head, "I wouldn't have."

Sakura seconds her own motion, "nor would I."

Reje calls out, "you need to go to the Mil, set it on fire!"

Jin looks to Odette, "what do you think."

Sakura interrupts, "That isn't Reje talking. The White Beast is talking through him."

Odette looks to Sakura, "how do you know that?"

Sakura explains, "Because I can hear its voice also."

Jin points to Odette, "follow me." He walks up the steps and slides into the bathroom, Odette follows him confused, he shuts the door, so the two of them can talk away from the others.

Jin folds his arms and lowers his head thinking, "Masumo is not the White Beast. It seems to me that the White Beast and Masumo do not get along."

Odette tips her head "are you saying that there is more than one monster?"

Jin confirms, "that part seems clear."

"Then what do you want to do?" Odette asks

"You and I are going to go up to the campsite and look around. If that was where Sakura was attacked, then it escaped into the river, I would guess that the monster sleeps somewhere nearby." Jin hypothesizes

"And what about Sakura and Reje?" Odette asks.

"We leave them here." Jin thinks aloud, "Sakura seems to be able to resist the monsters mind control, or whatever it is, and Reje is safely tied up."

Odette complains, "this doesn't sound like the right move to me, but…"

May 14th, 11:00am

Monks armed with staves and knives are threatening, but police with military training are even more so. Itchishin-Megami is brought to its knees. Inside in hour, monks are on the run. Dozens are tied up and brought before the constable.

Jo Kogotana orders, "Where is Nekoba!" No one is talking. Jo grows irritated, "someone bring me Nekoba!" no one talks. Jo cocks his gun and threatens one of the monks. "Where is he!"

Oso steps between Kogotana and the monk. "that man can't talk." Oso kneels down; he whispers with the older man, "open your mouth, please." The monk shows off the fact that he has no tongue. Oso explains, "many of the older monks have mutilated themselves to prevent themselves from infringing on the rules of the Buddha. Burning the palms of their hands, removing their tongues, the head of the penis, or cutting out their eyes if they feel they have committed a crime against their gods."

Useto comes into view, pushing ahead of him the Moji brothers, Tobi and Tami.

Jo grunts, "Well, I know those two can talk." Jo walks over, briskly, "where is Nekoba?"

Tobi explains, "he was asked to leave the temple."

"Why?" Jo orders

"He broke the faith," Tami explains

May 14th, 12:17pm

Odette and Jin walk around with their phones out. They take photos of the campsite that they have gathered at so many times in the past. Jin inquires, "See anything out of place?"

Odette calls over "spiderwebs, stretching between the trees. The whole canopy is a blue-black color…"

Jin confirms, "I can see that also. It is some sort of resin. I have never seen anything like it."

Odette points, "when Sakura left the camp to go… do her thing, she went this way."

Jin points, "that is the path that leads down to the river and to the temple." Jin walks alongside Odette as they follow the path before them, leaving the camp and starting on their way to the river.

Odette whispers, "so, did we consider what we are going to do if we find the White Beast?"

Jin giggles nervously, "I was considering screaming like a girl and hiding behind you."

As they walk down the path, they come to a tree with a ribbon tied around it and a dreamcatcher hanging from each of the low hanging branches. There is an old rotten wooden sign on the ground, it had fallen over long ago, and no one ever took the time to hang it back up. "the Kareki stretch." Jin explains. "1949, 99 men left their homes in the middle of the night one winters day. They all walked to this spot then…"

Odette looks up, taking a picture of the trees. She gasps and drops her phone falling over backward. She points into the treetops, "Jin, look!" Jin looks up, he can't see anything out of the ordinary, he then lifts his phone to take a picture also.

Jin shuts his eyes and breaths slow and deep to keep calm, he shutters as he shakes, finishing his story. "hung themselves by the ankles, and waited to die." Ten bodies hang from the tree just overhead, hanging by silk ropes, gagged, the eyes are sewn shut. The shapes gray, these men died of dehydration it would seem.

Disembodies eyes flicker in the shadows of the trees, hidden by thick shadows. One of them moves ever so slightly. A black-hand, grips a tree branch sliding forward only a few inches. Jin can see through the illusion that is hiding them for a moment, he gasps and falls over also. Jin grips one of Odette's hands; he picks up their phones and points backward. Jin keeps his eyes locked on the shadow, he doesn't want to blink, he doesn't want to lose sight of the beast.

A loud humming fills the air. The monster has noticed the kids. And it has noticed that they can see him also. Jin points as they are crawling away, "look there."

Odette scurries, "I can see it."

The living shadow runs down the tree face first like a lizard. It dashes on all six of its legs running at them...

But then stops short. The kids have slid into a gap in the canopy, the bright noon sky bathing them in harsh light. The monster dares not chase them another step. It runs away.

The noon light would shatter the cloak of darkness it wears, and without the shadow to protect it, it would lose its magic. But it has smelled them. As the sun slips lower in the sky, it will be able to sniff them out. It will find them. It will taste their flesh.

May 14th, 1:45 pm

Odette and Jin run back down the hill and out of the woods. They run as hard as they can, Jin grabs the first cop he can find and demands to know where his father is. They are directed to the school, a barricade is set up, the school is in lockdown. Jin and Odette getting in only do to Jin's relationship with his father.

Eight cops are patrolling the school. Jin is taken to the locker rooms, Jin shouts for his father. Jo is kneeling in the shower room, examining a burnt corpse on the ground. Jin freezes in places as Jo holds up a hand to silence him.

The ground has scorch marks on it, one wall has paint on it. The corpse is curled up into a ball, puffed out like a scorched marshmallow, the skin black and red, stretched and flaking. Anything that may have clued someone in on the identity of the dead by sight is gone, no gender, no hair, no clothing.

Jo waves over one of the investigators and points to the wall, "make sure you have a picture of that." He points to the writing on the wall. Jo looks to the wall and reads aloud what is written "Hannibal is at the gate, the nine keys to the knowledge he will not have. If it is a truth you seek, ask Agora. She will take you to where bears meet men. There you will find me."

Odette looks down with a gasp, "who is that?"

"Was," Jo corrects her, "Dean Gogiro, if I am not mistaking."

Jin has lost his train of thought as he is staring at the remains of the principal "what…"

"I have a feeling it wasn't accidental death." Jo lowers his eyes. "Hannibal, Nine Gate, Agora." Jo takes a long gaze at the wall. "Dean wanted us to see something, and I think I have some idea where he wanted us to look." Jo waves as he turns to walk out briskly, "come with me." He calls Jin and Odette to his side.

The three walk down the halls of the school; Jin on the left, Odette on the right, Jo in the middle.

Jo expresses, "Hannibal Barca was a Corinthian, he fought in the Punic Wars against the Greeks. When people say 'The Barbarians are at the gates' Hannibal is who they are talking about. The nine gates are the Greccio Roman gods: Mars, Mercury, Saturn, Urines, Neptune, Jupiter, Pluto, Venus, Gaia. Someone was trying to break into the astrometric lab, Gogiro saw them, stopped them. Agora was a gathering place. The center of art and history of the ancient Greece world. Gogiro hid something in the library for us."

Jo tips his eyes up thinking as they push open the library doors, "where bears meet people, that I have no idea what he meant by."

Odette cuts in "that part doesn't seem so hard. Natural Sciences. He hid whatever it was, in section SCI."

Jin looks between Odette and his father "Why do I suddenly feel like the slow one here?"

Jo nods in confirmation, "that makes sense to me. Look for anything that doesn't belong."

The group ransacks the library skimming books, moving around painting and sculptors on display. Jin calls out as he finds a folded-up note slid into the spine of a thick book. He unfolds it. "Zackary Edwardo Di'moor passed away May 13th at 11:45 am, death by incineration. He was found dead in the school bathroom the following morning; police have no leads. Linda, I am sorry, the key is under chimney rock. I will see you on the wall." Jin shoots his father a glance. "Chimney rock. I know where that is."

Jin runs off ahead, he shouts to his friends as he walks "Gogiro was a member of the national geological society. There is a photo in his office; he and some other guys hanging on the wall behind his desk. It was taken at Chimney Rock Carolina in 1990."

Jin throws himself at the office door, forcing it open, Jin runs around the small office and picks up the photo to show to his father "See."

Jo looks at the photo, then up at the wall, it was taken from. Jo leans in looking at the discolored paint. "the wall behind the photo was repainted recently." Jo rests his hand on the wall and gives it a soft push, the wall is made out of clay, it pops out of place. There is a hole in the wall only slightly larger than a human hand leading to a gap in the wall. Jo holds out a hand and calls out "Flashlight" as he looks around in the hole.

Jin and Odette both pull out flashlights from their back pockets. Jo takes the one from Odette, mostly do to her pushing it at him. Inside the gap in the wall is a small box hidden in the folds of the insulation. Jo pulls the box out and sets it on the desk.

Odette questions, "more old-world cop stuff?"

Jo nods, then Jin explains "how to best hide information. This is a balancing act, accessibility vs. security. A safe dipped in concert is very secure, but hard to carry around. On the other hand, it would be easy to reach tucked into your socks, but it isn't very safe."

Odette expresses, "so we have a box hidden in drywall?"

Jo opens the box. Inside there is a cell phone, a glass pendant with lesser etching on it, and a folder with a fist full of ID cards hidden in it. Jo looks in the envelope " Chow Norai, Chan Heduma, Chief Gunnery Sargent Andy Zuko, and Igaru Gogiro…" Jo looks at the kids "Gogiro was a government spy."

Jin speaks up, "he has been living in town for more than ten years."

Odette looks over, "Deep cover job?"

Jo looks down at the necklace and phone, "that would be why he knew to look for the hidden letter that lead us to L."

Odette looks to the ceiling and folds her arms in contemplation, "L wanted to be found."

Jo opens the phone. There is a text displayed on the screen. This phone was hidden here only a few hours ago. He read the text. "L, Inside, Fox owned umbrella décor, Intermediate tame, Ultimatum newborn dolphin edge regiment, Turtle helm endings, Monkey indeterminant laughter. - Zed-" Jo looks out into space, "I think it is time to give L a call."

May 14th, 2:20 pm

Nekoba has found his way back to the mil, back into the company of Sirosanto. Sirosanto is standing at a workbench, he is painting a coin-shaped wood chip. Ancient symbols, forgotten magic. Something from a lifetime so long past not even the dead remember where the image comes from. Sirosanto calls over as he smells Nekoba's approach "It would seem you aren't intimidated by me."

Nekoba inquires, "Sirosanto, how old are you?"

Sirosanto chuckles, "well, that is not easy to explain." The old man sets down his work and looks to the sky "this body hatched six or seven days ago…"

Nekoba is confused, "so, why do you look so…"

Sirosanto replies, "old? Beet-up? Sick?" the old man looks to the young preacher "I would ask why you aren't with Shi right now?"

Nekoba presses, "please answer my question."

Sirosanto drops his head "you don't pull punches, do you?" there is a moment of silence as the two watch each other. Sirosanto submits, "we stay young by shedding our skin. Under ideal conditions, we will shed once every 30 or 40 years. This will revert us to how we looked when we first become sexually active. But only so long as we wait until that time. If we get hurt, we can choose to shed earlier, but that will shave years off of our lives. And from that time on any time, we shed we will look older, and more of our scars will become permanent, following us even into our new bodies."

Sirosanto lets loose a tired breath. "I had a few bad decades around the turn of the last century. I got involved in a conflict... well, that part doesn't matter. What does matter is that I was forced to shed 10 times in as many years."

Nekoba inquires, "you were discovered, you were being hunted?"

Sirosanto grudgingly nods, "you and I, we are not alike, things that are not like you can be very not like you. Shi and I look like butterflies from this world on a surface level, but under the skin, we are nothing like you, outside of needing to eat and a need for companionship."

"Masumo, Shi, whichever name is right." Nekoba stumbles on his words, "she was saying that sometimes humans can become what you are."

Sirosanto agrees, "It has happened a few times. In the last 2 or 3 thousand years. It looks like it is becoming more common as our races grow more intertwined, we are effectively dissolving into one another. At some point, if things go on like this, you and I will become indistinguishable from each other. At least, that is what I would hope."

"And how does this come to pass?" Nekoba insists.

Sirosanto is becoming aggravated, "have you ever heard of Hobbits?"

Nekoba shakes his head, "I recall no such word."

"About 100,000 years ago, there was a tribe of protohumans, an animal that was a Hominidae, but not Homo Erectus. They were close enough to humans that they could breed with humans. They were living on the Galapagos islands before your race arrived there. When you discovered the island, you killed or breed with as many of them as you could. Now the only place you can find Hobbits is with a chromosome count. About 1 in 80,000 humans have non-human RNA. And that is why."

Nekoba looks for clarification "are you suggesting…"

Sirosanto cuts in, "I am not suggesting, I am saying, do to recent leaps in medical technology you and I are chemically compatible. The biggest obstacle now isn't genetic; it is anatomic."

Nekoba squints, "I don't understand."

Sirodanto turns back to his table. "I am not qualified to have this conversation. My blood was used to make an artificial butterfly a few years back, but I don't know how it works. Talk to Shi, she will tell you more."

May 14th, 3:30 pm

Jo, Jin, and Odette tinker with the radio, the dials have all been spun to see to it; the frequency is scrambled. Thankfully Jo had been taking notes and knows how they salved this puzzle the last time.

Odette pulls out her phone and shows it to Jo, "Kogotana-son, we came here to show you this."

Jo takes a moment to flip through the phone "I don't understand, what am I looking at?"

Jin explains, "the toxin that is causing hallucinations, it can fool our eyes, but not our phones. It acts as a filter between us, adding a layer that washes away the illusions. Odette and I went back to where Ri was found. Monsters are hiding all over the forest. And Ri was not the only person to fall prey to them."

Jo squints as he examines the pictures "by the gods." He finds the image of the living shadow, the disembodied eyes floating in the tree. Jo gets sucked in, leering forward entranced by the evil eyes. "this is like nothing I have ever seen."

Jin takes over programing the radio as his dad is talking to Odette. Odette explains, "that thing, I think if it bite someone, it fills their body with some sort of a parasite, that parasite lets them mind control people."

Jo looks over, "and how did you come to that conclusion?"

Odette explains, "Reje and Sakura had both been 'stung' Reje after sunset went seven flavors of fruit loops. Sakura, on the other hand, it seems to not be able to control so effortlessly."

Jo needs a moment to digest this information. He whispers, "people infected glow on camera? That means we can track them…" he starts to whisper, "…but what after that?"

The radio kicks in "This is L, can you hear me?"

Jo swoops over and grabs the microphone. "Yes, L, I can hear you."

L calls back, "what is your situation looking like?"

Jo responds, "Gogiro has passed away."

There is a moment of dead air before L replies, "That is disappointing. Would it be correct to say he died of natural causes?"

Jo with a trembling voice replies "I would not describe his death as having been 'of natural causes.'"

Again, it takes L a few seconds to message back, "did he have any last words, constable?"

Jo takes a deep breath, "he left you a message. 'L, Inside, Fox owned umbrella décor, Intermediate tame, Ultimatum newborn dolphin edge regiment, Turtle helm endings, Monkey indeterminant laughter. - Zed-"

"Thank you. I understand." L explains

Jo calls out, "I do not. What does that mean?"

L expresses, "Dean Gogiro was one of my assets. He was doing a job for me in the area. Constable, did he have on him a graphite stone and a wireless device of any kind with him?"

Jo growls softly to himself before answering, "he did."

"protect these objects, they are more valuable than I can explain." L request.

Jin picks up the microphone "L, I fear that things may be more complicated than we had first anticipated. Using my cellphone camera, I was able to see around the illusion cast by the monsters in the forest..."

L cuts Jin off, "And how did you come to conclude that there are in-fact monsters in the forest?" Jin freezes, he doesn't know how to explain the things he has seen. L continues her thought "until you have excluded the natural, it is not justified to invoke the unnatural. We are well aware of the idea that the human mind is easy to confuse, it is a simple feat to distract or misdirect someone, or pervert their perception..."

May 14th, 5:15 pm

A few nurses stand in the hallway outside the room Takashi has set up fort in. They whisper back and forth with each other. Even in the hospital, they are not immune to the madness taking root around the town.

The door slides open, Takashi slides out and locks the door behind himself, he stands slouched, his hair is uncombed, his skin is showing a faint hint of gray. He is under stress, to the point that it is no doubt taxing his health, both physically and mentally.

Arnaldo speaks to Takashi, "Doctor Tenzuma has not shown up for her shift, sir."

Takashi speaks in frank, "did you miss the memo? Tenzuma passed away."

Arnaldo looks shocked "when? Has she already been set off to sea?..."

If Takashi doesn't stop the boy, he is just going to keep talking "unless stated otherwise, the dead or to be cremated from now on. No services, no ceremony, no autopsy. The heart stops beating into the flames. Do you understand?"

Arnaldo looks to Iwata "what? Just like that? What about the families?"

Takashi slides his hands into his pockets and looms downward, "dead is dead, into the fire."

Iwata shouts, "I have had about enough of this Doctor! The sneaking the stalking, and the snap judgments. I need you to explain to me what is going on."

"you really want to know?" Takashi looks between the two, "do either of you have a cigarette? I am out."

There is a nod, Iwata checks her pockets "I am also out."

Arnoldo explains, "I have never smoked."

"enough games Takashi," Iwata explains.

"Fine, follow me to conference room three." Takashi takes them to the elevator then to the third floor. Takashi sets up the TV in the room and plugs in his camera. He looks to his coworkers. "do you both agree that this is one of the cameras from A.V. lab.

Iwata looks at the device and reads the code on the underside of it that was written in nail polish "PM04. This one was last rented out to post mortem. It is one of ours."

Takashi looks over, "and do you believe that I have the skill set needed to tamper with the footage on this tape in any way?"

Arnoldo expresses, "nothing I have seen would lead me to believe that you can alter footage."

Takashi nods, "then we are in agreement, the footage on this tape was most likely filmed here and is unaltered?"

Iwata sits back in her chair, folding her hands as she waits for the film to play. "I will second that motion."

Takashi turns on the Tv. The film plays, the three witness Takashi turning on the camera in the autopsy room. Laying on the slab is a flesh-colored mass with oozing purple pours, bioluminescent sludge drips onto the floor.

The watch as Takashi plugs probs into the mass then listen to his analyses as he starts to describe what he thinks is sitting before him. "Female, 30 years of age, mother of 2. Time of death, 10 pm…" they observe as he reads off the EEG numbers. Then as he recounts Dr. Tenzuma's notes.

A suddenly unnerved Iwata speaks out, "what are we watching?"

Takashi explains, "I was hoping one of you had some idea. That disgusting slime on the table at the time I was filming this was Setsuka Tenzuma. But when I went back to rewatch the footage, it wasn't."

Arnoldo is a man with mixed interest. At the same time, he was in medical school, he was also attending classes on art, photography, and criminology. Arnoldo stands up and sneaks up close to the TV. "rewind that a few seconds please." He requests.

Takashi does as asked, Arnoldo questions, "Takashi, was there anyone else in the room with you as you were recording?"

Takashi explains, "not as far as I am aware. Why?"

Arnoldo points out the lighting "the shadow on the ground there, that was being created by the surgical light, this one over here, that is the overhead lamp. But you can also see a shadow in the corner of the screen over here. I don't know what is casting that shadow. I would assume that is the shadow of the cameraman if this was staged."

Takashi explains, "I was using a tripod. There is no one holding the camera."

Iwata questions, "what is that viscus fluid on the ground?"

Takashi shrugs, "beats me. I couldn't see it, couldn't smell it, couldn't feel it."

Iwata thinks, "then we need to find out how to see it." Iwata leans forward in her chair. "Gentlemen. Whatever we do, I want this to be fast and clean."

Takashi taps his fingers on the table before him. He grunts as he thinks, "Arnoldo, I am having a thought here. I want you to walk around the hospital, I want you to take a photo of everyone and everything you can find. Print them and bring them here."

Arnoldo looks back and forth between the middle-aged doctor and the elderly nurses. "do we bring the rest of the staff in on this?"

Iwata shrugs, "what are we going to say? We need to collect more information. We need something to report before we call a staff meeting."

May 14th, 6:45 pm

Takashi stands over the remains of Tenzuma. The beast is wiggling about, thrashing, stirring. Returned form the Never. Tenzuma has shed her skin. She has grown two new arms, claws on the ends of her hands. Her skin is black, she has six eyes, a beak. Cartilage is growing over her skin, forming into armor. Splints of metal have developed around her claws and beak.

Any part of her that was once human is gone. Tenzuma is now something truly and whole inhuman. Takashi has gathered chains and ropes to tie her to the table. Takashi sets out his operating tools.

One hand reaches for a rib splitter; he cuts long her intercostal then pulls away the ribcage breaking it outwards, looking into her insides. Tenzuma howls. She tries to struggle, the ropes hold.

In the dim light, Takashi takes notes. He talks to the camera set over his shoulder. "The body is laterally symmetrical, two harts, six-chambered, in both hemispheres. Lungs attach to shoulder blades, hidden completely by ribs and heart, it would seem that the bone structure is hollow and there is segmentation between the shoulders. Stomachs are multichambered. The small intestine, kidneys, and pancreases all seem to be absent."

Takashi continues to dig deeper into the screaming monster's body. "Liver and sex glands are engorged, a secondary uterus is present, as is an unknown organ that seems to bridge the oval ducts. Muscular fiber is porous. A pocket-like protrusion can be seen within the chest cavity. And what I can only assume to be venom glands bleed into the esophagus. There seem to be a half dozen other organelles lined up along the spine and around the neck."

For some time, Takashi goes on, talking to himself as he hypothesizes over what the strange things in the monster's chest could be. Where the beast came from and how it lives.

There is a knock at the door. Takashi yells out "I need fifteen more minutes!" he pulls the bone splitter out of the monster's chest, the chest snaps shut like jaws, and several hair-thin tendrils shoot from the wound sowing the chest closed. Takashi stars with wide eyes "Well, if that isn't a useful talent...I may have some idea as to what one of those alien objects could have been."

Takashi changes his clothes, then steps into the hallway. Odette jumps forth and hugs Takashi, "I have so much I need to tell you."

Takashi rubs her head, "then let's talk. We can go up to the employ lounge, I will grab us something to eat."

The two head to the main floor. Takashi waits in line and grabs dinner for the two of them. Today the hospital's kitchen staff is serving quartered chicken with a beef marinate and radishes stir-fried with garlic and bean sprouts.

Takashi picks up a slice of fried garlic "I am told that this is huge out west right now. This is being served all over

France, Italy, and Central America. I hope it is as good as it looks."

Odette sets her phone on the table. "I was just taking a walk around the block."

Takashi asks, "Anything interesting going on?"

Odette turns on her phone and loads up the photo gallery, "have you taken a look out over the river lately?"

Takashi picks up the phone and looks at the picture in question. The water seems to glow, nearly invisible globules form a web reaching from one side of the river across to the other, a semi-articulate chain of mater grows from somewhere under the surface.

Takashi's head cocks to one side as he starts to think, starts to look for puzzle pieces. He thumbs through the phone, looking at other photos. He finds the tree with the swinging corpses, the photo of Reje covered in slime, the picture of the shadow beast crawling down the tree.

He continues to scan through photos. Odette standing around her room showing off outfits, pictures taken at the park, or in other places around town. his eyes are drawn into the corns of the screen, searching the backgrounds of images for anything out of place.

After a few minutes of silence, Takashi whispers, "how long has that been there?"

Odette understands what he means to say. "weeks, months. I have no idea… how much time do you think most people spend really looking at pictures they take. Most of us are egocentric and only really interested in ourselves and those related to us. Little things like mosquitos the size of large dogs somehow seem to escape or view."

Takashi asks, "where is Reje?"

"I have him tied up at our place."

"I recommend that you leave him there. Keep everyone else away from him also." Takashi request. Takashi has barely had time to finish his chicken before he lowers his head with a look of disappointment "I should get back to my work."

Odette reaches across the table, gripping her uncle by one arm. "you didn't come home yesterday."

Takashi nods, "yeah."

Odette continues, "or the day before that."

Takashi grunts, "so?"

"how long has it been since you have been home?" Odette inquires. Takashi shrugs and shakes his head. He knows that he slept in his office yesterday, and he thinks he may have the day before, but he can't seem to remember much before that. "Takashi, you need to come home, take a bath, and shave. We can watch a movie together, maybe 'Perfect Blue' or 'Lady Ninja.' I seem to recall you like low brow comedies like that."

"That reminds me, what about Reje? You say he is tied up; is he being supervised?" Takashi asks.

"Tomoji is with him, didn't I say that?" Odette looks confused.

Takashi nods "in that picture, you can see purple slime dripping from Reje's skin. I have seen that before. Soon, Leta will be that last Tenzuma."

Odette lowers her head and rubs her eyes with one sleeve. "I had a feeling. You know, I would like to be able to imagen that, whatever all this is just wasn't. I would like to watch TV. Go to school, think about boys. But. The suffering in the air is thick. The smell of hot death runs strong in the air. It is starting to weigh on all our souls."

Takashi pulls his hand back. "I need to go see Nurse Iwata. I will be back in a moment." Takashi departs, leaving Odette by herself sitting in the lounge.

May 14th, 8:10 pm

Odette and Takashi walk back to their house. Takashi stops at the river for a moment. He looks out into the water; he reaches into his pocket, drawing his phone. He takes a photo of the river for himself then looks at it for a few moments, "that pattern on the surface of the water. I have seen it somewhere else. What was it?"

A cop patrolling the street calls to the two of them, "Keep moving, Doctor, you need to get off the street." Takashi nods; he hugs Odette, and the two keep moving.

In short order, they arrive at home. Sakura Tomoji is still there. She has changed her clothes, having put on a pair of Odette's tights, she is still dressed in her white sweater.

Sakura explains, "I needed a change of clothes. I through my uniform in the wash." She speaks in a dry tone.

Odette's eyes run down her friends' body. "my clothes look a little tight on you."

Sakura starts to comment, "I also noticed that these pants tend to get sucked…"

Takashi interrupts, "Is Reje Tenzuma still here?"

Sakura nods as she points over her shoulder, "want to go see him?"

The three walk into the basement Reje's skin has turned blue and black, a shell has started to grow around his body.

Sakura comments, "He did not look that bad 15 minutes ago."

Voices call from the shadows in the basement. "Sakura, Sakura, Sakura. Tomoji, Tomoji, it is time, step into the shadows, come with us into the forest."

Sakura shuts her eyes and breaths deep; she forces the voices out of her mind replacing it with the swinging of a pendulum.

The voices turn their collective attention on Takashi, "Dr. Tsu, you can't protect them." the voice changes from shapeless to a very clear voice, the voice of Setsuka Tenzuma "you did nothing to protect me, you will do nothing to protect him."

Takashi looks between the girls, "I just want to ask, does anyone else hear disembodied voices right now?"

Tomoji nods, "I do."

Odette shakes her head as she pulls out her phone "no." she scans the room with her camera, only narrowly does she miss a white-haired beast kneeling before the window as it runs off.

The voice yells, "you will sleep! And when you do, your children die."

Takashi lowers his eyes as he thinks, "I will deal with Reje. Go upstairs, I will be there soon."

Odette's eyes snap upwards, "I think I know where you saw that web pattern you were talking about."

May 14th 10:45 pm

The voice of the White-haired beast shouts to Reje, "thou must Awaken! Theh enemies' draw nearer! "

Reje awakens, wrapped in a blanket lying on the floor. Takashi walks down the steps a butcher's cleaver in one hand. Reje shakes his head, he looks about in panic "Takashi! Takashi!" he struggles, "Takashi, what is going on!"

Takashi whispers, "I am sorry, Reje. I couldn't help you; I couldn't help your mother. But I will do all I can to protect your sister." Takashi stands over Reje. He pulls the ax back in both hands, and heartlessly he strikes.

It is not fast, it is not clean, and it is not painless, but Takashi strikes. He strikes time and time again, severing Reje into bits and bites small enough to shovel into the furnace.

This is the cure to evil, to burn away.

Sakura was awakened by the screams. She stands at the top of the steps looking down, Takashi now splattered with hot blood, makes his way back up the steps. Head down, one hand in his pocket, the other on his cleaver.

Sakura asks, "did you…"

Takashi nods, "I did."

"When the time comes…" Sakura starts

Takashi confirms, "of course."

Sakura hugs Takashi, "Thank you."

Takashi pulls his phone from his pocket; he hides it in the palm of his hand "why haven't you changed yet?"

The two stair each other down for a few moments Sakura can see the phone hidden in Takashi's hand, she can't lie, she can't run. Her choices are limited. She can attack Takashi, or she can surrender. The doctor is the spirit of humanity, and it's will to fight.

Sakura lowers her eyes. "you won't need that," she points at the phone, "I will comply." She leads down the steps "down in the laundry room."

Takashi leads Sakura down the steps and into a corner of the room with no windows, hidden from the door.

Sakura takes off her hoody, the scar from where she was stabbed clearly visible through her undershirt. She then steps out of her tights and undergarments. She lets out a soft breath. She is defiant, she wants to live. Maybe, just maybe, this will allow her to do so.

"I did change." She explains, "on the 12th, I shed my skin and became the thing you are now hunting." As her eyes open the illusion, she had been casting gives way.

Sakura is a black-skinned, six-eyed, six-armed monster. Four sets of translucent wings grow from her back, a blade grows from the center of her face. She has only three fingers and three toes, her legs are multijointed.

Takashi looks for his cigarettes. Looking at Sakura has made his heart jump. He chokes on his tongue struggling to keep calm and collected.

"I am still me, Takashi-son."

Chapter 8: Seven Days Remaining

May 15th, 12:15 am

Leta sits in the hospital, the door to her room is bard shut. In the last two nights, the maintenance staff has transformed the psychiatric ward of the hospital into a high-security prison.

Like so many others, Leta has found that it is a challenge to keep her clothing on. She has now been through two rounds of radiation treatment. She is sick, and she is sleepy all the time. After her first treatment, she was having trouble keeping food down. Still, one of the nurses recommended an experimental treatment that seemed to counteract the worst of the adverse effects of the radiation.

A nebulizer with cannabis oil and a hand full of other medications seems to have helped. The treatment is considered untraditional, but given the severity of things, as they are, much of the hospital staff seems Ok with using whatever tools are available to them to keep people as happy and healthy.

The night is not quite; screams fill the air. Deafening whispers echo from all corners of the hospital. Leta looks to the door as a voice calls her name. She then turns to the window as the sound comes from the other side of her.

Ri is floating outside her window. He smiles wide, "there you are, love. I have been looking for you for days."

Leta stands up; she walks backward, pressing herself to the door. She keeps her distance. Ri laughs, "Don't act that way with me. You are mine." He reaches a hand through the window, "come over here." Ri wave Leta forward

Leta shakes, "you are not Ri, Ri is gone."

Ri giggles, "I am right here. Come on, beautiful, give me your hand. Let us get out of here."

Leta shouts, "No!"

The beast becomes angered, he shakes the bars of the cage as his mouth drops open, and his spearing tongue rolls out of his mouth. The effects of death start to show through, his skin stretches and fissures his eyes cloud. "Give yourself to me. Give yourself to me before one of the others takes you!"

Leta shouts, "No!"

Ri explains, "I love you, I wanted you. I deserve to nest with you. Not one of them." he waves a hand about.

Leta looks about searching the room for something to protect herself with; there is nothing in sight. A pounding strikes the door behind Leta, Leta shrieks. The center of the room is the only safe place. There are monsters on all sides of her, and there is nothing she can do to fight. Leta can only hide.

Ri crawls up the wall, he hangs from the window above Leta's and looks into her room, upside-down. "my mother took your mother. She is one of us now. As for Reje, Takashi killed him. Leta, the only safe place is with me."

Leta shuts her eyes and lowers her head; she hides her head between her knees, pinching the sides of her head to drown out the noise all around her.

Ri grunts, "Fine, I can come back later."

May 15th, 12:20 am

The fire alarm triggers in the hospital, Iwata is the senior-most officer on staff. She walks down the halls of the hospital, charging as if she had a purpose. The storm shutters fall. The building is locked.

The old nurse makes her way to the tripped alarm to see for herself what is going on. Arnoldo chases after her with intent to do the same. "Iwata! What is going on?"

Iwata explains, "supposedly a fire on the top floor." Iwata looks to the boy as they start to run up the steps, "any news on your side of things?"

Arnaldo explains, "I developed the photos from Nobani. I think I know where the infection started. It is the flies. The plague of flies, they are the carriers. The heatwave woke up whatever this is and brought it into the town."

Iwata nods, "we will need to follow up on that."

The two reach the top of the steps, and Iwata throws open the door to the hallway vengefully. The top floor is a mess. Two dead nurses lay in the hall and three elderly patients. Cut apart as if by a woodsmen's ax.

Handa stands at the end of the hallway. One hand still on the alarm. His eyes are bulging; he is covered in blood. "Takashi shouldn't have attacked us. Things are going to get so much worse from here on out."

Iwata looks to Dr. Handa, "what is…"

Handa pulls out from behind his back a fire ax. His mouth drops open, and his tongue rolls out. It is brown and slug-like, thorns emerge from it as his jaw drops off, crab-like legs fester out of his chest. Iwata is stunned. The bulky man that is Handa runs at Iwata.

Arnaldo pushes Iwata off to one side. Handa barrels into the younger nurse throwing him across the room with the utmost ease.

Handa explains, "in payment for Takashi's sins; we will take from him ten times what he took form us." The voice is reverberating, echoing from all corners of the hall. It is as if it is not one beast in Handa's body but a dozen treating him like a puppet.

Handa swings his ax at Iwata, the nurse walks backward, staying inches out of reach. The monster grips the ax in both hands as he teases. "you could have owned this hospital, you should have. But you let Takashi have the job, why?" Handa gurgles. "is it because of the debt that you owed to his father? Or is it because you like him?"

The monster swings the ax again; Iwata falls over the receptionist's desk as she tries to keep away from the beast. Handa holds the ax overhead and slams it into the table, almost breaking the table in half with its supernatural power.

Arnoldo has regained his footing, he picks up a wet-floor sign and runs over, he swings the sing into the back of Handa to get his attention off of Iwata. The attack is meaningless. Handa looks to the small man; he reaches out to grab him with one hand and lifts him into the air.

Iwata makes a bold move, this alien, whatever it is. It is dressed in human skin, so maybe, human rules still are applicable. The small woman takes a knife from a serving tray and runs around to the other side of the desk. She takes the knife and runs it across the underarm of Handa.

A cut across the muscle linking the shoulder to the elbow forces the hand open. Arnoldo is dropped, relatively unharmed. Iwata gets backhanded for her trouble knocking her to the ground.

The sounds of the siren's still calling. Three police officers nearby come charging up the steps to investigate. The monster howls, black tentacles erupt from the cut in its arm. It can hear men in the stairwell; it turns to flee.

The police arrive only to find five dead and two injured. Quick thinking and cooperation prevent things from getting worries for a short time.

But the night is young, and the troubles that the hospital will see are only going to escalate. The white-haired beast and her slaves are growing more easily agitated. It would seem they are also becoming less concerned about being seen…

May 15th, 3:33 am

Oso sits up in bed; his head lowered into his hands. The night can be hard on the heartbroken. His sword returned to its cradle; his kimono hangs from the wall.

The lights are out; thick shadows dance maddeningly. The sounds of Reko growling in his sleep almost shakes the walls. But then all goes still.

"Father!" A voice calls in from the streets

Oso's eyes jump. He turns, looking about. The voice of a child, or siblings, are voices that one never forgets. A longs shadow reaches around the room. Almost human.

Oso stands; he walks across the room, taking his sword from the wall. Oso throws open the window of his room, looking out into the back yard.

Ri stands in the yard, his arms resting at his sides, he holds up a hand to wave. Oso's heart sinks, his mouth drops open, he struggles to breathe. To see the dead walk, glowing with angelic light, the fear, the pain, it is beyond words.

Ri calls over, "Dad, come out here."

Oso keeps his eyes locked on Ri for a long few moments, trying to decide for himself what he is seeing. He wants to drop his sword and jump out the window, but something in his soul tells him to stand his ground.

Ri beckons again, "Come on, hurry up."

Oso nods, he comes to a compromise with himself. He walks around the house and goes out the side door; he keeps his sword with him.

Reko Jet sees Oso make his way for the door and shouts at him, "what are you doing, you crazy old…" Reko tips his head, he watches Hanzo. Something is not right about him; the look in his eyes is one of hushed desperation. He is a man on the edge of losing his sanity. Depression rooted deeply; its hooks bleed out one's will to fight. Reko can feel Oso is struggling to hold on.

A hot wind blows as Oso walks around to the back of his house. The smell of rotting meat is thick in the air — the night wind carries with it death. Ri holds out his arms, inviting Oso to come to him.

Oso walks forward; he is shaking, crying silently. Oso drops his sword, he stagers, the image of Ri possessing his thoughts, forcing his actions.

Ri's mouth opens as Oso approaches showing his fangs, the boy's thorned tongue rolls out as he salivates, awaiting the moment when his father embraces him and he can taste his skin.

Reko grabs Oso as he is about to hug Ri, and using one arm as a fulcrum throws Oso across the field, demonstrating his valorous strength.

Ri sheds his skin, transforming into the winged beast that is his natural from.

The monster stoops and howls. Angered by the rejection of his girlfriend and the interruption of getting to embraces his father.

Ri pounces at Reko. Assuming he will be able to down the giant with one swing of his claws. But even for a Sanguine, Ri is small and weak. He is young, and his powers are limited.

Reko is not small or weak. The blacksmith is, in fact, mighty. One my think him one of the great giant warriors of Scandinavia if he were not Japanese. Reko takes the head of the monster in one hand, lifting it high into the air effortlessly then flings it at the ground.

Ri is stunned. He lays on the ground under Reko, Ri tries to crawl away from the giant. Reko rests a foot on the beast to hold him still. One hand reaches onto his belt. Reko pulls out his hammer and spins it to make sure he has his grip right.

Oso gains his footing; he looks up and tries to understand what has transpired. Reko drops the hammer onto Ri, splitting him in half with the hammer as if it had been a blade.

Oso shouts, "what? Why?.."

Reko thrust the hammer down a few more times, reducing the corps to little more than blue-red sludge on the ground.

"That wasn't Ri, Hanzo, it was a Baku. It was trying to confuse you. Draw you into the shadows with it." Reko looks to the quivering swordsmen "this is the third time I have stopped you from killing yourself. I think we are going to need to work out a payment plan of some sort."

Oso crawls over to the remains of Ri and looks down at the slime he left behind. "I don't believe it." he looks up at Reko from crouched, "how can this be?"

Reko rubs his neck with one hand, "I don't know." Reko looks out onto the streets, "but there is no hiding from it. there are monsters, after all."

Oso runs over and grabs his sword. "we need to do something about this. If Ri was a monster, he wasn't the only one."

May 15th, 6:12 am

Takashi doesn't sleep; only the maddest of the crazed could after what he had seen and done. Odette was on to something before she fell asleep. The entomology book he had been reading several nights ago rests under her head as she sleeps. A notebook off to one side of her checkered with her research.

Takashi slips the book out from under Odette's arm to look over her notes. "Drain Fly?" he reads her headline. "attracted to funguses commonly found in and around bathrooms. Less than a millimeter in length, these fur-covered bugs belong to the family of 'true insects'…"

Takashi falls back onto the couch as he watches Odette sleep thinking about what she had found. "yeah, that would make sense. That is the root of the infection. The common link. The infection started in the septic networks and worked its way up here. Odette, you found it, you found what Tenzuma was looking for."

Sakura comes in from the bedroom, she has redressed and makes her way to the laundry room to grab her school clothes "they are asleep. The voices of the ... whatever they are, have gone quiet."

Takashi turns his head, "Sakura, is there any way I can convince you to come in for some test?"

Sakura stands still for a moment, thinking, she then shakes her head "truth be told I would rather not."

Takashi tips his head back with a strained grunt "that is understandable."

May 15th, 8:20 am

Jo Kogotana stands in the observation room, watching an interrogation. The investigator knows his script and reads it just as it is meant. The man being questioned has nothing to say.

The female detective takes over. She is much more abrasive in her method. She gets in close; she shouts, she threatens violence. When the witness still refuses to talk. The woman shows her sword.

The male detective takes over again, as the two jump back and forth in an attempt to unsettle the witness. The door to the observation room slides open.

Useto walks in. Jo rests an arm on the wall as he leans on the glass, looking down. "DO you know what is bothering me right now?"

"No, sir," Useto explains.

"unless this scum confesses right now to having set that fire, I have to let him walk," Jo explains.

Useto changes the topic, "sir, I was just with Tomi in interrogation room #4. He wants to see you."

Jo nods, "alright."

Useto holds up a hand to stop Jo "Sir, if I may talk freely…"

Jo waves him on, "what is it you want to say?"

"I think it was wrong of us to go to Ichishin-Megami, the monks have been…" Useto starts to complain

Jo cut him off. "and that made them lawless and unruly. The monks are free to do as they wish, so long as the laws, they make for themselves so not contradict the laws that we live by. Ichishin made a mistake. They assumed that they would never be held to judgment."

Jo walks out of the room and down the hall to meet up with Tomi. The young monk waits in the dramatically under decorated interrogation hall.

Tomi smiles and takes a bow, "Constable."

Jo stands tall. He rests one hand on the desk and looks down at the monk demonstrating his position of power. "Talk fast." He orders.

Tomi explains, "you bringing us here was not a good move. You have endangered yourself; you have endangered us..."

Jo punches the table, "...Make a point!"

"you know the local myths and legends. The ghost stories that everyone in town has been repeating for the last several dozen generations. Well, there may just be a lick of truth to them."

Jo cuts Tomi off again, "I am not interested in talking to you about folklore." Jo points across the way. "my men dug up no less than twenty burnt bodies in your back yard. I want you to tell me about them."

Tomi nods. "this is not going to be easy to explain."

Jo shouts, "I suspect it will not be!"

"the fox demon." Tomi explains, "the ghost stories. They all date back to the same thing. Every few generations, they wake up…"

Jo pulls back a hand, threateningly "say something that makes sense."

"Tamamo-No-Mia, the fox demon, she has lots of names. And every time she wakes up, it marks the end of an age. The death of the old guard, the burning of the village. We have been trying to keep her asleep. Doing anything we can to make sure that she stays underground." Tomi tries to convey

"And" Jo questions, "How does the explains the burnt bodies?"

"Tamamo is awake. She has attacked us. We are trying to unearth where she is hiding. Everyone we have sent looking for her though has come back changed." Tomi elaborates.

Jo walks back and forth, he is deep in thought "Reductio ad absurdum, let's say just for a moment that I am willing to take you at your word. Where is Tamamo? Where is she hiding? What are you going to do when you find her?"

Tomi leans on the table, his head down "my feeling is that she is somewhere off in Shika woods. Maybe near Kareki stretch. Or the Northeast Summit. But, we have been seeing people all over the place that have fallen under her power. That is why we have been drawing magic seals all anywhere we go; we are hoping to herd the possessed away from populated areas. Jo, we are trying to help."

Jo has a heavy heart. A week ago, he would not have been willing to entertain this madness, but after seeing the things he has in the last few days, he feels inclined to except that Tomi thinks he is telling the truth. "I am gong to send my people out there. Have them take a look around. See if your story holds water."

"That may not be wise." Tomi comments

May 15th, 9:05 am

Oso Hanzo and Reko Jet are in the back yard of Oso's house. Hanzo had set up a funeral pyre and burned the remains of his son early in the morning. Hanzo has gathered his training blades. He needs to work out; Jet is happy to help.

The two men stand shoulder to shoulder, a blade in hand each like each other's shadow Hanzo slide-steps to the right, Jet to the left. Both men bring their swords overhead. Then slash, from shoulder to hip across the body. Jet and Hanzo box step reversing their footing to counter slash then is a three-step pivot step past one another into their next slash.

The dance is slow and deadly, a traditional exercise of professional swordsmen dating back generations. The dancing blades is old and part of ritual no longer in common practice. With Ri dead, Jet is the only person Hanzo will teach the blade dance to.

With Jet's family also missing, Hanzo's variation, 'the one-and-a-half-handed blade,' may well end this lifetime. The past can only live so long as someone remembers it.

Sakura Tomoji walks around to the backyard hearing the sounds of the men working out. Sakura drops Reje's broken sword on the ground. "Reko!" she yells out, "can this be fixed?"

Jet picks up the broken blade from the ground, "History and mythology are littered with broken swords. This one doesn't need to stay broken. I will fix it."

With that, Jet departs from the group. Oso watches him walk off, "Well, there goes my workout partner."

Sakura picks up a practice sword; she flips about the blade gripping it in revered-edge stances. "I am still free." Sakura explains. "if you are in the mood to do some sparing."

Oso grins happily, "I am a samurai, girl, are you sure you want to do this?"

The pair engage in a playful sparring match. Oso is taking it slow and easy at first, but Sakura demonstrates an uncanny skill with a blade. It is unclear who she trained under, be it her mother or father or officer Useto, but whoever it was, they must surely be a gifted swordsman in their own right.

The two spend a good part of the morning playing point matches. Oso, in the end, coming out on top, but given another few years of training, Sakura would be better than him.

May 15th, 11:10 am

One by one, the senior staff of the hospital are led into the conference hall. Takashi stands at the whiteboard. His arms folded as he watches, a level of dire concentration burning in his eyes.

Dr. Iwata is the acting head of the nursing department.

Jaki Yu is in charge of environmental services and housekeeping.

Professor Hugo Chon works in records and bookkeeping.

Ms. Chippa Nehan is running dietary and recreation.

And Officer Sensue Sie is acting head of security.

Takashi Tsu runs his eyes along his staff; most of these people are kids, only a few years out of school. But what is there that can be done? Day after day, he has people getting hurt, or worse. So, a few men that may or may not be field-tested needed to be pushed up the ranks. Takashi takes a headcount. Then whispers to himself, "why don't I see nurse Arnoldo?"

There is a moment of tension as everyone finds themselves staring at Takashi, waiting to see what the acting director called them for.

The door swings open, and Arnoldo staggers into the room, holding a large stack of slides, a folder filled with projector papers, and a polaroid camera.

Takashi addresses the nurse "out antiquing?"

"I ran across the river, stopped by my grandma's thrift shop. I found this." He holds the camera overhead, "I had to share it with you guys."

For a few seconds, Iwata mocks Arnaldo for his detention, but then Takashi intercedes on his behalf, "Hang on, I think I know what Arnoldo is getting at." Takashi waves, "come here, Arnoldo."

Arnoldo approaches, he starts to talk in a fast jittering voice, Takashi needs to slow him down. After a few moments, Arnoldo starts again "Sorry, sorry, sorry. Let me try again. I was thinking about you and the tape from earlier. Everyone here knows that you do not know about computers or editing. But I do. So, if we started passing around cell phone photos, everyone is going to think that I doctored them somehow. But with a camera like this one, if you want to do a trick, it needs to be 'in-frame.' So, if we are going to check our friends to see if any of them are an Alien-Life-Form, I think we should use an older camera."

Takashi thinks for a moment "you know people have been faking UFO sightings and Spirit Photography since the

1800's" Takashi slaps him playfully, "But I like the way you are thinking. Let's do this."
 Takashi takes the old camera; he whispers with Iwata to make sure she understands what is going on also. Iwata stands up to prime the staff.

"Listen closely. What Takashi is about to say is going to sound strange. But we are all educated people here, and we understand that extraordinary claims require evidence. So, evidence will be provided." Iwata has a hand set on her shoulder; she sits down as Takashi takes over.

"Since the start of the month, we have been on the defensive. A pathogen of unknown origin has been plaguing our town. Mr. Arnoldo, Doctor Iwata, and a hand full of volunteers have been working day and night to track our Nemesis. We have been losing. We have no aid coming from the outside, and we have lost Doctors Tenzuma and Handa along with others. But now, thanks in no small part to their sacrifice and courage, we are ready to strike back."

Takashi fires-up the projector "some of you have reported hearing whispers about some sort of ALF that is not off the table. It would seem that what we are fighting is a parasitic life form that lives outside of the spectrum of visible light as we see it. Odette Tsu and Orochi Arnoldo have been collecting photos of contaminated areas." He starts flipping through photos.

"this alien fungus, or whatever we end up calling it, can be perceived via video media. Why? How? We are still working on that. What I can confirm is that those that die from the 'infection' can be manipulated by it. It is my feeling that the infection has originated in the waterways under the town, possibly being transferred from person to person in part by drain flies or other household..."

Ms. Nehan interrupts, "...can you clarify what you mean by manipulated?"

Takashi waves to Iwata, Iwata stands up, "Shortly after the passing of Dr. Handa, Arnoldo and myself had encountered him. He was responsible for the riot the other night. Officer Sie will confirm this."

Takashi picks up again "I am not an expert of Entomology or Parasitology, but it looks as if the 'infection' has smoothing in common with a swarm of parasitic insects, they nest under the skin, incubate, copulate, divide then replace. At some point, the bugs are in control of the body. They seem to have some of our memories, or at least the ability to act human enough to confuse us. They walk around as us, find new host then…" Takashi's head drops, he turns off the side projector and walks away a few steps lost in thought.

The room has fallen salient as everyone is considering what was expressed. Nehan speaks out, "I was required to take classes in parasitology to get my tittle, and I would like to say 'controlling' one's host is not typical behavior for parasites."

Takashi whispers, "not common, but is it possible?"

Nehan replies, "there are a hand full of parasites that can do this, but not on something the size of a human. Not in that way…"

Takashi spins to face Nehan, "but why do it at all? what is the end goal?"

Arnoldo comments, "Isn't the points of life always the same? Proliferation."

Takashi shakes off his looming feeling of dread and suspicion as he waves to Arnoldo, "Please hand me the camera." Arnoldo does. Takashi takes a moment to look at it; he reads the camera specs off the base of it. He then turns his attention to the room again "here is the short and skinny of what I was trying to get at, these alien life forms like to play games with people. It takes over the body slowly. As you approach the point that you are contagious, assuming that is the right term, you start to glow purple, and if you are a full-on monster, you can see that also, using this." He holds up the camera. Takashi takes a photo of himself then sets the picture on the table for everyone to look at. "Now Sie, then Iwata…" he has his coworkers line up to have their photos taken.

Once satisfied, everyone is human. Takashi explains, "that is why we have been burning our dead."

Iwata Asks, "now, how are we going to fight this?"

Takashi explains, "that starts with sterilizing the building. Mr. Yu, would it be possible to raise the temperature in this building above 220°f."

Yu stars with his eyes wide as he considers it. Iwata interrupts, "That is lunacy!"

Takashi orders, "Can it be done?"

Iwata slaps the table "do you know what happens to the human body at…"

Yu cuts in "…not all at the same time! I could do it two floors at a time if I lock off the vents at the right junctions."

Iwata speaks out, "and what do we do after that."

"Heal the sick, kill the dead." Takashi orders.

May 15th, 12:10 pm

Jin and Odette walk to the park side by side. They approach the table that they have sat at just about every day for years. Only to find Masumo there, her head down reading a book, her umbrella slid into a knot in the wood to hold it up and open as if it were a beach parasol.

Jin sits down, he sets his book bag on the table and starts to shuffle through it, "and so six is now three." In pulls out a few bottles of juice and sets them out "somehow, I suspect there are not going to be many people at our graduation party."

Odette takes one of the bottles of juice; she pops the lid and drinks it fast. "Let's see if anyone makes it to graduation. I don't know about you, but I am still three years off in spite of honors credit."

Masumo speaks out, "do you know what an Ash Borer is?"

Odette nods "yeah, it is the little green bug we see all over the place. They attract monkeys and sparrows. They love the taste of them; it seems."

Masumo retorts the information she is reading "Ash Borer lay 70 eggs at a time sometimes as many as 200. And it seems that once they leave their larva stage, it only takes them a few days to reach their full size."

Jin remarks, "I guess you need to grow fast when you live at the bottom of the food chain in your ecosystem."

Odette squints as she thinks, "I heard my mom saying something about America having a big problem with Ash Borers. Apparently, there are no animals in the states that actively hunt them, so their population doubles every few years." Odette leans forward, laying on the table, "supposable woodlands all along the Rocky Mountains are infested, and they are pushing other animals out…"

Masumo comments, "how strange that such a small and weak animal can do so much damage."

Jin pulls out his phone; he shouts, "Smile!" he photographs Masumo. Masumo squeals and looks away.

Jin shows the pictures to Odette. "it is not the same." They both comment. Masumo's wings are visible in the pic, but unlike the other monster they have seen, Masumo's fur is brightly tanned, sometimes silver, her wings have textured patterns on them, some sections laced with colors, red, yellow, and orange.

Masumo regains her footing, "that was not nice of you!" she complain.

Jin looks to Masumo, "then you know what I was doing."

Masumo huffs, "of course I do. I have been watching the two of you out monster hunting all day."

Odette shows the blade she has strapped to her leg at this point "you killed Reje and Ri." She starts to draw the edge " you are the shadow monster that we saw hiding in the tree." Her eyes turn cold and hard "now is there any reason we shouldn't dismantle you?"

Masumo is unintimidated "if you kill me, you can't learn from me."

Jin holds Odette back, "wait; she isn't afraid of getting hurt." He goes on, "every animal has an instinct for self-preservation. If she isn't fighting back, that means she doesn't view us as a threat."

Masumo looks over her shoulder "have you two ever been to the A&W station? I was just there. They have fantastic ice-cream. It isn't like the ice-cream they have at the Mochi shop; it is soft and bubbly…"

Jin inquires, "Masumo, what are you?"

Masumo leans forward; her eyes turn intense, her voice goes deep and soft "I am your best chance of surviving. There is a war coming to this town. Butterflies, Sanguine, men, and everything between. This has all happened before, and it will happen again."

Jin leans in entranced, "what?"

"if they win, we die, if I win, we play again next century. Last time it was Nobunaga that was the champion of humanity, this time, it will be one of you." There is a short pause, then Masumo's voice goes high and happy "anyway, I want some more ice-cream."

Masumo stands up and runs off, holding her arms out like an airplane. Jin scoots in to whisper with Odette, "do you believe her?"

Odette holds out her arms in a shrug, "I don't know." Her head shakes "have you looked around lately? Do you see how weird everything is?" she points up the street "we have a wrecked ocean liner in the front yard of the temple, we have no phones, the school has been shut down... everything is wrong right now."

Jin takes a deep breath and shuts his eyes; he brings up a hand and bites onto one of his fingers as he is thinking. He whispers with himself, "take it slow, look around, think. Calculate the odds." He opens his eyes, "we have nothing to lose by pressing her for more information. Assume that what she told us is incomplete. But in every lie, there is some truth. She is a monster, but maybe we are useful to her."

Odette cuts off Jin's train of thought, "come on, Jin! We are going with her."

May 15th, 12:20 pm

Masumo holds up a cardboard cup catty with three cups of ice-cream in it. "they only had one flavor left, but it is a good one, it is cola-flavored."

Jin looks to the shop Masumo had just stepped out of. "I don't think I have ever been in there."

Masumo looks up at the sign, "what do you think A&W stands for?"

Odette shrugs "could be someone name."

Jin adds, "or two peoples names: Alan and Wright maybe, or Albert and Wriggly."

Odette comments, "Reje, I bet knows."

Masumo adds, "they are a western-style barbeque. They had one of these in England when I was there also. The food at this one tastes better." She takes a long drink of her shake.

Jin focuses, "Masumo, what are you?"

Masumo looks up to Jin through half-shut eyes, "you already know. I told you everything I can remember. Come on, put it all together."

Jin's eyes dart open as he thinks, he goes back, thinking about every conversation he has had with Masumo, what it all means. 'There are things in the world, strange things, old things, things we can't hope to understand,' 'boy 'Because you have done this, for you, I shall give you a gift.', 'The blood of the mosquitoes mixed with the blood of the butterflies'

At last, Jin remarks, "Shi, Queen of the Butterflies."

Odette looks between the two of them "I don't remember that story. Someone catch me up to speed."

Jin jumps to a conclusion "aliens didn't invade us; they were here before us. The Mil was erected on top of the nest of the butterflies. Tamamo-No-Mia, O-kami, Mr. Red Blue. These were all stories about times that people had encountered Shi and her children…"

Masumo looks bashful "that may be overstating the facts somewhat." Masumo turns and looks out into the woods "do you know where the old village is?"

Odette looks upstream, "give or take."

"Nekoba is there right now…" Masumo starts.

Jin cuts in, "how do the illusions you cast work?"

"the olfactory glands can be used to highjack the other senses." Masumo offers

Jin presses for more information, "what about cameras can bypass that?"

"Smell-o-vision doesn't exist yet." Masumo joke dryly

"can you fool both my sight and vision at the same time?" Jin becomes aggressive in his inquiry.

Masumo flaps her invisible wings, and the next time Jin and Odette blink, the three of them are standing outside the temple. The church is cleaner and better dressed; then, it has been in days as if they were setting up for a festival.

Jin and Odette both gasp in confusion, throwing their drinks as the change disorients them. Masumo demonstrates superhuman speed, balance, and foresight by catching two shakes in one hand and taking hers in the other.

She explains, "you would be shocked by the things I can do." She smiles, "evidence is not evident when the truth is not true, and facts are not factual." She hands them back their drinks "time can be warped, space can be folded, and the mind can be distorted."

Odette struggles to understand; she takes a deep breath to calm herself "if you have this kind of power. What can possibly threaten you?"

"something that has the same power."

May 15th, 7:10 pm

Sakura Tomoji is happy to share what she knows about the Sanguine with Oso and Reko once Reje's sword has been repaired. She tells them about how she was attacked; she tells them how the beasts try to invade people's minds. But most important of all, she tells them that the monsters can die and that she has some idea as to where they go to hide during the day.

As they walk through the trees, the sun is setting quickly, Oso comments "this looks like someplace I have been before."

Reko explains, "that is because you have been here; this is the Kareki stretch."

Oso nods, "that is right…"

Sakura interjects, "is there anything that you would like to confess, Oso-son?"

Oso explains, "this is revelation to no one. After my wife passed, I grew deathly sick as well. I came out here and called out to the kami to heal me, no matter what that means. The kami answered my call. They put a rope in my hand and told me to climb the hanging tree. They would heal me if I demonstrated my love for them by leaping to my death. I jumped, and the rope snapped from around my neck. I feel into Reko's arms as he was walking through the forest."

Oso looks to Reko, "by the way, what had brought you this deep into Sheka anyways?"

"I was out with Ahiru." Jet is brief with his reply.

Eyes in the trees watch them. One of the many forest beasts has spotted the hunters "Ki-Me," the yellow-eyed devil. Ki-Me has seen these three before. But in the case of two of them, it has not been for over a decade. He had bit Oso the last time he was in the forest and has free rein to read his thoughts. And even offer him suggestions. Ki-Me is older than some of the forest spirits but not the most powerful. That honor belongs to "Shirio-Kemono," also called Tamamo-No-Mia daughter of "Shirio-Oh-Kami."

Ki-Me flaps his wings; he fills the air with an intoxicating scent. Ki-Me reaches into Oso's mind, seeing if he still has the power to control him after all these years.

Oso smells the thoughts of the fly in the tree. His back straightens out; he stands tall. His eyes haze over. Jet calls out to Oso, "hay, what is going on? Do you see something?"

Oso turns to look at his followers; Oso reaches across his body, gripping his blade. He swiftly draws his sword. He is coming in at Jet with a traditional three-strike kill. A slash from the scabbard across the eyes, then flip the blade around to come down across the nose.

Jet does not let this happen, he back steps taking a cut to the arm, and as Oso comes in for the seconds hit of the combo, Jet attacks the attacker. Jet uses his good arm to grab Oso around the wrist and holds him still.

An old scar on Oso's neck becomes visible once more, a long red mark running down the throat and behind the collarbone. The old injury seems to burn, reinvigorated as if a freshly pulsating blister, filling with die blood cells.

With much anguish, Reko outstretches his bleeding arm and grabs Hanzo's other hand; the massive man starts to walk Oso backward.

Sakura's eyes turn upwards; she spots the bug in the tree. She uncases her wings and leaps into the branches with heroic agility.

Sakura shows Ki-Me her sword and speaks to him, "you are doing this. How?" she commands.

Ki-Me looks up, losing his concentration, "you are a moth?..., aren't you?"

Sakura is consumed by the need to hunt, the need to kill. In a brief moment of all-consuming passion, she draws the sword and strikes the monster. A slash across the wings, the beast falls from the tree.

Black snake-like tendrils spray from its back, searching for its broken bits. Sakura leaps from the tree, landing on the beast's chest with a sword plant. The blade breaks through the fly's body and darts out its back spiking the thing to the ground.

Sakura kneels atop it. With a hiss, Sakura chokes down her bloodlust. This monster could be helpful.

Oso shakes his head, his vision becoming clear as the beast loses its grip on his mind. Jet, fails to take notice as he takes action to disarm Oso, Jet cat steps to one side and pulls on Oso's arms, drawing the samurai across his body and into a knee strike. Oso collapses.

Sakura orders, "How does the mind control you have work?"

The beast buzzes and shakes its body side to side, struggling. Sakura mans it with the back of her hand "I asked you a question bug! How does it work!"

The monster grabs at her trying to force its way out from under her. Sakura is having none of it; she leans forwards straddling the beast and takes its throat in all four of her arms, throttling its breath. "start talking now!"

"I can't talk if I am dead." It gasps

"then, this does hurt." Sakura loosens her grip. "I have power, and I plan to live to see the end of all of this. Now, talk. What are you? How do we kill you? What is this power you have over us"?

Ki-Me explains, "you are one of us, the one that birthed you should have told you these things."

Sakura speaks out, "what do you mean, birthed?"

"you are awakened. Are you not? Your blood and ours are mixed. If not, you could not transform."

Oso sits up, "awakened? You mean to say not everyone can become what you are?"

Jet pulls out his hammer and stands over Sakura waiting, he can see what is going on, and he doesn't like it one bit.

Sakura explains, "my mother suffered an unfortunate fate. She told me nothing about this."

Ki-Me elaborates, "there are a dozen or more subspecies of us, we are each unique, but still one can see the resemblance between us, like dogs of a breed. You, a moth, you can mind control humans just like I do, maybe better. Flap your wings fill the air with skin dust, those that breath your dust, you can see them think." He continues, "sting them with the tooth on your tongue, and you can send them dreams."

Oso asks, "and how can one resist this?"

Ki-Me explains, "one cannot. Once one is in your mind, your mind is theirs, but only one mind can horrid many. Two Sanguine cannot share one human."

"then, if I share my blood with these two, you lose your power over them?" Sakura asks.

"no, so long as I live, I control all that I have stung." Ki-Me clarifies.

"so long as you live." Sakura sees the loophole; she exploits it. Sakura thrust herself down on the monster and takes his throat in her fangs. She crushes him, suffocating him in her jaws.

Jet holds his hammer overhead "tell me you are still you or I am going to…"

Once Ki-Me stops struggling, Sakura tips her head up "I am me. No one can control my thoughts; it seems. Maybe my mother somehow gave me immunity to them."

The sky crackles, a stiff wind picks up. More rain, every night it seems, rain. Have things always been like this, or has the awakening of these forest spirits somehow angered the world, allowing for these nightly storms.

Sakura can do nothing to hide her monstrous nature; rain pours down her body, her clothing turns translucent, the monsoon washes away the blood from her face, her eyes are wide and fearful. "I am one of them." she whimpers, "I always have been."

Reko Jet grips his hammer tightly. He watches Sakura, seemingly having forgotten the deep cut in his arm. He grunts in contemplation. The voice is right; her expression is understandable. Maybe she is telling the truth, or perhaps Sakura Tomoji is an exceptional actress.

Oso takes off his backpack; he looks to Reko, "Give me your arm." Oso pulls out of his bag: a sewing kit and a bottle of rum. "this is going to hurt a lot." Oso cleans a needle with rum then stitches up Reko's slash.

Reko points out, "that wasn't the only one of them." he growls. "Where are they, Sakura?"

Sakura crawls off of the monster. She points "that way. There is a fissure in the ground that leads into an underground waterway. I can smell them."

Oso looks up at Reko "are you good to keep pushing forward?"

"It is only one arm; I have another."
Reko proclaims
.

May 15th: 10:24 pm

Jin and Odette are walking hand-in-hand, Jin has his flashlight held out before him. He spins around, suddenly aware of his surroundings.

Jin jumps about to face Odette; she seems to be just awakening from having been sleepwalking. "Odette, where are we?"

Odette pulls out her flashlight and looks side to side "I don't know, I have never seen this part of town." the houses are old, burned, and crumbling under there own weight, half-covered in snow.

Masumo skips down the street; she spins her umbrella around playing with it "welcome to the old town."

Jin barks, "how did we get here? What did you do?"

Masumo stops spinning and looks up to the clouds, "which did you want me to answer first?"

Odette speaks up, "are you controlling us?"

Masumo explains, "you two can't be controlled. Your families have developed resistance to us over the years. I can send you thoughts, but I can't take full control of your bodies."

"Resistance?" Jin asks.

"The more times someone in your bloodline is bitten, the larger of a dose it takes to alter your brain chemistry. And if at some point you were one of us…" Masumo bites one of her fingers. "maybe it would be easier to have Nekoba explain that part…"

Odette cuts in "… Nekoba?"

Masumo points to a cave "he is at the sunken chapel, been there since he recovered." Masumo takes the two of them into the underground. Through the museum of lost things, and to a small room packed tightly with scrolls and books dating back hundreds of years.

Nekoba is slumped over a table, a pen in one hand, a blank parchment off to one side, and two others set before him and to his other side as he is translating.

Odette calls out, "Nekoba-son."

Nekoba looks up, "Tsu?" Nekoba stands up. He looks to the kids. Odette rushes over to offer Nekoba a hug.

Jin whispers with Masumo. "I want to say I am not thrilled by this."

Masumo whispers back, "do you think I am trying to hurt you still? I have been helping you since the beginning."

Odette questions, "Nekoba, what is all of this?"

Nekoba looks down at the scrolls "the lost articles of Ojoyoshu. It turns out that reading a 900-year-old book is not easy. Even if it is written in a language, you speak. The usages of words change a good deal over the ages."

Odette looks at the book "Ojoyoshu: the Path of Salvation, I have seen copies of this in our town library."

Nekoba picks up his pen and sits back down "you have seen copies of copies. But looking at older versions, you can find some essential things that change between them. The word 'brother,' for example, on this page, it is spelled differently, on this page. That is not a mistake. 'Brother' has two meanings." He points between the two spellings "this character means 'of flesh' and this one 'of arms' but in later printings, they only ever use the character for 'of arms.'" He moves on to another page. "now here. This word means 'birth' but so does this one."

Odette leans in looking at the page, "I don't know this character."

"that is because it no longer appears in common vernacular. The closest word we have to that is 'manufacture' or maybe 'erect.' Honen himself was having trouble transcribing this because he didn't know why the original penner of the scroll was using this spelling and not the more common ones."

Odette asks for clarification, "who is Honen?"

"12th century, he was an artist and a scholar, he helped build the modern Buddhist church." Nekoba expresses.

"what do you mean by modern?" Jin asks for clarification as he approaches.

"Everything morphs over time, Nothing more so than things that are enshrined in culture. One of the easiest ways to view this is through the lens of Judaism. Once a polytheistic church, like most of the ones around here. But after the fall of Judea at the hands of Iran, the survivors began adopting the ideas of their invaders. The Jews started to incorporate ideas like a god having an enemy, and the promise of eternal life in exchange for sufficient sacrifices or other holy gifts. These ideas come from the church of Zora, not from Judea."

"the same thing, of course, happened to us. Look around our church, see if you can spot anything that looks like it may have been brought in from somewhere else. Everything changes."

"so, by the time Honen lived, new ideas had been brought in, and old ones had been forgotten. Looking at early writing can give a good clue as to how things evolve."

Jin asks, "do you know about the monsters in the forest? about Masumo?"

Nekoba looks to Shi the Butterfly, "I do now, and it looks as if Ichishin-Magami has known for some time." He looks down at his books. "I had found a passage in one of these most revealing books, a conversation between Siddhartha and a kami, who's name I can't seem to figure out how to pronounces. The kami had told Siddhartha 'that which is to immerge from the flesh is more than that which is to immerge from lust alone, no elder that is from the sky would allow being born that which is not with …' I think that last word translates best to 'purpose.'"

Jin thinks aloud, "I think this needs some more context."

Nekoba nods. "I admire a man that searches for understanding so heroically. Buddha was trying to understand something. He wanted to know what use gods have for men. In light of the things I have seen of late, I think I have an idea of my own. Directed Panspermia. Life was created intentionally. Or at least is being guided."

Odette looks around, "Ok, I will say it." she takes a deep breath "what?"

Nekoba leans back in his chair, "we are not alone in the universe. There are things out there that could be described as gods — metaphysically speaking. Masumo's people lost their world. To some sort of accident and somehow, she and a few dozen others it would seem escaped. They immigrated here. But we are not them. If they want to live, they need to find a way to refresh the gene pool. They have been experimenting with us for generations. Trying to fuse us into one animal."

Jin cuts in, "so you are saying that the atmosphere is right, the levels of gasses and whatnot are not a problem, the bacteria and funguses are not deadly to them, and we somehow look-alike in spite of being independent creation events, and the only problem comes down to sex?"

Masumo speaks up, "I wouldn't say funguses weren't a problem. But to the bacteria on this planet, we were alien; our biology just isn't close enough to yours for earth parasites to latch onto us."

Nekoba adds, "if I am reading this right, Masumo's people have been working for generations to either make us more like them or them more like us."

Masumo elaborates, "amazingly, in the last few decades, your medical technology has exceeded anything we ever had. In fact, so has your information technology and understanding of physics. Your locomotion still needs some work, but given the limited parts you are starting with, I can understand."

Odette turns to look at Masumo, "started with?"

Masumo nods, "you are the first sapient animal on this plant as far as I can tell, on our world we evolved as the ninth sapient race. We constructed most of our machinery around the hollowed-out shells of the races that came before us. So, once we learned how to talk, we started evolving pretty fast."

Chapter 9: Six Days Remaining

May 16th, 2:45 am

With some effort, Oso, Reko, and Sakura can track down a cave hidden in the depths of Shika. The original plan had been to burn the place to the ground, but it turns out that setting fire to a cave 600' deep by ¾ of a mile wide is not such a simple task. So, it is time to come up with a new plan.

The three of them hide around the opening to the cove. Wait for the monsters to come back. Then depending on how many there are, come up with a plan after that. If there are only two or three, then perhaps the three of them can overpower them. If there are a dozen, then they will need to regroup and come up with another attack strategy.

Two are coming, moths, gray wings, yellow skin. Both female, one fully grown, one is adolescent. Sakura could detect them approaching from over a mile away. She calls out to the others what she can sense.

The two monsters land outside the cave, the adult is dressed in a red housecoat with black accents, the adolescent is holding a bag made out of a broken plush toy and dressed in the uniform worn by 8th graders, a red dress, white blouse, and red coat. Jet spots something in the hands of the smaller one...

... a plastic horse toy, blue and red in color. It is Ahiru's birthday present. Jet steps out of hiding. He is blind with anger. The small bug sees him, and she shouts, "Papa-son!"

The older of the two bugs takes notices; she grips the small one pushing her bake protectively. "Reko." The older one calls out, "allow me to speak please." She lowers her eyes.

Jet snarls, "don't try to confuse me, monster." He squeezes his hammer tightly "you are dressed in Kuma's clothes, but you are not my beloved. And that thing at your side is not my girl, that is not my Ahiru." He advances aggressively "I know you can use your evil spirit magic to control people, you will find it very difficult to control me."

Kuma pushes Ahuir "run child." She commands.

The monster that looks like Jet's daughter runs int the woods. Jet calls over to Sakura, "follow her." Sakura does as instructed and chases Ahuir.

Kuma walks backward away from her lover. "Reko, things are going on here that are difficult to explain…"

Oso stays hidden for a moment longer, his eyes dance back and forth between the moths and Reko. 'why does this one look so afraid?' he asks himself 'why has she not fled, or attacked?' he squints 'those two look more like Sakura then like Ri or demon at Kareki stretch.'

Oso stands up to protest, "Reko! Stop!" Oso commands

Jet pays no heed; he Dashes forward and grabs Kumi around the neck. With one massive hand, he lifts the ghoulha overhead. Oso jumps out to grip Reko by one arm to stop him from swinging his hammer into the monster. Jet complains, "Don't make this harder than it has to be."

Oso explains, "she might be like Sakura; she might still be in control..."

Jet cuts in "... then why would we be in Sheka woods and not back at your tea house?" he squeezes the monster, Reko is more than strong enough that with just a little more focus he can shatter bone with his bare hands. Kumi has no hope of struggling against the giant.

With a wave of his arm, Jet throws Oso off of him and, in the same motion, pushes Kuma into the nearest tree. He swings his hammer repeatably, pulverizing the small bug, he keeps swinging, waiting for her to stop trying to heal. It would seem that the regeneration of this monster has a limitation.

Oso can do little but watch helplessly. It is as if Oso can do nothing to protect anyone around him. Only avenge their deaths.

Sunrise will come all too soon, Sakura returns to the group panting and wheezing. She cradles her chest and complains "that one clearly has more practice at flying then I do."

Jet stands tall, splattered in blood. "I assume that you took care of it?"

Sakura shakes her head, "she outran me."

Jet nods "we will find her another time. Our homes are all tainted. I see nothing that can be done but for us to go door to door searching for the infected and slay them."

May 16th, 3:15 am

Machohero awakens sharply, something is in her throat, wiggling around in her chest. Her eyes spring open, she can't move, only gag on her own tongue.

Looming over her bed is a monster, no less than 10 feet tall; its arms easily reach across the bed, balancing itself. Its wings stretch out, darkening the room. Its hands are long, its arms are long. It seems the monster has extra joints allowing it an even more inhuman dexterity.

Machohero can feel the blood being drained from her body and replaced with something else. The jaws of the white-haired-beast encircle her head. Machohero can't hope to scream; she can't struggle in any way. She is in the mouth of the beast.

In a matter of moments, the world goes dark. Machohero is filled with fear, but not pain. After sucking the life from Machohero's body, the white-haired-beast sits alongside her bed.

The monster rests a hand on Machohero chest and pets her, comfortingly. "Have no fear. I have taken away your weaknesses. When you awaken, you will be younger and more fertile then you had ever been, and if you do as I tell you, your seed will live long and grow fast."

May 16th, 7:00 am

The heatwave is over, with the morning's sunrise comes a slow sprinkle of rain and a cold snap. The sharp drop in temperature with the rising sun calls in a stiffening breeze. The air is hardly over 40°f

Sakura walks into her house. Useto's house is modest, 1 story, 2 beds, a bath, a common room, and a kitchen. Useto never needed or wanted more. A shrine is set up in the common's room. A statue of an elephant made out of wood, a sword, and an ax, a few dozen smooth stones, and three incent sticks.

"Dad, mom, are you home?" Sakura calls out.

Useto steps out of the kitchen, he is dressed in his uniform pants but is void of a shirt. He dries his hands and slips one into his pocket as he replies, "Yumia, has gone to see her parents on the other side of the river." Sneakily he draws his phone from his pocket. "You didn't come home last night. Or the night before."

Sakura kneels down and unlaces her boots "I was with Odette, Reje passed away." Sakura raises her eyes; she spots the phone in her father's hand. "Dad, please don't." she ducks her head; she falls onto her knees, outstretching her arms in plea.

Useto explains, "I did know about Reje, Dr. Tsu told me."

There is a long moment as Useto thinks. He knows what he should do. What he doesn't know is, does he have the wear for all to do what must be done if he sees what he knows he is going to see.

Sakura sees the delay, she doesn't want to have to reach for her knife, but she will. She can take her father's camera from him if she must. She is faster than a human, stronger, she can overpower him. But she will not, not if she doesn't need to.

Useto shuts his eyes; he returns his phone to his pocket without taking a photo. "Between Takashi and the chief, it seems everything is so odd right now. I don't even know if I can describe some of the things, I have seen these last few days."

Sakura stands up, "Dad, are you home for a little bit?"

"yes." Useto explains.

"please. Let me cook for you." Sakura asks

May 16th, 9:13 am

In large, the monks are still in lockup. Jo Kogotana stands before the monk Tobi. "I have a proposition; I have 7 men here that want to search the summit of the mountain for any signs of alien activity. Now, I have been informed that you recently traversed that road, if you would volunteer to lead my men there, I can have you and your brothers released."

The fit young monk leans on the wall, he nods, "Yeah, I can do that job. But what do we do if we do find aliens?"

Jo explains, "they are to be purged. Included in your supply bags will be kerosene and swords." Jo steps away from the cage "my men will be ready to deploy at 11 am"

Jo makes his way from there back to his office, he bumps into another deputy on the way, a girl named Maaya Sakomoto.

"the radio's have been blowing-up since 5 am. Missing persons, vandalism, assaults. People are not happy."

Jo explains, "our grocer has now missed three shipments, people are running low on household comfort: hand soap, paper towels, beer. They are getting aggravated, uncentered. The only tool we have is to intimidate them into keeping up the social contract."

"how much longer can we expect before unrest turns into ..." Maaya asks.

"...Not much longer. If the lights stay on, people will continue to trust me for a month, no more, if the lights go out, people will be in revolt before the end of next week. Losing the phones is a problem, there is no help coming. Everyone can see that." Jo grunts.

Jin calls out, "Dad!" he waves. "look what I found." Jin points to Nekoba.

Jo bows to Nekoba, "Allow me to say, I am happy to see you. Where have you been?"

Nekoba lowers his eyes, "gathering information about our visitors."

"then perhaps it is time for us to go see Takashi." Jo turns his eyes to Jin, "I trust you are up to date on all your reading?"

Jin smiles and nods, "of course, just because I am not at school does not mean that I can neglect my studies."

Jo orders, "what is Philosophy?"

Jin explains, "the love of wisdom. A Greek word, it was the foundation of modern science and arithmetic."

"What are the disciplines of philosophy?" Jo presses.

"in order:

1.) Epistemology, the philosophy of how to search of knowledge,

2.) physics, the philosophy as to how knowledge is vetted,

3.) Metaphysics, the philosophy of predicting and hypothesizing what knowledge we expect to gain,

4.) Esthetics, the philosophy of quantifying beauty,

5.) Ethics, the philosophy of how people should relate to each other

6.) Politics the philosophy of how people and governments can and should behave."

Jo grunts as if he isn't impressed, "and what is a Ph.D.?"

Jin rolls his eyes side to side, he looks disappointed, he forgot something and is having no luck placing it. it takes him several seconds to reply to the following statement, but at last, does "Doctor of Philosophy?"

Jo nods approvingly, "what is the burden of proof?" Still staggering from knowing he got something wrong on the last question Jin chokes. Jo shakes his head, then orders "run home, check on mother."

Jin bows, he then runs off.

Jo and Nekoba make their way to the hospital.

May 16th, 10:00 am

Takashi bikes into work. Takashi stopped at the library on his way, he picked up: a collection of maps of the town. Blueprints of some of the houses as well as maps historical sights. Now, can Takashi read diagrams or a schematic? No, but he has friends with a diverse set of skills, hopefully, what he lacks they can make up.

Takashi walks swiftly, collecting

daily reports as he walks. The hospital is a well-oiled machine. Most of the people in it have secondary and tertiary training allowing people to pick up extra jobs and help out in a multitude of ways. But even with exceptional discipline and indomitable determination, the staff is approaching the limits of their resolve.

More then a hand full of teachers have volunteered to act as EMT's, the kitchen is running low bread and sugar, but the supply of cocoa powder seems to be holding steady. Takashi is determined to maintain his hospital to the last, and he has just the people to do it. For the time being.

One of the nurses ushers Takashi into a conference room, a hasty conversation playing out as she does "…let him know that he is clear to start floor six, we will need to wait four hours between burns, and turn off the lifts in all non-staff-only areas…" Takashi passes on a note he received as he was walking

"…it is all being worked on already." The two talk over each other.

Nekoba and Kogotana are waiting, "how is this place still so clean? Maybe we should bring you to the town hall, maybe you can get the town back under control." Jo jokes.

Takashi takes a set; he pulls out his lighter and starts spinning it in one hand "it is called delegating. I don't need to solve every problem; I just need to know that someone knows it and someone has a plan to fix it."

Nekoba leans back in his chair and folds his hands over his stomach. "Gentleman, I feel we all have places we need to be today, so maybe we should talk shop." He looks to Takashi, "are you aware of the alien invasion?"

Takashi taps his foot and looks up, thinking, "I don't know if 'Invasion' is the right word. 'occupation' is apter. I think."

"how many of them do you think there are?" Nekoba inquires

"At least two. And they are in a state of sub factoring." Takashi explains, "they are twin phyletic, two sister claves that integrated together and their offspring broke off to become something new. It is something like horse breeding, distant but related animals meet somehow and …"

Nekoba cuts in, "amazing, you are so close to right."

Takashi leans in, "don't keep me in suspense, what do you know?"

Nekoba continues, "If I understand my sources, I know two things, first, they are hybridizing, second, they are speciating." Nakoba feels for his glasses on his face; he drops his hand to his side, remembering he lost his glasses. "at one time, there were only two. A predator and the pray the predator was after. With the change in environment, they adapted."

Takashi steps in on that "well, I am pretty sure I have seen the predator. I haven't seen the other."

"I have. The butterflies. They are amazing. Eternally young, benevolent, they are looking for nothing other than love." Nekoba explains, "If I were the type of man that gave merit the idea of spirits, I would surely recognize them as just that."

Jo joins the conversation, "so, how come the predators are only becoming aggressive now?"

Nekoba elaborates, "the Butterflies have a method of controlling them."

Takashi locks eyes, waiting for Nekoba to volunteer more information, "and what kind of control are we talking about?"

Nekoba looks down at his hands "that part is unreliable, I would say. It seems to be something to the effect of bacteria. Something that the predators are born with that just sort of forces them to self-destruct after reproducing a few times."

Takashi's mouth drops open, "that sounds less than benevolent." Takashi turns his attention back on Kogotana. "I would like you to make another public announcement. I want you to announce to the public that we are aware of the alien life forms walking amongst us, and that you would like to invite the aliens to make their way to the hospital. If they do so, we will guarantee their safety in exchange for their assistance in treating the sick and injured. I want to know what they know."

Jo looks in concern for some time, "Are you sure that is wise?"

Takashi makes himself a cup of tea. "no, I am not. But I would like it if one of the aliens offered to let me examine them." he sticks his nose in his tea, taking a hard sniff "Sakura, is she one of the butterflies, Nekoba?"

Nekoba lowers his head. "I only know two for sure. EvaMasumo and Sirosanto, others were named, but I did not see them."

Takashi retakes his set. "we could also try to force people to come forward by calling for a public health emergency, which truth be told we could have done days ago, or we can start breaking down doors, call it a police action."

Jo cuts him off, "you don't have that authority!"

Takashi points at Jo, "you do."

Jo looks to Nekoba, "what are your feelings on this?"

Nekoba folds his hands and shuts his eyes as he thinks about what has been spoken. "I will help you write the request for the aliens to step forward. I have been reading their writings, maybe I can find some choice words that will facilitate this change. They have been hiding for a long time and will be skittish."

Jo looks at the bag that Takashi was holding when he stepped into the office "what do you have there?"

Takashi explains, "A hypothesis."

May 16th, 1:19 pm

Odette has biked up to the water treatment plant. She had left her house early in the day to get here, with the main bridge down it is now a 6-mile trail upstream to the next path that leads to the farming district.

In the last few days, the town has changed dramatically. There has been flooding, a dozen larger structures have started to sink into the soft earth. The farm district is transforming into something that doesn't belong on this earth.

The glassworks, the water treatment center, and the steelworks all being amongst the places being claimed by nature. This is where it starts, this is where the drain flies originate from. Odette knows it.

Odette also has a plan to keep them at bay. All she needs are a few pictures she can give to Jin, and tomorrow the whole police force will be here to put an end to this.

Odette reaches into her backpack and pulls out a car battery and a signal light from the shipyard. A 1M lumen bulb in that lamp. This thing will night into day when she turns it on.

The water treatment plant is a modern-looking building. Large and painted in warm colors. The pipes that run across the wall are wrapped in white plastic and labeled with long sequences of letters and numbers that Odette doesn't understand, but it is clear that these are meant to help someone find their way around.

She holds her lamp in one hand, her phone in the other, slowly she walks around, she scans the top floor first then moves her way down the building. The place is a maze, but Odette is clever, she has a plan. On the upper level, she can find nothing of interest.

But, reaching the lower floors, things change quickly. Shades of white give away to red and brown. Opening a door, she finds what must be an entrance to an older building that this one was built around.

Eyes appear in the depths as Odette approaches distilling vat. Odette shines her torch at the eyes, the fuzzy tentacled beast fleas from the burning light. Odette looks down into the distilling vat. Thousands of gallons of placental fluid boil, hundreds of half-formed semi-human-monsters swimming in it.

Odette takes a photo of the sludge "our town's monster population may just be higher than our human at this rate." A shadow passes behind Odette, Odette feels the motion and spins around, she pulls out her high-powered flashlight and searches for the movement.

She spots a small shadow rounding the corner, "you know, in retrospect, I would feel a lot better right now if Sakura, Ri, Reje, and Jin were with me. Or Masumo, maybe I could have asked Mosumo to come with me."

Odette chases the shadow. The monster has frozen in front of a door with an electronic lock on it, the beast seems to be having trouble reaching the key panel as it looks to be a nine-year-old girl. She has gray wings and fluffy fur poking out of the caller of her uniform. The monster has on a backpack with a nametag on it 'Ahiru Jet.'

Odette calls out, "Hey, I recognize you. Ahiru, you are in the drama club and Jr. Swim team. I was in Jr.'s swim two years ago myself."

Ahiru calls out, "would you mind turning off that light, it is bright."

Odette calls out, "promise not to eat me."

"I am not a Sanguine, I am Chromon or at least half Chromon."

Odette lowers her, flashlight, "what are you doing here?"

Ahiru replies, "I am looking for something."

Odette approaches, "would you mind elaborating?"

"My mother, she was hurt, I came here to get her cocoon, that way she can rejuvenate."

Odette looks at the lock, "do you know the code?"

"yep, 9,9,9, and 9." Ahiru explains

"I like it, short and pointless." Odette keys in the code for Ahuri, "so, are you about nine-hundred-years-old by chance?"

Ahuri shakes her head, "no, I am nine. As far as I know, us half Chromon can't regenerate the way that true-bloods can."

The door unlocks, behind it, there is a stairwell and what looks like a hospital. The place is mostly empty, the ceiling is lined with a blue, pink slime. A thick meaty scent looms in the air.

Ahuri lowers her head and covers her mouth "that smells worse than I remember it."

Odette nods, "smells like gym shorts after soccer." long shadow passes behind the two girls. Odette fails to notice, "so, how do these cocoon things work?"

"I don't know, I have never been cocooned." Ahuri looks up as if to search the lights for an answer.

Odette questions, "you just know that you need to find your mothers?"

"yeah." Ahuri nods enthusiastically.

A tall, dark, image towers over the two, only once it speaks, do they become aware of it. "that isn't how it works. A cocoon can only be used once."

Both girls spin to look back. A white-haired beast towers. Ahuri pulls her hands up to her mouth and backs away, whispering, "Shirio-Kemono."

The white-haired-beast slouches forward, it locks eyes with Odette, "call me Ten-feet-tall." The monster laughs.

Odette pulls out her flashlight, she flips it on swiftly, Shirio turns her head looking away from Odette, she snaps forward a wing pushing Odette. With the torch no longer holding her at arm's length, the beast steps forward and swings out and arm to grab Odette.

Ahuri bounces forth to grab Shirio, Shirio is a monster, more than three times the size of Odette or Ahuri. Shirio holds both Odette ad Ahuri in the air with two hands each. "You are Odette Tsu, Takashi Tsu's niece. Your family is in debt to me, and I want my retribution."

Odette struggles, she flails and lashes her body about. In a stroke of luck, Odette lands a kick to the beast breast making her loosen her grip. The two kids squirm and are dropped. Odette lands on her knees and, in a frantic rage, kicks off the ground and jumps at Shirio talking her.

Shirio is shocked to have gotten stuck, Odette sits up on her chest and punches at the moth a dozen times before the moth regains her senses. Shirio grips Odette's arm and twists off to one side reversing their positions.

Ahuri takes off her backpack and flings it at Ahuri as a distraction. In the moment of confusion, Ahuri pulls all four of her arms into her chest then stomps forward, thrusting out with all the mass she can muster shoving Shirio away from Odette.

Ahuri shouts at Odette, "Fly!" Ahuri folds her wings and calls on her butterfly magic to bend light around her body and become transparent.

Shirio shuts her eyes tight and hisses to restore her focus. Odette swoops down to grab her flashlight, she grips it to the back of her arm then delivers a crushing backhand to the side of Shirio's head, knocking her onto her back.

From there, Odette affects her escape, Odette runs. The beast is powerful, and all she had done is dizzy it. The best thing Odette can do is find a place to hide until she can escape from the waterworks.

May 16th, 5:45 pm

Tobi makes his way up the hillside, he talks to himself as he and the seven cops walk "it is funny, twice in two weeks I have made this trip into forbidden lands. May the kami have mercy on me."

The trip is restless; all the way up the hill, the group is followed: antelope, monkeys, and wild dogs shadow them menacingly.

The voice of a female phantom shouts to them. "Tobi, was I not clear last time? The ground you stand on is cursed, you must not walk this path."

Tobi calls to the cops, "arm yourselves." Tobi opens his coat and pulls out his mace.

But the words of the monk go unheeded. A howl comes from all around them. White-gowned monsters rain from the trees, the Sanguine are upon them. The police are outnumbered three-to-one.
In a matter of moments, the black-skinned monsters have disarmed and overpowered the men Jo had sent to investigate the old village.

The child-like god of death teases, "I tried to tell you."

Tobi was at the front of the group; he had a moment's warning, of the monster's charge. Tobi had taken measures to keep himself out of their reach.

The child-like god continues, "your father warned you also, why did you come?"

Tobi does the only sensible thing, he runs into the forest.

May 16th, 8:15 pm

Machohero awakens, the events of the day are gone from her memories. She is at the beach, she is dressed in her old competition swimsuit. She hasn't worn then outfit in 15 years as far as she can remember, she has her old surfboard with her. She must have gone out to her locker in the industrial district and dug it out.

Machohero wades out into the water, she feels inclined to try to surf again. It has been so long since the last time she has done this. She feels healthy, stronger then she has in decades. The night sky empowers her.

A voice whispers to Machohero from the deep. "enjoy the night. It is now a part of you." The winds are strong; it is a beautiful night to surf. "but still, of all the things you will be able to do, there are still rules you must follow."

"you must spread your seeds; you will find after only a few days this need will become most all-consuming. You must feed on raw meat; no cooked foods will satisfy you. Eating the heart of a beast will be most satisfying."

"fear not for nature has equipped you will all the tools you will need to find what it is you wish for. As your hunger grows, your beast will become greater."

"you have powerful jaws for breaking bones. You have a lashing tongue for cutting flesh, and your skin produces a hypnotic miasma. You can heal overnight from near-fatal wounds. You are an apex predator. You can hunt any pray you wish, and nothing will hunt you."

"by midnight tonight, your strength will be at its fullest. The first hunt is always the best. You can strike off on your own if you like, or you can hunt alongside me, if you chose to do so I could teach you much."

"embrace the night, it is a part of you now."

"you may think that you are dammed, a cursed thing, never to walk in the sunlight again. But that is not true. You will wish to sleep during the day, the sun is hot, and it drains our power some, but it is not unlike the moon is to man. It will be a struggle at first, but you will find that you can walk in the sun all the same as you can walk in the moonlight."

"But why do we act as we do? Why do we kill those that were once our friends? Why do we prowl the night? Invade the homes of others? The query is not as hard as you may think. Why does the scorpion sting? Why does the fly bite? Or the spider spin webs? It is because that is what why are. No one tells the spider to eat the fly. It simply knows that is what it must do. You and I are the same."

"with one change. If we wish, we can invite our friends to join us. Give your seed to anyone you would like to join us. Not all, but some will become like us, and we will be all the better because of it. What about those that can't or won't turn? Well, the night was not meant for everyone."

"Embarrass the night, for now, she is you."

"come midnight, I will show you how we hunt, how we kill. To take life from one is to give life to you, that is the price of immortality."

May 16th, 9:30 pm

Takashi arrives home before Odette, but not by much. Takashi has his head dipped in the kitchen sink washing his hair as the door opens and Odette staggers in, winded but otherwise not any worse for it.

Takashi calls out, "you are late? What happened?"

"I need a bath," Odette makes her way up to her bedroom. She shouts out to her uncle, "not much, found a hidden underground hospital, a vat of ten thousand gallons of bug eggs, got chased by a monster birthed from my nightmares. You do anything fun today?"

"microwaved the top two floors of the hospital…" Takashi turns on the sink to rinse his hair and gets nothing but a dry hissing sound as the pipes shake, "…oh, this doesn't bode well…"

From the top of the steps, Odette calls down, "Looks like we lost water!"

Soap dripping down his face, Takashi lowers his head and folds his arms, "if Tokyo saw fit to cut the main water line then…" A massive popping sound echoes from every direction as the lights all around Takashi burst "that is what I thought.'

Odette shouts again, "and lights!"

Takashi takes a deep breath, "crap."

May 16th, 11:45 pm

Useto cares Sakura back to her bedroom, he lays her in her bed and offers her a kiss. Useto walks out of Sakura's room and makes his way down the hall to his, he has a hooded lantern to light the way.

Useto undresses. The massive shadow of the White-haired-beast looms just out of sight. Useto's eyes are drawn to his bedroom window, which is swung open, then to a bottle of lighter fluid set on his bed.

The middle-aged cop crouches and pulls the nightstick from his belt. The white-haired beast steps out of the shadows; it swoops forward and lifts Useto with one hand; it crushes his larynxes as it choke-slams him onto the bed. It uses one of its other three arms to pin Useto's hands to his sides.

The White-haired-beast looks to Mashohero, "this one. Take him, take him, and your power will grow."

Machohero shakes her head "I know this man, he is an honorable man, I don't want to…"

The White-haired-beast cuts her off "then you can breed with him, it is all the same to me. This man has committed crimes against us and I want retribution. I give him to you, my child, one way or the other."

Hunger stirs in Machohero's body, she sheds her skin and approaches the bed, she crawls forward on all four climbing over Useto, her mouth opens, and her tongue slides out of her mouth.

The White-haired-beast explains, "if you wish to feed off of him, slide your tongue into his chest under the floating rib. From there it is easiest to reach the heart. If you wish to mate him then slide you stinger into his mouth and down his esophagus, your body will know what to do after that."

Machohero is under the White-haired-beast power; she runs her tongue up Useto's chest and, in a swift strike, spears him. Her tongue fishes around in his body and pulls out his heart. Her mouth opens wide and engulfs the muscle.

The scene is grizzly and over quickly. The white-haired-beast spills the bottle of oil onto the bed. Then orders her minion. "light a cigar, throw it onto the bed as we leave. We will come back tomorrow night for his child."

Chapter 10, Five Days Remaining

May 17th, 10:15 am

Jin and Odette sit in the hospital room Sakura is in, the fire brigade showed up to Useto's house quickly after the fire had started. Sakura was not aware of anything. The flams seemed to have a strange effect on her body. The soft light, the deathly heat. Her body did nothing to inform her of the danger of it all.

Sakura slept peacefully through the fire, not even chocking on the smoke. Iwata stands over Sakura checking the interments.

Jin asks. "what is her condition?"

Iwata writes down a note "well, she isn't breathing, she has no heartbeat, and her dermal temp is 105.7°f. That aside, I would say that everything else looks stable."

Odette wonders, "how do you get a skin temperate of over 100°f without a pulse."

Iwata expresses, "I assume she has a heartbeat; I just don't know how to check it."

Sakura's eye dart open, she looks side to side then jumps to her feet. Iwata grabs Sakura and pushes her back onto the bed.

Sakura orders, "what is going in?"

Jin replies, "there was a fire, I was able to see it from my house. Useto, your father, he…"

Sakura asks, "Is he dead?"

Jin nods, "honestly, there wasn't much left of him by the time the EMT's arrived. You look to have gotten lucky on the other hand."

Sakura looks between her friends "it is less than 30' between my bedroom and my father's. I should be just as dead as he is."

Iwata explains, "you have your alien blood to thank for that, I assume. You had 3-degree burns covering half your body 4 hours ago. Now you look perfectly healthy."

Sakura looks up, "am I free to go?"

Jo Kogotana leans on the doorframe as he is entering the room "That is up to me."

Sakura stands up, this time Iwata sidestepping to allow it. Sakura has been given a hospital gown, it is short, cold, and uncomfortable, but she will live with it "Kogotana-son, I should like to be dismissed."

Jo expresses, "this is the second time that there has been a murder, and you were withing spitting distance of the victim." He grunts, "Sakura, how old are you?"

She keeps her head down, "I am 15."

"and when is your birthday?" Jo orders.

"June 9th," Sakura explains.

Jo exclaims, "are you sure? Because I think your birthday is May 9th, and you are 16."

Sakura looks up, as does Jin, "Sir?" Sakura asks.

Jo explains, "I have a lot of paperwork to do. And a fifteen-year-old orphan miner on the scene doubles it. What is worse is if you tell me you are fifteen, I am going to have to bring you into protective custody, you are going to be living in our juvenile facility until you are 18, or until Tokyo says otherwise." He pauses for a moment "if you are sixteen, on the other hand, you can couch surf, I think is the right slang, until you are on your feet."

Jin looks to Sakura with a smile. "I just did the math on that, you are ten months older than me."

Sakura gets then hint, "my birthday was May 9th."

Jo nods, "I have an extra bed, you can stay with me for a few weeks if you like."

Odette adds, "or me."

Jo steps out into the hallway, he wasn't joking about having work to do. Jin chases after having just noticed something that his father had let slip.

"Dad!" Jin shouts

Jo stops, he pivots to face his son, "what is it, boy?"

Jin questions, "do you think that Mr. Useto was murdered?"

"I do." Jo explains.

"why?" Jin asks

Jo elaborates, "sitting near the body when I arrived was a copper ring, with an engraving on it. one that I just happened to know where came from." He asks, "have you ever noticed the cigar box I have on my nightstand?"

Jin nods "yes, you got that as a gift from someone as I recall."

"Odette's mother. She got it from a mutual friend of ours that moved to Pakistan a few years ago. She gifted to me knowing that I like a smoke now and again. They are not cheap cigars, and most certainly not ones that Useto is likely to have been smoking in bed," Jo postulates.

"the ring is part of the packaging for the cigars?" Jin lowers his head and thinks, "I don't understand."

"the person that killed Dean Gogiro is the same person that killed Useto. I suspect it is someone I know, someone that is close enough to you and I that they had been in our house. I think they are challenging me, challenging my authority." Jo looks agitated.

Jin shakes his head, "no, you can't draw that conclusion from that data. I think what the killer is trying to tell you dad is:

Fist, they know that you are following them.

Second, they know who you are.

Just because they have been to our house doesn't mean that we had to invite them in.

Hitchens's Razor: when evaluating evidence, the proposition that requires the fewest number of unfalsifiable claims is likely true."

Jo laughs happily, "good boy. Always follow the evidence. You are right, all I know is that the killer knows who I am."

Jin drops his head backward, thinking allowed, "the killer likes to burn his victims, why?"

"as soon as we know that we will be much closer to finding them." Jo proclaims.

May 17th, 11:58 am

Takisha waits in the conference room. Iwata steps in and drops a folder on the table. Takashi has his head tipped back and his arms folded across his chest as he stares at the lights.

Iwata announces her arrival, "Doctor."

Takashi is not feeling up to small talk, "I assume that is inventory."

"Yes." Iwata explains.

"water, gas, and batteries are all listed amongst our assets?"

"If they are not, we will need to get maintenance to do a check." Iwata expresses. "Doctor, we are not going to be able to keep our door open for much longer if we can't get resupplied."

Takisha grunts, "I understand that."

Iwata rest her hands on the table and leans into Takashi, "so what are we doing?"

Takashi opens his eyes and leans forward, getting nose to nose with his would-be partner "We keep working, we keep working even if all we have left is cold water and soothing words. We are responsible for this town one way or the other." Takashi turns his head looking to the window, "how well-stocked do you think the chemistry department is at the school?"

"are you recommending looting?" Iwata asks.

May 17th, 1:20 pm

The remaining of the police walk around town, hanging up bulletins. Masumo taps one of the cops on the leg as he is hanging the note. "excuse me, would you be so kind as to read me the announcement? I am too short to see it."

The cop reads the note aloud "the chief constable would like to inform the people of Chīsana-Mura that as of 8am, it has been confirmed that the main water line running through our town has been compromised, and the electric grid has been turned off. Anyone in possession of portable gas, or an emergency generator, is encouraged to offer these items to the needing amongst you."

"it has been brought to the attention of me, the chief constable, that there are gaijin living amongst us. People with extraordinary training and knowledge from afar."

"concerning the sickness that so many of us have been exposed to, it may be possible that these gaijin, should they be willing, could offer their unique perspective in resolving these concerns. Should anyone offer aid at this time, they will be honored, and protected. If you are amongst the gaijin and wish to step forward, please make your way to the constable's office at your next convenience."

"I ask that we all continue to act with the best interest of our neighbors and the community in mind. Thank you." the officer lowers the note.

Masumo bows, "thank you so much."

May 17th, 3:25 pm

Sirosanto steps into the police station. The cops are on edge, after losing so many of their ranks over the last few nights, everyone is nervous. The murder of Useto Habiki being the most upsetting of all. Sirosanto surrenders his sword to the guard at the door. "I am told that you are searching for a gaijin. I am a gaijin."

Detective Sakomoto leads Sirosanto to Constable Kogotana. "Sir, I believe this is the man that we were looking for."

Jo looks up, "Mr. Masumo, is it?"

Sirosanto bows, "sometimes."

Jo sets his phone on the desk and taps it. "so, are you willing to show yourself."

Sirosanto holds out a hand in protest as he shakes his head, "that will not be needed, I openly will offer you anything that you want."

Jo calls over to Maaya, "bring me, Orochi Arnoldo."

Maaya bows and walks out of the room. Arnoldo is already in the office, everyone had hoped that someone like Sirosanto would step forward, Arnoldo is there to collaborate the information offered. Nekoba is also close at hand.

Arnoldo sets up some recording equipment. Then the interview can begin.

Jo starts off, "are you or do you know who is responsible for the deaths of Dean Gogiro and Useto Habiki?"

Sirosanto shakes his head, "do I know? No."

"are you aware of the alien virus that has been plaguing our town?" Jo continues.

Sirosanto nods, "yes."

"was it engineered by you or someone related to you?" Jo questions.

Sirosanto nods, "yes."

"Is there a treatment?" Jo leans in interested.

"Before asking that, you would need to understand what it was we were doing. The idea was not to forge a deadly parasite, it was to find a way to make humans and Chromon more alike. It is shockingly amazing, the things we have learned in the last thirty or so years. It was your species that unlocked the genome."

"We had been performing genetic experiments for centuries, eons maybe. But there had allows been something blocking us. It was you that showed us how to tweak the allele frequency."

"at that point, all that was missing was an intermediary. We needed something that was, on some arbitrary level, chemically parallel to both of our species."

"for some time now, we had been performing controlled experiments. Using native-born parasites to transfer ribosomes between my people and yours."

"We were trying to make our races chemically cross fertile. We had some middling successes; our females have on a half dozen occasions successfully bread with your men. We haven't been able to go the other direction yet as far as I have been told."

"But then there was a security breach a month or two ago. We lost a number of our test subjects. Now we have mutated parasites lose in the wild."

"under controlled conditions, if a subject started to experience any sort of side effects do to our testing, we were able to abort the test by exposing our patents to a low-level radioactive isotope. You have the same drug we were using in your hospital. D-38."

Arnoldo joins the conversation, "If I may ask, some people seem to think that, you, have some sort of magical powers…"

Sirosanto shakes his head, "let me assure you that any perceived magic you or anyone else may have seen is a result of technology, not witchcraft."

Jo gives Arnoldo a disappointed gaze then turns his attention back to Sirosanto "were you aware that there has been a string of murders wherein a key factor was the removing of the heart?"

Sirosanto shakes his head, "no, I was not aware of that."

"are you aware of any purpose it may serve for one of your people to perform such an action as to remove a heart?" Jo adds.

"yes," Sirosanto nods, "but we would be talking about some ancient superstitions and a time before my people moved to this world."

Jo squints, "but you are saying that such a thing is not without warrant?"

Sirosanto folds his hands on the table and sights, "if anyone were doing such a thing in the world today, and they very well could be, that person could only be described as a psycho."

Nekoba, who had been sitting in silence up to this point, cuts in. "Sirosanto, something I wanted to ask, but seem to have neglected to do so. What is your relationship with EvaMasumo?"

Sirosanto needs a moment to think, "between hibernation, rejuvenation, cloning, and rebirth, things like relationships tend to become complicated. But I think the most correct thing to say is Shi the Butterfly is my mother. I, as well as my sister, are both made up 88% of her."

Arnoldo looks up, "88%?" the number having caught him off guard, "not 50%?"

Sirosanto explains, "your species is sexually dimorphic, ours has more than two genders, there are 93 if I am not mistaking. Before we were able to clone if one wished to mate, they needed to find a partner that produced the same or a greater number of ribosomes. Ribosome count being the largest difference between the genders."

Jo coughs, "Gentlemen, let's try to get back on topic."

Nekoba pushes the conversation forward, "Sirosanto, what do you know about the rogue amongst your ranks?"

"what do I know, or what do I think?" Sirosanto comments, "I know nothing, but I have thoughts."

Jo commands, "let's start with, do you have a plan to get all this back under control?"

"The Sanguine can't stand cold. As soon as the temperature drops below 30°f they will all fall asleep and no one will hear from them again until the temp gets above 108°. Back in the 700's, we poisoned them. Forced them to sleep, but it looks like they are not going away so easily this time. As for the GMO," Sirosanto shakes his head, "I have no idea if they even can be brought under control."

Jo looks angry, "there were no safeguards in place?"

Sirosanto clarifies, "There were, they were compromised."

Jo struggles to control his frustration, "and what about this psycho we were talking about? How do you recommend dealing with them?"

Sirosanto nudges his head up, "you are the constable. If anyone knows how to deal with psychos, it should be you."

"arrest them?" Jo questions

"shoot them." Sirosanto recommends. "I do have something that can help with that, though." The old man reaches a hand into his pocket, he sets on the table a bottle filled with a thick white jelly. "Kuma dreamed this up. It is an inoculation, it will interrupt the connection between your nose and brain, if it works the way she told me, it will block us from influencing you."

Jo hands the bottle to Arnoldo, "bring this to Takashi. Find out if it does what it is meant to and if we can make more of it."

May 17th, 4:15 pm

Reko climbs out of bed. He makes his way to the front of the shop; he looks about noticing the doors are all locked and Oso is sitting quietly in the dark a wet stone in hand as he had been cleaning a knife.

Reko points, "door are shut."

Oso bobs his head, "I have no food left to cook. No tea left to boil. I have nothing left but a box filled with coins and no place to spend them."

Sakura comes in from the second floor. "Maybe I have something that will make you happy." She jumps down the steps and slaps a book down on the table.

Jet looks at the book, "and this is?"

"the names and home addresses of everyone that died in the last 36 months."

Oso looks confused, "how?"

"Took it from Takashi." Jet and Oso both look to Sakura sternly, she notices the disapproving stares "I didn't kill anyone if that is what you are thinking."

Reko picks the book up, he turns to the end and starts flipping the pages backward "So, are you thinking we should start sniffing around, starting with the most recent death, and work backward until we find our bugs?"

Sakura nods, "Yeah, that was what I was thinking."

Oso looks distracted, he drops his eyes looking at his hands. "Reko, who would you say are the most influential people in town right now?"

"Depending on what the word influence means. Jo Kogotana, Takashi Tsu, and Setkura Nekoba." Jet whispers.

Oso nods slowly. "I just remembered a story my grandmother told me. I am sure I am forgetting some details but. Something about it seems right to me."

"Buddha walks around a lake with a single swan sitting on the water. The swan is unmoving, silent. Then three men walk up to the edge of the water, each bosting about the great works they have done."

"The first man explains, 'I am strong, my feats of strength inspire men everywhere.' "

"The second man boost, 'I am powerful, under my guidance walls have been built and fortunes have been amassed.'."

"the third man adds, 'I am clever, I have drawn maps, and brewed life-giving tonics.'."

"Buddha smiles to the three men, he says 'you are all mighty; indeed, you have strength, money, and power to spare. But what if I were to ask you, can you use your powers to convince that bird to sing?' Buddha points to the swan.

"The first man says 'that is easy, you need simply tell the bird, you will sing, or you will be punished.'."

"The second man he explained, 'If you wish for the bird to sing, you must offer it women and silver as payment.'."

"But the third said 'you need only wait; the bird will sing when it is ready.'."

There is a moment of silence as Oso freezes, he squints and looks off into space. "I don't remember the rest of the story."

Sakura waits, she watches the men, "so, if this story is an allegory, who is who?"

Jet shrugs, "without knowing the end of the story, it doesn't matter."

May 17th, 7:00 pm

Word reaches Jo Kogotana, Reko Jet is on a rampage. In the two hours, he has publicly executed five people. His actions a cold and calculated, systematic, one may respect and honor him if they were crazy.

It was the same thing each time. Reko knocked down the front door, Oso, and Sakura watches the other exits. Reko grabs his victim by the back of the head and pulls them out onto the street.

In full view of anyone that may be watching, Reko then throws them at the ground and with one foot holds them there. He pulls a sledgehammer from the sling on his back and throws three swings down on them.

Reko leaves the broken and twisted body on the ground as he then re-enters the house of his victim. With the help of Sakura, he tracks down a massive egg-like ball of flesh hidden under the floor. Reko cuts it apart and shows the people of the town the half-formed body of a pod-person waiting to be hatched.

The next name on his list. Nena Kobayashy, forty-three-years-old, died nine weeks ago. An accident at the glassworks, people say, lights in her house still come on at sunset.

Reko knocks down the front door and just as he suspected. There Kobayashy is, sitting in an armchair reading a book, twenty years younger than anyone remembers her.

Nena drops her book when the door opens, she jumps to her feet and starts to back away from the giant marching into her den. Jet proclaims, "Kobayashy. You are a baku, but have no fear, I am here to purify your spirit."

Nena shouts as she makes her way for the back door, "You don't know what you are talking about! Keep back!"

Nena throws open her back door only to come face to face with Oso waiting there.

Reko grabs Nena and drags her out the front door. "That was what the other said too. But only Baku age younger." Reko lifts his hammer over his head.

Jo pulls back the hammer on his revolver and shouts. "Stop right there!"

Reko looks up, "I am doing good work. I am cleansing this land of evil."

Jo shouts, "Are you going to tell me that you think that girl is some sort of and Ona, or Oni, or Onryo."

Reko nods "This is Nena Kobayashi, look at her, she has turned into a child." Reko pulls back his hammer, reading himself to strike.

Jo points downrange, "drop the hammer, or I will shoot you."

Jet relaxes for a moment "when was the last time you shot someone, Jo?"

Jo explains, "It was some time ago." He walks forward a few steps "that girl is not a monster, she is an animal, not so unlike you or I."

Jet looks between Jo and Nena, "I let her up, she kills us."

Jo offers an ultimatum, "you let her up, and I arrest her. Does that satisfy everyone?"

Reko shakes his head, "Bars can't hold spirits."

Jo orders "Grab him!" four police that had been flanking Reko jump out.

Reko is powerful, but for any man holding up the weight of four full-grown men is near impossible. Reko is pushed off of Nena and rolled onto his stomach.

Reko throws an arm back to elbow a man off of him, he pushes himself up to kneeling then grapples with another cop. Reko pulls back a fist to pummel. The third cop breaks a nightstick over Reko's head, only after he is dazed can they chain him up.

Sakura comes out of hiding to aid Reko. She sheds her clothing and transforms into her moth shape. Sakura demonstrates her exceptional strength by grabbing two men at once and tossing them into the air.

Reko stands up and howls like an animal; he pulls on his chains, shattering them with his bare hands. Nena flees. Jo aims his gun, he is running out of options.

Sakura approaches Jo, "Do it, kill me, if you think that you can." Sakura grabs Jo's gun and presses it to her breast. "DO it." she requests again.

Oso grabs Reko and sneaks away.

Jo stands stunned. Seeing photos of monsters is one thing, seeing the real thing nose to nose is another, to feel the hot skin, to feel the warm breath. Jo knew Sakura was a Chromon, but he had no idea what she would look like in all her splendor.

Sakura shakes her head, "you aren't strong enough." She lowers her wings; two of her four arms drop to her sides. "I am sorry, Kogotana-son. I must do what I think is right, we all must. Reko, Oso and I, we are going to keep killing monsters. If any wish to be spared our vengeance. Tell them they must walk around openly. Show their wings. From now on, that is what I will do."

Sakura steps away from Jo, she flaps her wings and leaps into the air vanishing.

Leaving Jo alone on the street. Jo walks around, helping his men up.

Chapter 11, Four Days Remaining

May 18th, 1:25 am

The hospital is in panic. The reserve water tank above the hospital has ruptured, releasing 600,000 gallons of water spraying onto the roof. The sheer volume of water has caved-in the top floor and is threatening to destroy the rest of the building in short order.

The stairwells are flooded, water seeps in through the walls, drains are backwashing. The scene is nightmare-esc. Takashi has taken command; it is time to evacuate.

The dead are mounting, injuries are incalculable, A hundred or more people are unaccounted for. Takashi does his best to do a headcount as nurses are escorting people away from the building.

Takashi spots Jaki Yu stepping out of the hospital, Takashi grabs him, "Any idea what happened?"

Jaki shakes his head, "there is no getting up to the top floors, the stairwells are coming apart, best guess, something cut a hole in the reserve tank."

"is that possible?" Takashi asks.

"It wouldn't be easy; I will tell you that," Yu explains.

Takashi runs for the building, he has noticed a large group is missing, no one from the cantonment area has made their way to the courtyard. Those that were being treated for the alien parasite, all of them are still inside, they must be.

Takashi pushes his way to the stairs, ankle-deep water cascades down the steps. Takashi drags himself up, slowly, he struggles with each step.

The third floor, the door is open, the ceiling is warped, water pours through the creaks the bodies of a dozen dead nurses and patrons lay face down on the floor. But that is hardly the most horrific of things that can be seen.

Arnoldo is laid on the nurse station desk, Machohero holding him down. She is in her bestial shape: translucent wings, her skin fading to black, her eyes shine with a metallic glow. Machohero's tongue is slide into Arnoldo's throat, she is in the middle of injecting her seed into his body.

Takashi searches his surroundings. He spots an I.V. stand on the ground, and he swoops it up. Takashi sprints over to Machohero and thrust the I.V. stand like a spear at her.

Machohero is forced off of Arnoldo, her tongue being ripped from his body. Arnoldo rolls over gagging and vomiting up blue slime.

Takashi pushes Machohero into a wall with his makeshift spear... and that was where his thought process had ended. With the monster pinned to the wall, Takashi has no idea what to do next.

Machohero screams. From a nearby room, the monster that was once Handa appears. From another, the White-Haired-Beast emerges.

Machohero claws at the air and lashes out with her tongue, the other two monsters stalk ever closer. Takashi considers his options. Outfighting, the three of them would be challenging for the best of fighters. For him, the prospect is impossible.

Takashi looks up, he notices how the ceiling is sagging. Takashi makes a bold move, he slaps Machohero with the I.V. stand to stun her then stabs the spear into the roof. Water starts to rush into the room, and the drywall splits. A veritable waterfall monsoons down as the fourth floor starts to drain into the third.

The monsters are stunned by this. Takashi picks up Arnoldo, nearly dragging him with one arm. Takashi quickly scans his surroundings. It is all to clear what has happened. This was all a distraction. The Sanguine engineered this disaster to capture the infected that have been locked up here.

A dozen more bugs are hailing away those that had been bitten before. Only one door seemingly remains locked. Leta Tenzuma. They aren't interested in her anymore. Arnoldo sees the same thing that Takashi had.

The White-Haired-Beast is furies. She sends out a call to her underlings. 'Kill

Takashi Tsu.' She flaps her wings. Bugs all around the two men turn to look.

Arnoldo forces himself upright. He discards his coat. "Dr. Tsu. Get Leta." Arnoldo pulls his hands into his body, taking a fighting stance. The young nurse throughs himself into the fray. He fights for all he is worth to hold the bugs back, giving Takashi whatever few seconds he can to unlock Leta's room and make for the exit.

Takashi understands what Arnoldo meant for him to do, and so he does. Takashi breaks open Leta's room and picks up the teen girl. With one hand wrapped around her rump, hugging her to his chest, Takashi runs. He stumbles down the steps. He dares not look to see if he is being chased or not.

Arnoldo made a sacrifice. So many of Takashi's friends have. All of it seemingly fighting to delay inevitability for only hours or days. That seems to be the life of a doctor taken to its utmost extreme. Years of work to add moments to the end of one's life.

As Takashi makes it outside, the entirety of the hospital seems to start to sink into the underground waterway. Takashi runs only a few more steps before he falls to his knees and drops Leta. He slouches forward onto all fours looking back at the remains of the hospital.

Iwata kneels alongside Takashi, propping him up "Doctor, are you alright? Are you hurt?"

Takashi shakes his head "it is gone…" he mumbles "everything is gone…" he struggles to breath "we lose…"

May 18th, 3:15 am

EvaMasumo and Sirosanto stand atop the roof of the Ichishin-Magami temple. Evakicks her feet as she sits and watches the night sky. Evaturns her head looking to Sirosanto "it was her, wasn't it?"

Sirosanto stands alongside his mother, "my sister, yes."

Evadrops her head in disappointment "I was hoping she would never wake back up."

Siroansto grunts as he is thinking, "I can't blame her for hating us after what we did."

Evalays down, sprawling herself out on the roof "I never would have expected that one of us could do such a thing."

"I might have done the same all thing considered." Sirosanto sits down, folding his legs "we changed her. We made her into what she is. We took a science we didn't fully grasp, and we used her to test the limits." Sirosanto moans, "an what is worse of all, the results were not outside of what we expected."

Sirosanto places a hand on his mother's stomach, patting her playfully "you can see as clearly as I can. It worked. She is what you wanted to be."

Evaturns her head and sits up sternly "there is a difference. I cannot, will not, bring harm to a sapient lifeform. Not them, not us."

"is what she is doing harming them?" Sirosanto questions.

"Is there any harm more profound than to take away another's free will?" Eva asks.

"Isn't life preferable to death?" Siro santo counters.

May 18th, 8:05 am

After several hours of sitting in Jo's offices, filling out papers, and explaining what he saw this morning, Takashi is sent home.

Odette finds some of her older clothes that are in Leta's size, give or take. Odette watches Leta dress and questions, "so, you are human again?"

Leta looks to Odette, "what do you mean again?"

Odette nods, "that is right, you have been MIA for almost two weeks, let me tell you, you missed one hell of a week. School burnt down, the dean was killed, power is out, water is out…"

Leta tightens her belt and looks at herself "I didn't notice before, you have some sharp hips. How does a nerdy girl like you get into such good shape?"

Odette explains, "Boxing. Last fall Useto was hosting a class on Fridays and Sunday mornings. Jin and I were both there. Reje was going to be, but he couldn't seem to get out of bed at 5:15 am."

Leta looks back to Odette "I was kept up to date on some of that. No one told me what happened at the school, but I guess not many people knew about that."

"Do you know about Reje?" Odette asks in a reverent voice.

"Ri told me. Or his ghost did." Leta explains.

Odette nods slowly, "I am sorry."

Leta shuts her eyes, thinking, "everyone in town has experienced a death in the last few days. It seems the dead are angry."

Odette refers back to what she was saying before they got sidetracked. "you had the alien virus. I thought you, like Reje, were turning into a bug."

Leta holds out her arms showing off now that she is fully dressed. "what do you think?"

Odette smiles, "I like it, I used to have the same outfit."

Leta turns her head to look at her back in the mirror "it seems I recovered."

Odette rubs her neck thinking, "I think that makes you the only one." Odette waves, "lets head downstairs. I will make us something to eat."

when they get to the front room Odette wave. "Takashi! I am cooking, what do you want?" Odette starts digging around "rosemary rice, egg noodles, Saulsberry beef, mushrooms, ramen…"

Takashi has one hand slid into his belt; he is slouched over, staring forward into a blank wall. He can't seem to mutter a coherent thought, instead just grunting.

Odette shouts, "Takashi!"

After waiting a few moments, Odette shrugs, "Fine, mushrooms and carrots it is."

Takashi mumbles "heat to 212°, Setsuka, read 500mg ..." Takashi falls onto his side, he is both tiered and injured. He is running out of strength.

May 18th, 2:30 pm

The monk Tami is brought before Jo Kogotana. Jo looks up from his desk, "I have been led to believe that you have recently been promoted. You are the new chaplain, right?"

The monk nods, "yes."

"you know what day it is on the 20th, I assume." Jo commands.

"The Feast of Nobunaga, most people call it the Festival of Drums." Tami explains.

"That is two days from now, and do you know what I have just noticed." Jo asks. Tami shakes his head. "I don't see anyone in the town colors."

Tami expresses, "you have no doubt noticed that things have not been going according to plans."

Jo sets down the pen he had been holding "now do to the honorable behavior of your siblings, you and the other monks have been offered forgiveness for the crimes you have committed. Now I want something from you."

Tami tips his head, "how may I be of service Constable?"

"I want you and everyone else to dress in full festival gear for the next three days. I want to see no less than 4000 candles set up at the delta. I want a banner drawn 40' long and 8' high strung across the temple gate. I want to see Obon set up at the town square before sundown. I want everyone to remember, this is Chīsana-Mura."

"That will be challenging to set up in such a short time." Tami explains.

Jo orders, "then you will need to work hard. Every town in the province has a ritual and a festival that is theirs and theirs alone; this one is ours, and I want people to remember it."

Tami bows, "then I will need to get to work at once." Tami departs.

Jo picks back up his pen and continues writing. The door opens, a cop steps in "Constable."

Jo looks up. He doesn't know this patrolman. Jo squints, "I can't seem to recall you, are you one of the deputies?"

"Constable, I have a concern about the PSA you just mailed out…" he starts. Jo leans in looking at the uniform closely, the pen over his breast, it reads Habiki… "you say you want the gaijin to walk around 'openly', if they are honest people, they 'have nothing to fear.' Right?"

It suddenly strikes Jo what is going on, Jo is being manipulated, this man is a shapeshifter. "Sakomoto!" he calls out into the hallway.

The face police officer discards his mask and transforms into a black-skinned Sanguine; the windows burst inward, and two more jump into the room from the street, pinning Jo in one corner of the room.

The black-skinned monster grabs the desk and throws it off to one side. The best runs at Jo, Jo draws his revolver and shoots. The beast takes the shot to the chest, it staggers then charges again. Jo shoots two more shots at it.

    The other two rush in to join the fight, Jo turns his divides his attention between them. Before they can get into arms, reach Jo has taken three more shots at each of them. The revolver seems to have no stopping power at all against the Sanguine.

    One grabs Jo around the shoulders and shoves him into the wall; Jo flips around his gun like a hammer and swings it down, splintering the beast skull with it.

    The second grabs him from the side. Jo throws two elbow strikes into it monsters face then a double cannon punch to the ribs to throw the beast into the wall.

    Officer Sakomoto runs into the room, ninjato in hand. The third beast spins Jo around and grapples with him from behind. The monster shows its fangs. Sakomoto wraps a hand around the monster's eyes and tips its head back. She delivers a stab to the side of its neck to make the monster drop Jo.

    The second has regained its balance and is pushing itself back to its feet.

Sakomoto slashes the monster across the cheek splitting its mouth open. Jo grabs his sword from off the wall then jumps in, taking a cleave severing its body in two from shoulder to hip.

Jo and Sakomoto take a moment to look between each other and silently agree on what has just transpired. The Sanguine are becoming ever more aggressive. Even going so far as to attack the chief midday.

May 18th, 5:45 pm

Nekoba had been sitting at the park for some time, the day is getting colder. It is relaxing. So many people right now are walking around, playing at the park, picnicking. Seemingly unaware of the horrors that have been happening all around them.

The wind howls, the flapping of leathery wings echoes form all sides. Nekoba finds that the park has faded away, and he is sitting in the hidden treasure chamber under the old church. Sitting at the same desk, he was sitting at for days reading the writings of the Chromon.

Eva Masumo sits alongside him. She leans forward, placing her hands on his legs as she looks up at him from a low angle. She grins and shuts her eyes. "So."

Nekoba looks around, considering what he has just seen, "I assume this is an illusion."

Eva nods, "you are still at the park."

"this is very convincing. Can anyone else see this?" Nekoba ask.

Eva shakes her head. "Just you. No one can hear you talking either." Eva continues, "but we need to talk."

"About what?" Nekoba asks.

"you and I." Eva wiggles in place. "in a few months, I will be fully grown. And I want to know if you want to become one of us or not."

"you need my consent?" Nekoba ponders.

"of course, I do." Eva explains.

"what about the others that have been turned, did they give consent?" Nekoba looks concerned.

Eva goes silent. She pulls her hands away from Nekoba and leans backward, resting her hands behind herself for balance. "no. not the ones that have been changed by Shirio."

"Are there others you are talking to about this?" Nekoba inquires

Masumo nods "there are others that are eligible. But this year it is only you. In five years, Jin Kogotana will be considered."

"Five years?" Nekoba questions

Masumo clarifies, "Jin was always on our list. Even before he was born. His great grandfather had a relationship with me, he set the gears in motion as to what is happening today. Just like your grandmother, the change isn't fast, it is done in small steps. Taking a lifetime to complete. Often needing to be done generationally."

Nekoba looks determined "that doesn't make sense. Not in light of what Sirosanto told us. You didn't have this technology at your disposal until only a few decades ago."

Masumo huffs, "I don't know what Sirosaanto told you, but these experiments have been going on for a very long time. Set up for what we are going began over a hundred years ago."

Nekoba stands up, "you can't both be telling the truth, but you can both be lying to me, and I would like to know why. What are you trying to conceal?"

Masumo stands threateningly it is clear she is upset, but she shuts her eyes and breaths deep to stay in control of her feeling "I can see you still need time to think. That is ok, I have forever." Masumo vanishes, and Nekoba finds himself back at the park.

Nekoba stars at where Masumo had been. "no, you don't, if you did, you wouldn't be in such a hurry."

Chapter 12, Three Days Remaining

May 19th, 9:00 am

A sound that has not been heard in several days calls to the town. the ringing of the bells at Ichishin-Magami.

The monk walk the street dressed in robes made of yellow, orange and black silk. Sashes and scarves with the name of the town cut into the fabric. Criers walk the streets with bells calling to the town. "36 hours until the The Feast of Nobunaga begins! Ready your homes! Ready your bodies!"

Tami approaches the home of Oso Hanzo. Tami pounds on the door. Oso opens it, his eyes heavy, his clothes splattered in hot blood.

Tami holds out a festival garb to Oso, "The Feast of Nobunaga is at hand, wash your face and join me, we need your hands."

"I am in no mood for dancing today." Oso explains.

"That is often the best time to dance." Tami retorts. "Besides I think Ri..."

And that warrants a surprise hooking punch, Oso strikes Tami across the chin knocking him onto his back. Oso stands over Tami, he picks up the robe Tami brought for him. "Don't speak to me again." Oso orders.

There is a moment of contemplation before Oso reaches down and picks Tami back up. "I am sorry, I am still feeling raw." Oso makes Tami look side to side "I don't think I did any long-term damage."

Oso steps back into his shop, "I will get dressed and help you with preparations for the ceremony. I want to stop by Tsu's house on the way. I need a few words the doctor."

May 19th, 10:17 am

Jin arrives at Takashi's house, for the first time in a long time dressing down, Jin has traded his coat and slacks combo for shorts and a loose-fitting shirt with anima influence.

Jin knocks on the door, Odette opens it in short order, Jin smiles "excuse me, do you happen to have a pound of wild rice, I seem to be running low."

Odette has chosen to were a pastel skirt and tank top equaly brightly colored. "High Jin, you missed breakfast."

Jin points out, "the monks are out in force today. Maybe I just never noticed before but those guys can sure move quick when there is work afoot."

Odette waves Jin in as she expresses "I think that this is in no small part do to how much things have changing in the last few weeks. There are no distractions, nothing to do but look around and enjoy the company of the people around you."

Jin continues her sentiment "no computers, no phones, no movies. No lights. That is a change. I can't remember any time in my life where I didn't have a phone or a laptop in arm's reach."

As they step into the entryway Jin discards his shoes. Odette questions "How is mom?"

"she is extraordinarily happy that the church has unlocked its doors. She says she is behind on her prayers." Jin comments.

"I don't remember your mother being invested in the church." Odette adds.

"one thing that may be paying a factor in her enthusiasm, the monk's crier announced that 'in reconciliation for lost time, the coffers will be opened and gifts of wine, cheese, and candy nuts will be offered to all worshipers today and tomorrow.'." Jin explains

"Candy nuts?" Odette questions "Maybe I have some prayers to offer also."

"Is Leta still here?" Jin asks.

"She is up in my room, last I saw she was checking out that new magazine I just got." Odette expresses.

"and Sakura?" Jin stands up after unlacing his shoes.

"haven't seen her since the hospital." Odette laments.

"Talking about the hospital, how is Dr. Tsu?"

Odette points, "hasn't moved from the couch since yesterday."

Jin nods "that is understandable, he had invested more in the hospital then you or I will ever know."

Takashi mumbles softly "Arnoldo, can I get you to join me in room 109?" he waves a hand dismissively, "let Iwata know that I still need to see the report from last night…"

"I don't know… should I hit him or something?" Odette shrugs.

"I think it is best if you leave him to rest." Jin comments. "Can we go up to your room?"

Odette laughs "My mother would have a fit if she heard you say that. I am not supposed to let anyone upstairs."

Jin remarks "I don't think I have seen your mother since she got that job at the aeronautics development firm."

Odette shrugs again and waves Jin to follower her, she dashes up the steps playfully. Odette knocks on her bedroom door and calls out "Leta, are you dressed."

"Yeah." Leta calls back.

Jin and Odette step in, Leta is laying on the bed holding a magazine up looking through the photos, Leta comment "what is the point of a 'Skin Magazine' when all the skin is black boxed?"

Odette giggles "I think I said the same thing."

Jin finds a place on the floor to sit down "you know, I was looking forward to this. Some excuse to put down my books and go out and do nothing."

Odette opens her window and sits on the frame, one leg in the room the other outside of it. "SO... anyone have any idea what we should do with the afternoon?"

Jin smiles "anyone have any stories to share?"

Leta speaks up "you want to do that? I thought that was a thing we only did out in the woods after school."

Odette rationalizes "well, the woods are less than safe and there is no more school so... sounds fine to me?"

Jin looks to Leta "Do you have any stories you like?"

Leta tips her eyes up thinking "I remember one or two."

Leta turns so she can see both of her friends, hiding the magazine she had been reading behind her back. She folds her legs tightly and rest her hands on her knees as she tips her head back trying to remember the smaller details of her tale.

"If you walk into the woods an hour before sunup, then take the hillside path until you reach the gate shaped stone and turn to face the sun. soon you will find a shadow cast on a stone. A stone with hole in it."

"once resting on this stone there was a pearl, set there by a kind kami. Lifetimes ago, that stone was taken. It was given to a man and he was told to take it, and another matching stone and turn them into earrings."

"the kind Kami used these earrings to make a magic gate, the gate would seal a door, leading, filled with more silver then any man should ever want."

"'The Kami one day saw a man walking through the woods. He had no shoes and a robe that hardly fit. He held on his back a large bag and he gripped in one fist a scroll. The goddess asks 'why are you so far from your home?'."

"the man explained to the goddess 'I have a sick daughter; I am searching for a magic flower to brew a potion with.'."

"the goddess asks 'I have been to your home, your village has many potions and many magic flowers growing all around it, how can you not have the flower you need already?'."

"the man tells the goddess 'an old man has taken all the flowers and all the potions for himself, he tells me that if I want a potion I most being him silver or brew the potion for myself, I have no silver so I am looking for the magic flowers here.'."

"The goddess explains to the man 'there is no need for you to walk deeper into these woods, let me offer you a gift.' And so she hands him her earrings telling him 'Just over there, you will see a magic stone, set one earring on that stone and a door will open, but be sure to hold onto the other earring tightly, if you drop it, the door will lock behind you and never open again.'"

"she continues 'behind the magic door you will find more silver then a man should ever want. Take a hand full, buy the potion for your child, then buy wheat and rice and a new pair of boots with the rest.'"

"and so, the man does as he is instructed. He opens the magic door and takes as much silver as he can fit in one hand. Be buys his potion, his boots, and his rice. Then the old man who had taken all the magic flowers asks him 'where did you find so much silver as to buy all these things?'."

"the man explains to him 'I meet a kind kami, she gave me here earrings,' he shows the earrings 'she told me of a magic door, to unlock it I must set this earing on a magic stone, then the door would open leading to the room filled with silver, then...'."

"but the old man doesn't wait to hear the rest of the story, he takes the earring from the man and runs off into the woods in search of the magic door."

"after much searching the old man finds the door and opens it placing both earrings on the magic stone. The door opens. The old man runs in to see the room full of silver. Then the door slams shut."

"and the goddess takes back her earrings, never to see the door opened again for behind that door is a room filled with more sliver then a man should ever want."

Jin claps, "that was amazing, I hadn't heard that one before."

Odette speculates "the goddess wanted the man to spend the money to root out anyone in the village that would be so selfish as to hurt those around them in search of fortune."

May 19th, 10:45 am

Odette hands out to her friends a few cans of soda "it is hotter than piss, but it is what I have unless someone wants to walk do to the water pump."

Leta bows "thank you."

Odette grins, "I want to go next."

Jin waves her on "go right ahead."

"The Emperor has five sons, and four daughters. Maybe you didn't remember though, the papers had announced that the emperor had six sons once."

"but no one talks about the sixth son. The emperor's sixth son like to fish. He had a boat and he liked to use a net wen fishing. But fishing of the west port isn't always the best. Everyone likes to fish down there so there aren't many good fish left."

"this makes the emperor's son angry. So he goes to the library and he grabs some maps and starts looking for a new place to fish. He finds a place, a place called Koi Lake. An elderly woman sees him looking at the map and where he had pointed on it."

"the older women explains to him 'if you want to visit Koi Lake, you have to remember, you can't approach from the south gate. Your grandfather promised the forest baku that no one would use that road anymore.'."

"the sixth son kisses the old women and thanks her then runs off to gather his nets and rods. He can't wait to see Koi Lake."

"when he gets home to gather his things he calls out to his sisters 'I found a new place to fish, I am going to Koi Lake."

"the oldest of his sisters asks him, 'do you know about the south gate?'. But he says nothing, he runs out the door and to the road he reads his map and pick a path, it is a long walk and he wants to be home before sundown."

"on the road the sixth son passes a fellow fisher walking home, he must have been fishing overnight. The fisher explains to him that the water is good today, he picked a fine day to go out. This excites him even more and he hurries his pace."

"a samurai crosses his path also. The samurai tells him 'the road ahead is hexed, he should tread better weathered roads'. But the sixth son shews him away. There is work to be done, and besides he is the emperor's son, no one is going to be trouble for him."

"even a fox sitting in the road calls out to the son 'Boy, this road is not for you. This is the path walked by spirits.'."

"the son laughs off the fox's words 'still you and I walk this way. Perhaps the spirits aren't looking right now.'."

"and so the son cast his net and soon drags up eight fish, eight fish so huge that they are all he could lift. The son ties the fish to his body and walks home. No one stops him this time. Until he gets home."

"the boy sets down the fish and he tries to call to his family to let them know he has made it home but it seems he can't rase his voice. He makes his way to his sister's chamber as he can hear her singing."

"the emperor's eldest daughter looks upon the face of her brother and..."

Leta calls out "stop!"

Odette looks over "what?"

Leta shakes her head "I don't want to hear the end of the story."

Jin drinks his drink "then let me take over." He waits for Leta and Odette to look to him. "Numbers have power, this isn't so much a story as a warning."

"sometimes, the forest becomes angry. Time and time again, throughout the pictures we have taken, strange shadows pass through our vision. Looks to close at any one and maybe you spot the face of the forest."

"the face collector, is amongst the names that have been given to him, but not my favorite, I like Noropobo. The tree man."

"Noropobo like to play games. If you see him and he sees you, he will send you a dream, in that dream you will see eight objects. Things lost in the forest. Then you will hear him humming, because that is the only sound, he can make."

"the humming is a timer. It will count down 16 hours. If you know the story of Noropobo you know to start looking for the lost things. Find them and you win. The spirits of the forest will gift you some… thing, that part is unclear. People don't talk about what the gift is."

"but once the humming stops then nature of the game changes. Noropobo is now playing hide-and-seek with you. Any time you are outside, or near a window, or looking at a picture where you can see trees or water, Noropobo walks closer to you."

"the power of the spirit eats light, and overheats electronics. As he approaches, you need to look away, shut your eyes. Stand facing a wall. Because once he can see the color of your eyes the game is over, he wins."

"when Noropobo catches you, you will see why he is called The Face Collector by some. That is what his clothes are made of. Human faces, and once you have seen him, your face is added to his robe, and he grow ever taller, so no matter how many faces are added to the tail of his coat it always fits perfectly."

"to this day he may have 100,000 faces on his coat, but not one is his own. Apparently, lifetimes ago, Noropobo had stollen something from the Baku and they took away his face in payment."

"so, should you see a shadow overlap your own, do not turn to face it, do not look at it. run. Noropobo may be looking for you."

Leta shouts "that story was horrible!" she throws her arms up in proclamation "what is that story meant to teach, Good people don't get rewarded, bad people don't get punished, it is all arbitrary! Find lost things, run away!"

Odette whispers to herself "evil doesn't need a reason."

May 19th, 11:07 am

There is a pounding on the door. Odette stands up and brushes down her body straightening her shirt "be right back" Odette walks off.

She opens the front door "this is Odette your door man. How may I be of service?"

Oso is behind the door in his festival outfit "I am looking for Tsu."

"I assume you mean Takashi," she points, "he has been on the couch pretending to be a daikon since yesterday."

Oso walks in, he talks a set kneeling in front of Takashi, he whispers, "Takashi, I need your help. I need you to do something for me."

Takashi whispers, "Hando, patch the call though my office, I will take it there."

After listening to Takashi talk to himself for minute or two Oso speaks up, "Takashi, I need you to sober up really quick like." He takes a deep breath, "the festival is upon us, tomorrow night for all of an hour we are going to have the ears of the hole town, you are one of the town elders, when you talk people pay attention."

Takashi isn't paying any attention. Oso thinks, "do you have some peroxide and wasabi pepper?"

Odette shakes her head, "I don't like wasabi, I think it smells bad."

Oso nods "ok, plan B, we can do this the hard way or the really hard way."

Odette looks up, "so, what changes between hard and really hard?"

Oso shrugs "well, hard is I try to shock him awake with a slap or two across the ear."

Odette asks, "and really hard?"

Oso lowers his eye, "how do you feel about public displays of affection?"

Odette shakes her head "I really don't think I like where this is going."

Oso confirms, "then you see my point." Oso crawls in closer to Takashi. Oso sets his hands on the sides of Takashi's head "one more chance Doc, sober up right now or this is going to get unpleasant."

Takashi is still talking to himself nonsensically, Oso sighs and nods, "ok, I am sorry Takashi."

Oso pulls his hands apart only a few inches then slaps the sides of Takashi's head clapping his ears.

Takashi screams and reaches up gripping the sides of his head. The air pressure resulting from the clap has dizzied him, scrambled his vision. An ear clap is an experience many times more disorienting then one would think.

Takashi once he has gained his equilibrium back reaches out to grab Oso threateningly. Oso hooks both arms out then thrust both hands into Takashi's chest to push him into the couch.

"Doctor, are you with us again?" Oso asks.

Takashi calms down, he feels around in his pockets looking for his smokes and huffs as he remembers he ran out days ago. "I am awake."

Oso explains, "tomorrow is the festival."

Takashi shakes his head, "I am not much of a fan, people tend to drink too much and act silly."

Oso explains, "I had an idea that my just end all this madness. I want you to put on a speech, tell the good aliens to come forward and help us hunt down and kill the bad aliens. We could end all this in three days if all goes well."

Takashi rolls his eyes side to side considering the proposition. Is this ethical, is this moral, could this work?

May 19th, Noon

Sakura watches the sky, Reko Jet by her side polishing a collection of blades that have been dropped off for him.

Sakura points at a passing plane "Reko, what type of Airplane is that one?"

Jet looks up "some sort of a prop flyer, I think. It is too small to be a passenger jet."

Sakura nods "that is like seven of them in the last hour, what do you think is going on?"

Sakura watches Reko work, she struggles to find something to talk about, "how many other people do you think known what is going on?"

Reko snarls then drops his sanding stone on the ground, he has been struggling to avoid eye contact with Sakura, "DO you have to walk around all day in your beast from? I find it very disturbing."

"and why should I hide myself? I am not running from anything; I haven't harmed anyone." Sakura protest.

"Can you at least put on a skirt and coat? You having your... fur showing is very distracting to me." Reko complains.

Sakura tips her head thinking "is it because I am a girl?"

Reko shouts in frustrations "I bludgeoned 15 bugs to death last night and your standing around talking, looking like one of them is provocative. My wife and daughter were turned into beast like you..."

Sakura cuts him off "not like me! I am still human!"

Reko growls "are you? Am I?"

Sakura stretches her wings and stands tall "stop it Reko! We can't question each other, we cant doubt ourselves. Alone we are weak, together we are strong."

Reko abruptly calms down "the things I have done, they hurt me."

"I know." Sakura steps into the giant man and wraps her arms and wings around him hugging him.

Reko places a hand on her breast and pushes her back to arm's length. Sakura nods in understanding as she notices the twisted look of pain on Reko's face.

Reko tries to find something to talk about to keep his mind occupied. "what were you doing the night that you changed?"

Sakura laughs slightly "struggling with my sexuality. I was part of a group that got together a few nights each week. Told stories. Mostly I was there because Odette was."

Reko misses the confection that Sakura just offered instead focusing on the part afterwards "I know a story if you want to hear it."

Sakura nods and smiles. She folds her legs and sits down; she leans forward in a butterfly stretch resting.

"I met a man from a town out west 'Dan-mark' I think was the name of the town he was from. They have strange gods there, strange spirits, and just as strange of stories."

"some of the words he used we he talked I didn't understand, so I will substitute them for words I know to try to keep the story going."

"four bards join forces to play a powerful song, the song they sing was so powerful that it awoke from a hundred-year-long-sleep a mighty earth kami. The earth kami comes to them in the shape of a women with a buffalo head. She speaks onto them 'your song is so beautiful that I have fallen in love with all of you. Now I command you to keep singing.'."

"so, what can the bards do but keep singing? And they sing, and sing and sing, for a day without sleep. But then they can sing no more."

"and the earth kami orders 'you must not stop singing, you must sing more for me. Forever.'."

"and so, one of the bards cries off into heaven 'kami of the wind, will you not give us the power to stand against the beast for surely, she wishes us to die.'."

"but the wind is unmoved"

"and the second bard declares 'the wind has not heard us cry, we have but one chose, we must take up: blade, and bow, and ax, and fist, and if we wish to live, we must fight.'."

"with those words spoken aloud the wind stirs. With the body of a bear the sky opens and the kami of the wind makes himself known."

"the kami of the earth calls into the past and draws forth the dead to protect herm honor. But the kami of the wind calls on the power of 'Dova' and uses his super breath to blow away the past."

"it is clear to the kami of earth that she and the wind are equal in power. So, she reaches into the earth and draws a spear and a knife, and with them she wishes to slay the sky."

"the wind kami can see also that the kami of earth is mighty and so he draws from the sky a hammer…"

Sakura cuts in "the wind god has a hammer? Not a bow or a fan or anything else that a wind god may want?"

"apparently the wind god has a hammer." Reko explains. He then continues his story.

"the sky and the earth clash, the wind god is powerful, but his hammer can not break the armor of the earth god. And the earth god strikes the wind god, the wind god is crippled."

"the earth god gloats, 'you are a small kami, your power is weak, I am the earth, I am unmoving. All things return to the earth after death, so now I shall take your life and add it to my life, and I will take your power and add it to my power.'."

"as the earth god taunts the wind god the first bard kneels before earth god, he strips from his body the chain from around his neck and rest it on the neck of the god declaring 'alone we are each a man, together we are two men, take this and add my power to yours.'."

" then the second bard steps forward, he takes the kota from his arms and places it onto the arms of the wind god saying ' alone we are each one man, together we are three men, take my power and add it to yours.'."

"then the third bard steps forward, he take the coat from his back and gives it to the god 'alone we are each one man, together we are a four men, take this and add my power to yours.'."

"And then the last bard steps forward and places his ax into the hand of the wind god announcing 'alone we are each one man, together we are many men. Take this and let our power know no limitations.'."

"then the wind god stands up, empowered in a way he has never been. The god takes the strength that the men have gave him and he has become greater then he has ever been. The earth kami goes to strike the wind kami again but now, emboldened the wind god throws is ax into the air and breaks open the sky, water and fire spill from heaven and frighten way the earth god."

"on that day the wind god declares onto all that follow his 'Steel is the symbol of courage, any man that proves his strength in life need not fear death, brave men from now until forever will be reborn as gods.'."

Sakura starches "you are right, the gods of that land are not like the gods of this one."

Reko explains "the way I see it, the moral of the story is simple, man created god, so we shouldn't fear spirits."

Sakura shakes her head "But you are afraid."

May 19th, 4:23 pm

Oso pushes a set of Obon onto the stage at the heart of town, a hand full of other monks, Tami included carry Taikyo drums onto stage creating a ring of drums thirty feet wide.

Oso is handed a set of staves wrapped I silk knots. Tami waves Oso on. "hit the drum, make sure it still works."

Oso nods, he runs at the large Obon and cartwheels into it, he drops to kneeling then takes a hand full of swings playing a few knots.

The thundering sound of the drum can be heard from almost anywhere in town. the low rumbling, the ground shaking power of the drum is something to behold. Monks and bypasser's alike cheer at the sound of the first mighty cord. Only hours remain until the feast can begin.

Takashi makes his way out onto the street, he follows the sound of the drums just like a hundred or more others wanting to see the stage being dressed.

The sound of the drums call to Sakura as well, Sakura jumps houses and crouches atop a house watch the crowed from afar.

As the drums beat, the voices of the Sanguine whisper loudly. Sakura rotates her antenna following the voices, as she becomes more accustomed to her new shape the voices become less painful to focus on.

"That is Takashi Tsu."

"Takashi must die."

"No, I want Takashi and his girl, give them to me."

"you mated only a few hours ago and you want to mate again?"

"I did as you told me, and now I am hungry."

"you are as twisted as me, I like it."

"tonight, give me Takashi and Odette."

"very well, then at midnight, they will be yours."

Sakura goes wide-eyed as she hears the voices whispering. "Odette, Takashi." Sakura whispers to herself. "I have to protect them."

Sakura looks about remembering "once bitten, no other Chromon or Sanguine can claim ownership of one... isn't that what the bug in the woods said? So, if I bite them then the others can't." she rationalizes.

Sakura sniff out Odette, she is with Jin and Leta. Sakura can smell from here already that Leta's blood is passions, no one is going to attack her again, but Jin they may. Sakura spreads her wings and jumps into the air, she flies off to find her friends.

May 19th, 4:38 pm

Sakura jumps up and sits on the window seal of Odette's room. the three kids are all streached out on the floor talking about whatever seems to be coming to mind.

Sakura calls out to the lot of them "Hay!"

All at once the three kids jump to alertness. Leta rolling over and falling off the bed hiding between it and the window. Odette hops the other way and grabs her coffee tumbler off the table as an improvised defensive tool.

Jin stands up but then holds up a hand to hold Odette back, "It is Sakura." He explains

Leta, nor any of the other kids have seen Sakura fully transformed but something in the way she stands, in the ways she moves, is enough to inform Jin of who she is.

Odette questions "SO, why are you wolfed-out?"

Sakura explains "I don't want to have to hide who or what I am." Sakura walks slowly over to Odette "Odette, monster are going to be coming her tonight, they are going to hurt and Takashi, but I can protect you, I can make you immune to the drug they use to control people." Sakura takes a deep breath to calm herself "I need to bite you." She explains

Odette pulls back the coffee cup and questions, "what did you say."

Jin cuts in, "wait, I think she is telling the truth, I heard my father and Mr. Arnoldo talking about an inoculation that had been dreamed up."

Jin steps between Odette and Sakura "tell me how it works." He orders

Sakura is becoming more animal like, it is subtle but anyone attuned to watching the way people move could spot it if they are sharp enough. Sakura takes a sharp breath tasting the air. "it is some sort of an enzyme in our salvific glands, we can 'mark' people, it lets us read their minds much more easily and even send them ideas, enough so as to control their actions with a level of focus."

"And how would your biting Odette proctet her?" Jin orders.

"the drug is tuned to specific people. Once bitten, no other bug can inject you and take control... from that point on only the first bug to bite you can send you commands. So, so long as I don't tell you to do anything it is immunity in a can."

Jin takes off his shirt "Bite me."

Sakura looks confused, "you are not in immediate danger. Odette is."

Jin explains "I want to see how it works." He then looks to Odette "if she bite me and I vamp out, I want you to slay me. If I am no longer human I don't want to be alive, do you understand?"

Leta calls out "wait, I don't understand"

Odette nods coldly "Thank you Jin, I understand."

Sakura looks between Jin and Odette "and how do you think you are going to kill us with a coffee cup?"

Odette reaches around behind her bed and pulls out her father's sword "do you think this will work better?"

Sakura nods "make sure you hit the heart or sever the spinal column , anything else and I will stand right back up."

Leta is the voice of ration "Wait, wont that turn you into a bug, Jin?"

Jin thinks "Sakura, will it?"

Sakura shakes her head "No, I don't think it works that way. I don't need to 'infect' everyone that I bite. I haven't worked out the details yet, but a bite alone wont do the job."

Odette steps forward. She pulls the flashlight out of her back pocket, "Sakura, sit down, I want to see something."

Sakura sits with her lower arms folded across her legs her upper arms around her stomach. Odette points "Jin, grab my library books."

Jin grabs the books and drops them on the bed. Odette flips though setting the book down on a diagram of a dragonfly, another book she sets down of a picture of a snake, a third on a deep see fish.

Odette request "Sakura open your mouth please." Sakura does as she is told, Odette shines the flashlight in her mouth.

Odette points out to Jin and Leta as they gather around, "Ok, so, there is some strange stuff going on here but I think I can see something interesting. Look at the shape of her teeth,"

Jin point out "they are sooth."

Odette uses a pencil to tip Sakura's head up and look at the roof of her mouth "the front set are, but look there." In the roof of Sakura's mouth there are two burrows, under her tongue, there are hidden fangs, the fangs slide into the holes in the roof of her mouth when her mouth is closed.

Off to the sides of her mouth there are venom glands, and a second set in the back of her throat. Leta asks, "why is her tongue rigged?"

Odette points at one of her books "because it isn't a tongue, her tongue is in a pouch in her chest, that is a stinger."

Jin asks "and what do you think those two galangals on the underside of it are?"

Odette shakes her head "I don't know."

Leta arbitrarily comment "the sides are pinching and it is somewhat diamond shaped, like a urethra."

Sakura mumble "this is getting somewhat uncomfortable."

Odette whispers with Jin thinking maybe Leta maid a fair point "on the dragonfly diagram, it shows that the dragonflies' reproductive parts are on it's tail. maybe it IS some sort of a sex gland…"

Jin steps away and folds his arms thinking "the important part is, teeth are one thing, tongue is another, a bite and a sting are not the same thing."

Sakura stands up, she needs a moment to roll her tongue around her mouth to wet it is as she was getting dry with three examining her.

Jin orders "Bite me."

Sakura steps up to Jin, she lowers her head onto the side of his arm, she feels up to his shoulder. The feeling of hot skin on her lips has a strange effect on her, she quickly grows short of breath as she looks for the spot she wants to bite. She shakes slightly and her body tightens up. Sakura pays it no mind. Her fangs expose, she opens her mouth.

Sakura slowly slides her fangs into the soft meat of Jin caller bone, this seems to case no pain at all, Jin stands still waiting. The bite is nothing more than a needle stab and the saliva she leaves seems to burn the wound shut. When Sakura pulls her head back it leaves little more than a red and white discoloration of the skin.

The blisters that had been seen on the infected before seem to be bite marks, not stings. It would seem that the Sanguine don't always want to kill and eat their food all at once, sometimes they want to program the infected to come to them.

Odette looks Jin over, "how do you feel?"

Jin thinks, "I don't think I could describe any particular discomfort at the moment. I suspect that your hypothesis was right. A bite isn't a sting."

Leta speaks up "ok, I will sign up, do me next."

Sakura shakes her head, she is still slightly short of breath, extending her fangs seems to require a level of focus more so then Sakura would expect. "no need, you are inoculated already."

Sakura looks over to Odette "Odette, take off your shirt please."

Odette questions "why bite my arm? why not my hand or leg or something?"

Sakura speaks up "I could but do you know how much more sensitive the hand is then the chest? You will be suffering muscle cramps for weeks."

Odette nods, "I see your point." Odette undoes her shirt and drops it onto the bed. Sakura's breath hitches as she looks at her school friend. Sakura struggles to swallow for a moment, she then regains control of her body.

Slowly Sakura steps up to Odette, she places two arms on Odette's sides, the other two on her arms. Sakura searches for the spot she wants to bite.

As Sakura does, she whimpers and chirps, she sweets and her body becomes tighter. Her legs shake and her stomach twist. A cold buring feeling overcomes Sakura as she holds Odette. After giving a quick nibble to the base of the neck Sakura drops to her knees.

Jin and Leta rush over to see if she is OK, Odette seems to be unaware of what has happened at first. Jin calls out to Sakura "what happened?"

Sakura holds up a hand to keep him back, she is quivering, clearly suffering an unexpected pain as one arm folds across her underbelly holding herself. "Stay back." She orders.

Sakura gains her footing but her equilibrium is shot. She stumbles into the bathroom holding herself up to try to find a drink, most disappointedly. Instead finding herself curled up on the floor in a ball struggling to regain control of her senses.

Leta follows, she shuts the door behind her as she steps into the tiny bathroom lit by a single window.

"what are you feeling right now?"

Sakura tries to explain "I feel both hot and cold, for a few seconds every part of my body felt tense then it let go and now I feel sick and tired."

To Leta this sounds familiar, she throws a thought in the air "Sakura, are you a virgin?"

Sakura seems to not understand what was asked "what?"

Leta offers a paraphrase "have you ever had sex?"

"no" Sakura states dryly. "why?"

Leta explains "Just sit up and focus on breathing, this will pass in about ten minutes."

"what are you talking about." Sakura struggles to speak.

"I acted the same why after the first time I had an orgasm." Leta explains.

"why would I ever want to do this again?" Sakura explains.

Leta sits with Sakura waiting for her to recover "it is a good deal more fun the second time. Or, it was for me." Leta thinks, "but, why Odette? Are you attracted to her?"

Sakura laughs, "I would have thought everyone knew that."

May 19th, 5:30 pm

Jin, Sakura, Odette and Leta track down Takashi at the promenade of town. the four of them struggle to explain all at once what they have learned.

After serval attempts, the kids take Takashi up the road to Oso's shop so they have a place both close by and quite to try to talk again.

Takashi tries to paraphrase what the kids have been tripping over their tongues to explain. "The White-Haired-Beast, whoever that is, is coming to my house tonight at 11pm to kill me, or mate with me. The elixir that Arnoldo had been studying was Sakura's saliva, and Sakura is a lesbian. Did I catch all that?"

Leta nods "that sounds right to me, did that sound right to you?" she looks to her friends.

Sakura lowers her head abashedly "why did you add the part about me being gay?"

Leta drops her head "oops."

Takashi picks up, "Jin, you signed up to be a human lab rat, and you let Sakura inject you with her venom?"

Jin nods, Sakura explains "only one person can 'linked' to a bug at a time. With my venom in his body, no other bug can take control of him."

Takashi taps his foot as he places his hands on the back of his head "and you want to bite me also?"

Sakura nods "that way you have some defense from the bugs."

Takashi nods in understanding "ok, then what?"

There is a long moment of silences as clearly Sakura had not thought that far ahead. Jet calls out, "Maybe I have a thought."

May 19th, 10:45 pm

The streets are alive, tens of thousands of candles burn lighting ever corner of the town. for the first night in many nights people walk the town well after dark.

This makes it challenging for Shirio-Kemono to travel without being seen. But never the less she manages. Her and Machohero have places to be.

The two land on the roof of Takashi's house and crawl down the walls looking in windows. Shirio sniffs the air. She can smell something is out of place. But can't seem to pinpoint what is bothering her.

Machohero points out "Takashi is in his room." she laughs. "Odette is with him. Maybe she is afraid of the dark."

Shirio explains "we should me slow. Takashi and Odette both have hidden strength. They are fast, lucky, and smart. They have drawn the eyes of the sprites. They protect them."

Machohero salivates, she wants Takashi so bad, she can feel a boiling in her stomach. "what do we have to fear? We are spirits."

"but we can still be banished. Remove the heart, sever the spine, and our bodies crumble away." Shirio comments. Shirio looks in to the front room and counts the shoes sitting on the steps "the Tenzuma child is here with them, do you see her?"

Machohero walks around the house searching "no, I don't see her."

Shirio commands "then don't waste time. Plant your seeds in Takashi's chest and run before he awakens." She looks to the streets "I should find my other children. Arnoldo, Handa."

Machohero comments "we can be quick, come with me mother."

Shirio has not laid eggs in a few days, not since the hospital, she is temped, she agrees "then we can share Takashi, your seed and mine will fill his chest."

Machohero opens the window and climes in, Shirio only a few steps behind. The two creep slowly forward. Machohero grabs the blanket from Takashi and pulls it back to look on her soon to be lover.

Takashi is wide awake, he sees the spector standing over him and clicks on the flashlight he had hidden to his chest.

Machohero squeals and falls backwards away from the light. Shirio grabs Machohero and turns to the window to flee, somehow Takashi knew they were coming.

But the window is being protected by Reko Jet, a two-handed hammer held high ready to strike as they turn.

Shiroi call "fly." She pushes Machohero at the door and away from Reko. Reko's hammer oms down. But Shirio is older, smarter, and stronger then the thralls she has birthed, she twist her body off to one side to get out of the way of the first swing.

The matriarch Sanguine sends out a cry to her slaves to come to her aid. Odette steps into view and holds up her flashlight to the beast. Shirio pulls a wing across her face to protect herself.

Reko thrust his hammer upwards coming in for a second swing. Shirio thrust down with two of her arms in a cross block pinning the hammer down. Shirio slaps Odette knocking her to the ground. Reko drops his hammer and punches Shirio across the face staggering her.

The Sanguine stumbles to the door falling out of the room. windows all around he house start to break in. six more bloodsucking beast smash into the house.

Odette, Reko, and Takashi chase Shirio out of the room and into the hallway. The elder monster runs down the steps and into the kitchen. Takashi parkours over the banister to catch up with her first.

As Machohero runs for the front door, Shirio goes for the back door. Machohero opens the door and finds blade suddenly splitting her ribs open. She looks up to see Sakura waiting.

Sakura reaches onto her hip and pulls a second blade. "that was Ri's sword, this is Tenzuma's."

Machohero is stunned, she can't believe one of her students would attack her. Someone she has fought for, protected...

Sakura takes the sword in both her upper arms and lifts it overhead, she cross steps inwards and takes a horizontal slash down at Machohero. The blade bus from shoulder to hip before it is to tide up in broken bone and muscle to be drawn.

Machohero collapses, slain by the sneak strike. Sakura picks up the two swords and examines them, the edge is rolled on Reje's sword, it will not cut again until it has been retempered.

In the kitchen Takashi pulls a meat cleaver from a magnetic hanger over the stove. Takashi grips the blade tightly and dashes forward.

Shirio snaps outwards with a wing to stager Takashi. The back door burst open and Oso Hanzo sprints in to Takashi's aid.

Shirio pivots to face Hanzo, Oso draws his sword and thrust out for an eye strike. Shirio holds up one arm and the blade bounces off her armored skin. Oso reverses momentum and goes for a slash to the neck. Shirio rolls her hands in a windmill guard to push the blade off line.

Takashi grains his footing and goes to stab Shirio in the back with his meat cleaver. The monster screams as the blade breaks her shoulder. Shirio is hurt, but still strong enough to fight. She grabs the caller of Oso's robe and throws the smaller man at Takashi. Takashi is knocked out when he hits the sink.

Oso, is not Oso reaches into his coat and reveals a string of knives tied to his chest. He pulls out four of them and starts throwing knives like dart.

The monster Handa howls as he smashes through a wall to come to his mother's aid. The darts strike the mammoth of a bug with little effect.

Shirio knows she is the king on this chess board. The death of a knight and a bishop will be painful, but the game is still on. She runs away leaving the hunters to fight her pawns.

But her escape is not clean. Sakura sees her fly away. Sakura chases after her.

Reko and Odette catch up. Handa throws his arms in the air and yells proclaiming his strength. Reko switches up his stance, he holds a knife in one hand his sword in the other.

Handa runs forward to grab Reko and Oso in his oversized hands. Odette flashes her flashlight. The monster freezes in place.

Oso takes the lead this time. A stab to the stomach with the knife, a slash to the leg as he cat-steps past the monster, a slash to the back and a stab from caller bone into heart and the monster crumbles. Oso in a matter of moments proves his training.

The bugs that had crashed thought the windows upstars have made their way to the kitchen, they circle their pray.

Reko, Odette and Oso move into position to protect Takashi. Odette is shaking, she talks fast trying to keep herself calm by chattering "Sakura told me these things aren't any stronger then you or I, Oso, Reko, you are both as strong as ten men, we can handle this. There are only twelve of them."

Oso scans the room, "I see six."

Reko points to the hole in the wall "the condition of your living room would seem to dictate these things may be slightly stronger than the average man."

Oso comment, "I just remember something. That thing you use Reko, for measuring nuts, I still have it in my shed."

Reko jest, "we will pick it up on the way to my place, I can hang it up over my bed, do you want to grab a beer on the way home?"

May 19th, 11:06 pm

Shirio comes to a landing at the hunted tree only a short walk from the kid's camp sight. Sakura lands and draws her blade.

"Face me Demon!" Sakura orders.

Shirio looks up and down Sakura's body, "I remember you, you are the Useto child."

Sakura corrects her "My father was Useto, I am not, I am Takimaki."

Shirio throughs her head in laughter "You are Takimaki? That makes you the emperor's brother-in-law's granddaughter." Shirio giggles "that explains a lot."

Sakura comments "you hurt me, you hurt my father, now I am going to hurt you."

Shirio watches the girl "isn't that the way it always is? I don't want to fight you my girl. I don't like fighting Chromon's" Shirio watches the way Sakura walks.

Shirio tips her head off to one side noticing something off about Sakura. "you are limping, your shoulders are slooutched, you can't stand up all the way, can you?" Shirio thinks "you haven't eaten or slept in three days. And you haven't seeded. Your body is about to cave in on itself my child. You need to cocoon or you will die, your own seed will burn a hole in your body."

"why do you keep saying 'child'?" Sakura orders.

"you havne't worked it out yet? You are the decadent of Tamamo-No-Mia and Nobunaga. In other words, me." Shirio explains.

Sakura shouts, "Nobunaga didn't sleep with you, you have no royal blood."

The matriarch laughs, "you know so little, my girl." She walks side to side as the two star each other down. "the emperor's brother had deviant taste, and it turns out that I could fulfill those taste." Shirio shapeshifts several times showing off the idea that she could mascaraed as dozens of women. "but the shape of mine he licked the most was this." She takes the shape of a mighty white wolf.

Sakura knows well that all these shapes are nothing more than an illusion, Sakura rushes forward and slashes her blade.

Shirio takes her true form. She traps the sword with her forearms then twist downwards to make Sakura drop her sword. "you are slow, tired, but I will help you, make no mistake of that."

Shirio thrust an arm out to grips Sakura around the neck, she uses her other arms to hold Sakura's arms to her body. The great bug chokes the child for a few moments as she explains, "cocooning starts with learning how to open your second set of lunges. I will help you."

Shirio drags Sakura to the water and drops her in the river holding her down. "you will learn, or you will not, there are no other options."

Chapter 13, Two Days Remaining
May 20th, 7:50 am

Takashi awakens to the sound of a hammer pounding on the overhand of his house.

Takashi looks about, he feels groggy; still, his head is pounding, he is having trouble putting together where he has been the last few hours. He sees he is at home. He is in his bed; Odette is asleep in the bed alongside him. Both are fully dressed. Takashi has a makeshift bandage around his head.

Takashi walks out onto the balcony, he looks down. Six dead Sanguine are hanging off the front of his house, and a sign is painted onto the wall that reads, "Consider yourselves warned."

Reko hooks his hammer onto his belt and clears the sweat from his brow. Oso is standing at the end of the walkway leading up to the house. One hand on his blade, the other dead at his side.

Reko calls up to Takashi, "It looks like you lived through the night."

Takashi nods, "I don't know if I care for your decorating sense."

"After what we did last night, anyone looking to pick a fight with you would have to be dumb or suicidal," Reko explains. "But if you are awake, then it is time for us to part ways." Reko waves and walks off.

Reko and Oso share a few words, but Takashi can't hear what they are saying. The conversation ends in a hug between the two men, then Reko continues on his way.

Takashi walks outside the house and looks up at the hanging dead. Takashi rubs his neck, his eyes are drawn to a hand full of markings on each of their bodies. He moves in close to one.

A hand reaches out and feels up the chest of one of the monsters. Takashi whispers to himself, "oh no," he pulls his hand away and rubs his eyes "I am so sorry."

Oso runs up to Takashi, "something on your mind, doctor?"

"There are only a half dozen people in town that have had open-heart surgery. And only one of them was a woman. This is Orin Iwata." He points over to another of the monsters, " and that is Orochi Arnoldo," then to a third "Muro Handa, these were all friends of mine." Takashi drops his head as he is thinking, "I suspect this is not by mistake."

Oso shakes his head, "doctor, I …"

Takashi holds up a hand to silence Oso as he stares at the dead, he picks up and tugs at one of the wings. "Oso, what do Sakura's wings look like?"

Oso looks to the sky and folds his arms as he considers the inquiry, "mostly clear, dark fuzzy spots near the top and base of her wings, red and yellow splotches around the veins."

Takashi nods, "I thought so." He takes a few steps back as he. "do you see what I am seeing?"

Oso holds his arms out in a shrug then squints and nods, he remembers the other night, "I noticed this a few days ago, the feral bugs, they have no color to their wings, it is the smart ones that do!"

May 20th, 8:16 am

Jo and Jin sit at the park, the park is filled with people dancing and making merry, today is a holiday, and spirits are high. Music is being played by those with the skill to do so, singers, guitarists, drummers play around leading the festivities in an unorganized sort of way.

Jo has his notebook in hand, he reads over his notes. Jin looks over his father's shoulder-

"L, Inside, Fox owned umbrella décor, Intermediate tame, Ultimatum newborn dolphin edge regiment, Turtle helm endings, Monkey indeterminant laughter. -Zed-"

Jin questions, "that is the note off Dean Gogiro's phone?"

Jo nods, "it is."

Jo starts trying to reorder the words to come up with some sort of a hidden message. Jin moves in close and tries to help "maybe it isn't full words, what are we left with if we only take the first letters?"

Jo reads aloud "L, I, F, O, U, D, I, T, U, N, E, R, T, H, E, M, I, Z" Jo stops and looks again, "what. Some of the letters are capitalized." He rewrites the letters with capitalization "L, I, F, o, u, d, I, t, U, n, d, e, r, T, h, e, M, I, l, Z."

Jo starts to read again, "Lifoud…'

Jin cuts in, "Each capitalization marks the start of a new word. L, I found it under the mil, Z."

Jo looks to his boy, "I think you are right. Gogiro left something at the mil for L."

Jin jumps to his feet and grips his father by the arm, Jin tugs at his father, "come on, let's go take a look." Jin lets go running across the park, making his way to the bridge.

Jo points and calls out, "wait, we can take my car." But Jin is already mostly out o earshot, Jo stands up and chases after his son.

May 20th, 9:30 am

Jo stops his car outside the Mil, he looks side to side, the road is slanted, the trucks once used to move logs have sunk into the soft earth. The Mil looks even worse than Jin remembers.

Jo looks about with a grunt, Jin nods in understanding. The two approach the main house. The paint has flacked off the door. The hinges of the door are rusted open, pulled away from the frame.

Jo puts on a pair of gloves and pulls open the door. The two walk inside. Jin moves to the center of the rusted shop. The saw has broken apart, and the ground is covered in shattered machine parts.

Jin snaps and points off to one side. "Dad, wasn't that where the ladder was that went up to Eve's room?"

Jo pulls out a laser pin and points off to the other side of the shop, "and that was where Mr. Masumo served me a glass of wine."

Jin shakes his head, "everything has changed."

Jo explains, "that was because we were hallucinating last time we were here."

The floor under Jin starts to crack, Jo grabs his son with one hand and pulls him back several steps. The ground falls away, revealing a stairwell leading into an underground storage room. Jin grips Jo by the sides of the face and gives him a quick kiss, "Good catch."

Jo pats the boy on the back and starts down the steps. The basement is filled with degrading eggshells, a strange slime covers the ground. Inhuman skeletons hang from the wall.

Jin points at one of the dead bodies, "is that?"

Jo shakes his head "no, that isn't a person, it is a shell, look at the way the bones push outwards. There was something else in there that escaped."

Jo hypothesizes, "what if they are caterpillars? At some point, the old body breaks apart, and the new one comes out."

Under the Mil, there is a passageway that leads into the underground of the town itself. The ecosystem of the underworld they have discovered is almost wholly unlike the world above.

Heated by geo-vents, boiling water, and thermal exhausts. Strange sponge-like lifeforms grow from the walls, mushrooms that have taken on the role of trees seem to clean the air. The smell is something unholy. But it is breathable.

Jin thinks aloud. "this is what Masumo was protecting with her illusions."

Jo adds on "Gogiro was a member of the national geological society… how much do you think Gogiro knew?"

Jin asks, "do you think it was Masumo that killed Gogiro?"

"I don't know what to think." The two walk around for some time, looking around the haunting place. After some time of snooping, the two follow the pitch of the ground, it leads them to the center of the strange situation.

Hidden by overbrush, a metal object, it is unlike anything the two have seen; it is egg-shaped, mostly smooth. Bone like appendages grow from one side, holding it to the ground.

A round door is on one side, left open haphazardly.

Within the egg is a computer-like device. It seems to have a chair attached to it that is pod-shaped, Jin guesses that the pod requires someone to sit in it to turn it on.

Jo won't let him get any closer. Near the heart of the device is what seems to be acting like a battery. An approximate fist-sized blue metal stone. Jo can't stop himself; he touches to stone.

The lights in the room flicker. The computers blink, and audio starts to play. Jo's eyes roll back into his head. The incomprehensible voice gives him instructions, and Jo complies.

Jo pulls the stone out of the device and hides it in his coat pocket. Jin grips Jo by the coat and shakes him, "Dad!"

Jo wakes up. He pats Jin on the side and nods along with him, "Everything is ok, I think. Maybe, it is time for us to find a way out of this cave."

May 20th, 12:15 pm

The Obon hammers, one thundering strike, three echoing beets. The festival silences. Everyone knows what that beet means. One of the town elders has an announcement to make. People start to crowd around the stage.

Behind the stage, waiting to be waved forward by the monk Tomi, Takashi talks to Oso. Takashi whispers. "I do wish that we had more time. I don't know if this is going to work."

Oso reassures the doctor, "Everyone in town loves you. Everyone owes you a debt, you talk, they will listen."

Takashi scans the crowd, "I don't see Jet or Useto."

Oso explains, "no one has seen Sakura since last night. Reko went out looking for her, Odette thinks she may have gone to the waterworks. There is something out there that the bugs are attracted to."

Tomi waves Takashi forward "without another moment of delay, I give you Takashi Tsu!"

The crowd thunders, everyone loves Takashi, just like Oso had said. Tomi hands over the Megaphone. Takashi struggles at first to get the tool to work for him, but, at last, seems to work out how it works.

"I would like to take this time to thank all of you. Many of us have relationships with each other, which seems to be the charm of this town. everyone knows everyone."

"or so we tell each other. I see a few faces in the crowd I can't seem to place names with. As Jo Kogotana would tell you, some of us live lives above and beyond that which we are comfortable talking about."

"on a day like today, I would like to lift that vale of fear and confusion. Today is a day of hardship. A day of loss and confusion. But also a day of rebirth."

"it was on this day three hundred years ago that our town was given its name. Three-hundred years ago, we were honored by the emperor. Many of our family still hold on to relics handed down to us by the royal family."

"our history, if you choose to believe it, talks about wizards and knights, and demons doing battle in our front yards. Right there on the steps to Ichishin-Magami, the mighty Nobunaga did battle with the child of Amaterasu-No-Okami."

"in this town, Man declared itself free from the chains cast onto us by the gods. We split heaven asunder, and we saw the birth of the first Baku. The first dead god. All in one voice, we declared, 'we are men, and we will fight!' and half of heaven knelled down to the might we demonstrated, and heaven vowed to serve man."

"some of those gods still walk these streets, some of us have seen them, some of us know them. I would like to invite any gods living amongst us to join me on stage. On this day that we celebrate the birth of our town, I would love for you to reaffirm your vows as we reaffirm ours."

Takashi looks side to side, waiting. "I know you are out there. Is there not even one of you brave enough to take the stage with me? I know at least some of your names, are you waiting for me to call you out?"

Be it frustration or aggravation, Takashi pulls out his lighter and starts to flick it open and shut with one hand. "Very well, then I would like to ask … "

A voice from the crowd shatters the stillness overpowering even Takashi on the megaphone, "Doctor, Please Stop!" Mr. Masumo walks forth. He climbs up onto the stage.

Masumo explains. "The doctor is right; gods walk with you. I will not ask my brothers, or sister, or mother or father to show themselves. But I will show myself. I am the spirit you call once called Din, the protector. I was the spirit that guides lost travelers, I was the spirit that nursed sick children."

The crowd seems confused, there is mumbles of skepticism. Din Masumo grunts and nods "I see you are not convinced. Was Din not the child ghost? Was Din not a fox spirit?" Din Masumo claps then bows, "you are right to not take me at my word. After all, foxes are well known as tricksters. Perhaps I would be easer to except if I looked more like a ghost or a devil."

Din takes off his rob showing off his woodsmen's build, he throws his rob off to one side then stomps his foot and howls, in the blink of an eye the old man is gone and in his place stands a burning white fox, Din announces "is this not what I look like in your scrolls and paintings?"

Din then stands on his back legs, he discards the illusion of the fox and becomes a butterfly, "Is this what I look like when I come to you in your dreams?"

Din next shows his true colors as a Chromon, "I have a thousand and one more faces I can show you and three times as many shapes I can shift into, how many would you like to see?"

Takashi squeals and falls over. He jumps back to his feet and brushes himself off "truth be told, I wasn't expecting you to show up." Takashi takes a deep breath to control his emotions. "After what I had seen, I was under the impression that you were night spirits and couldn't take your true form in the day."

Din turns to look at Takashi, "now that I am here, what did you want to talk about?"

Takashi asks, "the evil spirits. The bugs with transparent wings, do you have some way to trace them?"

Din nods, "we can track each other by scent. Another butterfly passes with two miles of us; we know it."

Takashi walks around Din looking him over, "and would I be right to asses that the ones of you with colored wings are in some way not like the ones with the uncolored wings?"

Din explains, "Colored wings are born, uncolored are genetically enhanced. Incomplete Ribosome strains introduced to a living body, unstable by design, the chemical breaks down and overwrites the DNA of inflicted."

Takashi nods as he considers the possibility "some sort of a weapon perhaps?"

Din shakes his head, "that wasn't what my mother had in mind when she manufactured the drug."

Takashi pushes his hands into his pockets and lowers his head darkly, this is the part he did not want to see come to pass, but time is running out, "then do you see any objection in finding the sick, and 'healing' them?"

Din looks shifty, "I assume by heal, you mean, kill?"

Takashi inquires, "Is there another way?"

Din denies "not after the infection has spread to the heart or brain. Once that has happened, there is no longer enough human left to reverse the process."

Takashi agrees halfheartedly, "then we will do what we need to do, tonight, no one sleeps, tonight, we take back our homes."

Din expresses, "I would recommend starting by crossing the river. When the infection first started, it fanned outwards from the water treatment center." Din looks around the crowd, "I told you all, I wasn't going to call out my brothers and sisters, but if any of you would like to help out, we are going to war."

Twenty more butterflies spring out of the crowd. Things are being set in motion, lines are drawn, teams formed. Din was right, it is time or a battle. The village rises up. The people will protect their homes.

May 20th, 3:25pm

Jo Kogotana arrives back in town, the park has seemingly been transformed into a battle station. Takashi Tsu at the center of it all. Radios and flashlights are being handed out to everyone, team leaders are being chosen. Weapons of all sorts are being distributed: spears, knives, bows, and whatever makeshift tools can be dug up: ice pikes, axes, and hammers.

Jin and his farther push their way through the crowd. Jo, once he has spotted Takashi points accusatorially, "what is this? Did you do all this?"

Takashi turns dramatically. "this is war."

Jo shouts, "I am out of radio range for three hours, and you start a war?"

Takashi explains, "no. The war came to us."

Jo points around the crowed, "and you intended to march into battle with kids and old women?"

Takashi is handed a pack of smokes by Maaya Sakomoto as she walks past helping with the organization. "me? No, I am not marching, I can't fight to save my life. I will be staying here with my maps and radio, and let someone else do the marching. As for kids and women, your wife recommends that we send them to the church to wait out this storm." Takashi lights himself a cigarette. He mumbles, "my god, that tastes good."

Jo shouts over to Maaya as she walks past, "and you let him do this?"

Takashi asks, "so, what can you do to help out?"

Jo moans in hindrance before his training as a cop starts to kick in. Jo is the chief constable, and he needs to act like it. "Maaya, find me Oso and anyone else here with a military background. Let's do this, right!"

Takashi smiles, he knows this couldn't have possibly gone better…

May 20th, 5:00pm

The monks of Ichishin-Magami have set up a temporary barricade around the church. Anyone to old, young, or sick to help out the militia have been lead into the chappal. The monks and some of the teens have taken it upon themselves to arm up and ready themselves to protect this place. The one and only safe place in Chīsana Mura.

Nekoba has been invited back into the church, but he is not permitted to take in official actions in the name of the church.

Jin is amongst the last of the people let into the chappal, he quickly finds his way into the company of Leta and Odette. Eva Masumo slides over to the lot of them as they are trying to work out what has transpired.

Eva smiles and tips her head, "well, it looks like we are all together again."

May 20th, 10:50pm

Shirio kneels on the roof of the water treatment plant. She squints off into the distance. Torches are lit, men walk the streets in ceremonial robes. Houses are being broken into in mass. Sanguine and Chromon are dragged into the streets and put to the sword.

Shirio watches with delight. This is so much better than she had ever hoped it would be. The evil bug grins, "We deserve this, you deserve this mother. Oh, what tangled webs we weave." She starts to giggle madly. "if only I had more blood to shed."

Shirio smells she can be seen. She jumps across the way to the glassworks; she is being followed. Who would dare chase after Tamamo-No-Mia?

Shirio needs to keep moving; after all, there is much work left to be done, and so little time left. She needs to make one more stop before midnight. She needs to see

Izu one last time, make sure everything is going to go down just as she wanted it to.

How easy humans are to control, how simple Chromon are to manipulate. Tomoji was the hardest thing to deal with this time around. But what else could she have expected from one of her own eggs?

The age has ended. It is time to watch it all burndown. The air fills with plains, cars circle the town. The NDF has arrived ...

Chapter 14, The Last Day, The Heart of Brutality

The Way of the Spirit

Gas bombs rain from the sky, chaos issues. Din has traced Shirio to the hillside leading to the old village. The flames of the burning town brighten the night sky.

Din's mind is filled with the last words that his mother had shared with him. 'You can't do this again.' She had told him, 'you are not strong enough to survive that a second time.' She had continued, 'what have you done?'

Din responds to the voice only he can hear, "I have done what I have always done. I have protected you."

Shirio walks hunched over all four of her arms pulled into her body, ready to attack "hello big brother." She hisses.

Din produces a naginata from behind his back, which had been strapped to his body with a leather belt. "Shirio, it is time for you to go back to sleep."

Shirio laughs, "no, not this time. This time I think I want to stay awake."

Din starts to stalk his sister, his pole-arm held low and ready. "why must we go through this every century, Shirio?"

Shirio stomps and throws her arms out, showing her comparatively huge size off, "Look at me, Din! Can you not taste my sickness in the air? No matter how much I eat, I am still hungry; no matter how many eggs I lay or who I sleep with, I don't feel satisfied! I can't stand the scent of dead flesh that hangs in the air around me, my body rots, and my parts break way, then in moments, they spring back. I feel uncontrollable drives, irresistible desires, I cannot tell if I am awake or asleep. They both feel the same. You took a newborn Chromon, and you transformed her into a half-man half-butterfly beast. Did you know that the human blood was tainted when you injected it into my heart?"

Din explains, "I can't undo the past, but the future you can still choose to change."

Shirio throws her head back and howls, the ground almost quivers at the sound of her voice as she cries. She leers forward and shows her fangs, "if you want a better world, heal me, throw your spear and cut out my heart. But if your first stab doesn't slay me, I will slay you. This time, in a way that mother won't be able to bring you back from."

Din shakes his head, "don't make me do this, Shirio, go back to the church, go back to sleep, and this time don't wake back up."

"I will kill, eat, and lay eggs until I feel satisfied, and if you don't stop me, no one will." Shirio reaches her arms back and extends her claws. She dashes forward as Din braces himself for the charge.

Din stabs his sister, Shirio has strength, but Din has reach. Blood spills down the front of Shirio's body, her head slumps forward. Din shakes and pants as he holds up the limp body. Din shuts his eyes; he struggles to stop himself from shaking.

Shirio lifts her head and locks eyes with her brother. "you missed my heart." She whispers.

"I know." Din whispers in return.

Shirio grabs her brother by the sides of the face. Her jaws wrap around his head, and her tongue spears into his chest. Shirio pushes her brother to his knees and floods his body with her seed.

The diseased eggs fan out across Din's body. The royal blood in his veins quickly turning toxic. In a matter of moments, the passion will replace all that is Din, and all that will remain will be another pawn.

The game goes on as long as the queen lives.

The Way of the Butterfly

The doors of the church are sealed, the sounds of bombs exploding in the distance are earthshaking. Leta looks between her friends "what on earth is going on?"

Jin shakes his head, "I have no idea."

Odette approaches the door. a monk stops her, "no one leaves the chappal until the chief gets back." The monk explains.

Odette orders, "what is the situation?"

The monk shakes his head. Odette returns to her friends, "looks like no one knows."

Another explosion, this one so close that the walls of the chappal splinter. Masumo looks to the broken wall "well, that sounded a lot closer than the last one."

Someone shouts, "the church is burning!"

Jin reaches over and grabs Eve; he commands, "Do something!"

Leta questions, "what makes you think Masumo can do anything?"

Masumo nods in agreement, "ok."

Eva discards her human skin transforming into the Matriarch, Shi the Butterfly. With a flap of her wings, the room turns to gold with fluttering particles of pollen thick in the air. A sudden wave of warmth and calming floods the chappal.

Nekoba looks around with wide eyes as the supernatural stillness sets in. The sounds of fighting have been silenced, the heat of the flames just outside the door is no longer noticeable.

Jin, Leta, Odette, and Nekoba seem to be the only people not standing around in a drunken haze. Leta whispers, "what is this?"

Jin explains, "it is Masumo."

Masumo walks over to the door guard "can you please open the door for us?"

The guard does so without a word. As Masumo steps into the courtyard, it is visible that all of Chīsana-Mura is on fire. A wave of towering flames forty feet tall can be seen circling the town and moving in from all sides. The strange gold dust produced by Shi the Butterfly seems to keep the danger at arm's length.

Shi flutters her wings, the majority of people in the church walk out behind her without her needing to speak a word. She leads them around to the monk's village and into the house of the elder. She pulls open the floorboards and shows off a tunnel leading under the town.

As people start to file into the underground, Leta comments, "Masumo, that is amazing. Where are we going?"
Eva is starting to pant as she is running low on breath, "this may be hard to believe, but this body is underdeveloped, and using my pheromone dust in this way would be hard even if I was in top shape. Let's move fast."

Nekoba beings up the rear of the group, he places a hand on Leta's back and helps her down into the tunnel then he helps Masumo down.

Nekoba explains, "in their native land the Chromon never needed to talk to each other. They could convey complex idea's through smells alone. They didn't need to start talking until they move to this planet. What Masumo is doing right now is to the nature of shouting her will at others."

Odette remarks, "this is absolutely magical."

Nekoba counters "alien, not magical. To her, this is natural; to us, it is not."

The group walks through the tunnels, safely, quietly. Serval miles, guided by the light of the queen butterfly.

The tunnel exits high up on the hillside, only a short sprint to the old village. Consumed by time and nature. The beast of the wild see the approach of the queen and bow their heads in her grace.

As they make their way to the old church and the sanctuary of lost things thereunder. Eva whispers for help. Her wings are creaked and braking. She has used too much of her pheromone dust. She is exhausted.

Leta and Jin catch Evaas she faints. The effects of the dust wane. Monks and citizens alike shake off the effects. There is a moment of panicked confusion as few have ever been this far up the mountain.

Nekoba takes charge, he points the group onward. "the church down yonder.

We hide there until the fires clear. Then we march onward to Tokyo." Nekoba has no plan, but the illusion of control can be almost as useful as the real thing.

The Way of the Samurai

Mass melee has erupted on the streets of the industrial district. Chromon flutter over the hoards of swordsmen to guide their actions and prevent Sanguine from flanking them.

The fighting is savage. The Sanguine do not fight like men, they fight like beasts. They claw the drool they pounce. But also like beasts, they can be intimidated: shouting, flickering light, these both force a moment of hesitation.

The people of Chīsana-Mura had only just taken advantage when the first of the NDF bombers fly overhead.

The first bomb to drop strikes the iron foundry resulting in an explosion that is unlike anyone has seen. The burst of flames, the green light of flaming salts in the ground flare around it. A creaking sound echoes off the landscape like the laughter of the dead.

The displacement of oxygen, as the air-fuel bomb ignites, likely killing dozens on all sides of the battle before anyone even saw the flash.

Oso Hanzo and Maaya Sakomoto had just chased a group of Sanguine into the water filtration plant barely a mile away when the first blast went off. Rocks and sand rain from the sky. Everyone freezes in place.

Oso thinks about what Izu had told him a week or so ago. Oso whispers, "oh, that was what he meant."

The shock of sound forces the bug Mayaa was fighting to back away. Mayaa does not reengage, nor does he. "What? What did He mean?" Mayaa orders as she grips her sword at ready.

Oso explains, "the government lost a weapon near our town. They were awaiting clearance from the Emperor to purge the hole place. the Emperor would rather lose a town then admit he lost something."

"What sort of a weapon calls for that level of response?" one of the Sanguine asks.

Oso ushers a hand at the bug and goes wide-eyed in a silent proclamation. A nearby butterfly offers a nod of acknowledgment "that makes sense on some level."

The roof starts to cave in Mayaa spots a door leading to the lower levels and an exit, the exit is quickly covered by falling pipes. Mayaa points, "this way."

Mayaa opens the door, the butterfly is first through, one of the Sanguine next. Oso rescues a second as he runs thought he door also. Mayaa is last, she falls down the stairwell as she is pushed by a wave of falling garbage.

The underground is dark, with no lights, no power. Mayaa finds her sword and jumps to her feet, ready to continue the fight. Oso holds out his arms to stop the two sides from fighting "are we really going to continue this? We are all Japanese, and we were just bombed by the NDF."

The butterfly explains, "those two are Sanguine, murder is part of their essential nature."

One of the bugs stands with his fangs ready. "I can keep my teeth in my mouth if you can."

The other Sanguine, a girl, lowers her head to Oso, as he had pulled her out of harm's way. "we are predators, but predators are capable of cooperation and gratitude."

Mayaa lowers her sword, "I am willing to wait until we are back outside to kill each other. Do you two have names?"

The female Sanguine offers "Aki."

The male hides his fangs, "Sura."

The butterfly gives his name, "Ebis."

Mayaa and Oso follow along, offering their names. Oso follows up by asking, " Is anyone acquainted with the layout of this building?"

Ebis nods "this leads into a place called 'the Rookery'; it is the only place in town where sick Chromon can go to find treatment. Assuming it is still standing after this."

Sura adds, "I was born in this building."

Mayaa looks between the two of them "are you two the same race?"

Aki asks, "are Asians still human?" she adds on "the mutation in our digestive tract is in many ways the same as the decolorization in your skin. Minor alteration in your bodies allele frequency caused by a shift in environmental condition."

The group stroll, carefully approaching the door to the sub-basement.

Aki falls back as Ebis takes the lead. Aki tries to whisper with Oso, Ebis calls her to the front of the group. "I would feel a lot safer with you up here with me."

Sura complains, "do you have a problem butterfly? Sacred ground, remember? The hospital is a safe space."

Aki explains, "that is why we were here in the first place, we were told that hunters were coming and we were looking for a place to hide."

Mayaa whispers, "sanctuary is only safe if everyone if everyone agrees that it is."

Aki walks backward so she can talk to the others "you wouldn't bring a knife or a gun into a hospital, would you?"

Oso looks up, thinking, "I might."

Aki places a hand on Oso's chest and leads him into a wall wanting to whisper with him. "Oso Hanzo, you are the grandson of Mokono Hanzo?"

Oso nods. "yes." Aki clearly means to make a point, but it would seem that Oso doesn't understand what she is getting at.

"you are the great-grandson of one of the original chosen. You are an honorable man." Aki starts to lean in, wanting to touch her beak to the side of his face affectionately.

Mayaa sees what is going on and is unimpressed. She places a hand on her sword and rattles the blade. "Keep moving."

Aki steps away, she locks eyes with Oso to the best of her ability "it would seem that tonight is not the night for what I wished to talk about. Should we still be alive come tomorrow night, perhaps things will be different."

The underground hospital has caved in, the road ahead is gone. This leads to a moment of consiliences between the three aliens.

Sura ushers off in one direction, "there is another way around." He points, "we will need to crawl through the service tunnels assuming that they were not damaged."

Stumbling through the darkness, the lot comes to a porthole. Mayaa takes the imitative to turn the crank that unlocks it. Serval Sanguine wait on the other side. They brandish their claws. Oso holds up a hand to call for them to stand down. Ebis, Aki, and Sura step in to protect the samurai.

Everyone is frightened, everyone confused. But it is the way of samurai to seek peace in times of conflict. Men, Chromon, and Sanguine alike are willing to fall behind Oso.

As they crawl through the sewers and waterways into the mines, a small army gathers behind Oso Hanzo.

No path leads to the Rookery. The place that marked the center of the world for the aliens is gone. So what can be done but for them to keep walking.

They walk until it is almost sun up, looking for a way back above ground. But when at last they find salvation. They are not alone.

Two dozen men dressed in NDF uniforms armed with napalm throwers and gasmask wait for the lot of them at the mouth to the cave. Someone tipped them off.

Oso alone steps into the light. The army stands and threatens Oso. Oso offers a glance back to Mayaa, his hand moves for his sword smoothly. Oso promised that the lot of them would reach the outside, one way or the other.

So, what is a man to do? Soldiers shout to Oso, but Oso cant hear them. His other hand reaches across his body, and in a divisive move, he pulls his blade and holds it overhead.

The way of the samurai has meant many things to many people. To Oso Hanzo, the way of the samurai is the will to fight, the intention to protect. Oso will clear a path, Mayaa, Edis, Sura, and Aki will get to see the sunrise one last time.

The Way of Mercy

Planes pass overhead, the roar of the engines shatter the stillness that is a way of life for people in the countryside.

Takashi Tsu covers the side of his head with one hand as the other grips the radio he has been using to organize the hunting teams.

A plane flies low. The tent the command station was set up in starts to buckle under the wind. Takashi shouts to try to hear the voices in his radio. "number six, you need to make your way to E-7 number four will meet you there!"

Jo Kogotana throws open the flap and rushes in. he grips Takashi and takes the radio way. "It is time for us to leave…"

Takashi argues back, "…we need to maintain order."

"Time is up!" Jo explains. "We are going to the temple." Jo drags Takashi out the door.

A bomb hits the ground, not more than feet away from the tent. Jo turns to face Takashi and holds him to shield the doctor from the blast.

But then the impossible happens.

The explosion freezes in place. The fireball seems to be removed from the flow of time-space. The flams wrap around the two men but leave a fifteen-foot-wide bubble for them to stand in where everything has stopped moving.

Rocks are trapped in the shell of displacement. Fire flams but docs not burn. Electricity bounces off of Jo as water in the air turns plasmatic.

Jo looks at Takashi with wide eyes; Takashi looks back in equal confoundment.

The two walk to the church. The bubble of force continues to follow them until they are at a safe distance from the park. Then everything returns to normal.

Ghastly whispers shout to Jo:

"the church down yonder. We hide there until the fires clear. Then we march onward to Tokyo."

"using my pheromone dust in this way would be hard even if I was in top shape. Let's move fast."

"I have done what I have always done. I have protected you."

The church is ablaze. Takashi falls to his knees; he cannot believe what he sees. The center of town. The church, which has stood for almost a thousand years, is now burning. And with it, everything that Takashi has ever known.

Takashi comments, "I told Odette that it was safe…"

Jo grips the side of his head, trying to make sense of the voices in his head. "I don't think she was in there." Jo points "this way, to Shika. We will find our families there."

The Way of Vengeance

The door to the old church buckles as something strikes it serval times. The door falls off its hangers. Reko Jet, covered in cold think blood, half-frozen, his hammer gripped in his fist.

Reko scans the old church. Almost a hundred people are hiding in the shadows of the collapsing building.

Reko orders "give me Eva Masumo."

Eva is lying on the ground, her strength sapped. Nekoba kneeling over her. Reko stomps forward. "Give her to me now."

Jin picks up a spear off the wall of the ancient church and stands between Reko and Eva. "Reko-son, that is enough."

Reko explains, "you got balls kid, but I have killed ninety-nine ghosts with my bare hands. You aren't going to stop me."

Odette steps up, and she holds up her hands in a kickboxing stance. She stands with Jin "Reko-son, please stop, Eva has been protecting us."

Reko expresses as he is getting closer, "Eva was the first to die. She was the one that brought the evil here."

Reko grips the spear Jin is holding in one hand and uses it to throw Jin across the room. "I won't stop until I have killed every ghost."

Odette steps into a side kick. The strike is pointless. Odette doesn't have the strength to stop Reko. Reko smacks Odette, and she faints.

Reko looks side to side. "anyone else?"

Leta runs forth; she holds her arms out to block their way to Nekoba and Eve. "they aren't monsters…"

Reko cuts her off "I am a MAN!" he proclaims "what god or devil was ever so powerful as to stand toe to toe with me? True men rise, true men build nations. Weak and tiny things like these ghosts, there is no room for them in our world!"

Reko pulls his hammer overhead to threaten Leta, Leta brings her arms overhead cowering at the sight of the blacksmith.

Bang!

A gunshot.

Reko drops his hammer as he is struck in the shoulder. Reko walks backward a dozen paces, his back rest to the wall.

Nekoba stands, the revolver he got from Din in one hand. Nekoba scoops up Eva in one arm, he squeezer her to his chest as a mother may cradle a toddler.

Reko growls he grips his arm to stop himself from bleeding. "Please forgive me," Nekoba speaks out. "I can not allow this to continue. I will take Shi, and I will leave. We will vanish into the hills. Never to be seen again."

Nekoba sidesteps around Reko, he slides out the door keeping the revolver fixed on Reko. Nekoba vanishes into the shadows of the snow-covered hillside.

The Way of Shadows

Jo and Takashi dash throw the first, Jo is drawn by the sound of the voices in the darkness. The two witnesses a fight between a union of Chromon and Sanguine fighting a group of NDF operatives.

But this is not Jo's battle, Jo must make his way to the old village. To find Jin, to find Odette. Takashi chases after only steps behind.

The path is not unobscured. A helicopter follows them. The flag of the CDCI painted on its fin.

The old town is in sight. they fighter there way up the hill. At the top, within sprinting distance of the church, the sources of the voices, a group of men wait for Jo and Takashi.

The NDF has found them. Jo and Takashi witness Nekoba sneaking out of the church and making his way around the mountain. The helicopter comes in for a landing.

Jo and Takashi are held at gunpoint. The two men hold up their hands in surrender. Two old men against a dozen soldiers is suicide.

A young chinses girl steps out of the helicopter. She shouts over the helicopter, "Jo Kogotana, Takashi Tsu, you are to be taken into protective custody by orders of CDCI. Get on the ground now and assume the position." The women produce hand binds from her pocket as she approaches.

The women kneels down as she ties up Jo; she whispers with him, "Watory stands with you."

Jo's eyes dart up in sudden actualization...

Epilog

[Mission Update.]

[document sent from CDCI, Honk Kong, China. ███████ ███████, Wales, England, ███ ███ ███████, New York, New York.]

[Secure channel confirmed.]

[Sender Operator code verified current and up-to-date.]

[Report filed by Operator Lin.]

███████████████████

Chīsana-Mura, Japan.

February 6th.

Institute approves research funding for ███ ████. First contact team includes civilian assets ████████  particle physicist, ████████, Electrical engineer, ████████ Biochemist. Team lead by Institute operative CODE NAME: Zed. Ph.D. Geologist. Supervisor, Agent L.

Standard containment and retrieval protocol are in effect. Electrical disturbance detected. Reported by Hijoji R&D Tokyo. The affected area is isolated to Shika Woods.

Low-level radiation exposer can results in damage to sciatic never, visible, and audible hallucination have been linked to prolonged exposer. An investigation is underway.

April 16th.

As the team moves closer to ▓▓▓▓▓, the group experiences what the particle physicist describes as quantum particle field disruption.

The team unearthed an underground passage leading through the hillside outside of the Ichishin-Magami temple. Throughout this passageway, the rules of mater seem to be in flux.

For brief moments, inertia, mass, and even gravity become irregular. Water flows uphill, objects traveling through the air may become trapped in space. Objects on the ground may lose momentum. On one occasion, it was explained that an object moving through water lost bouncy.

The events never lasted for more than several seconds, but a spike followed each event in background radiation.

It was reported to me at this time that Hijoji R&D had made contact with an NGO-military. It is suspected that they (Hijoji R&D) may wish to procure the specimen for themselves.

We have contacted local police and military officials to look into this mater.

May 3rd

███ researchers have had a "type 3 encounter" with a hostile life form. It is supposed that the effects of ███████ have altered the life form.

A team member had made his way to Chīsana-Mura Health and Wellness Center. It is believed that assistant director Takashi Tsu may have had prior contact with the life form, and copies of his notes could be valuable to us.

This resulted in a confrontation between our researchers and Chief Constable Jo Kogotana.

The information that we had failed to confiscate was offered to us openly only days later.

Against the advisement of Operator Lin, Agent Zed has contacted several people of interest across Chisana-Mura to collect local folklore and access to sensitive locations. It would seem that the investigation is leading the team ever closer to the Ichishin-Magami Temple.

People of interest include Lt. constable Useto Habiki, ▮▮▮▮▮▮ ▮▮▮▮▮▮ and ▮▮▮▮▮▮ We had attempted to contact an expert on local history, Setkura Nekoba, but it seemed he was unavailable to take our call.

Local church official ▮▮▮▮▮▮ had shared with us some pieces of interesting information. The township, so it is told, had once been located higher up the hillside. But a group of rogue monks, that had taken to nature worship were possessed to set fire to the village. The survivors of this had relocated to the current location.

The rogue monks had a symbol, an object to their obsession: A stone, fist-sized, egg-shaped and smooth, silver in color. This object, if it is real, maybe the artifact in question.

There is another shape that is inspiring concern in me. A butterfly, time, and time again, we see this shape. Spray-painted on walls, cut into trees, the shape whispers to us.

May 9th

The electrical engineer has requested access to thermographic software from the NWS. It has been noted that the weather in this area seems to be anachronistic to that of the surrounding locations.

Analyzing the data at hand, it would seem that the artifact is generating an EM field 40.02km2.

Agent Zed has taken an interest in a local ceremony being conducted. He describes a man being nailed to a raft, his body painted white and dressed in linin, then pushed into the river that cuts through the town. There was a time when pagan rituals like these were prevalent everywhere. But today it seems only people living in isolated communities still do.

A child had gone missing, several members of our team overheard. It may or may not be related to our case. More information is being gathered.

May 10th

███ ██████████ at the Health and Wellness Center has provided us with a blood sample. From Ri Hanzo. This blood contains aspects uncommon of humans. Including, but not limited to:
1. Two complete RNA strands
2. Nuroreactive chemicals
3. Abnormal high white blood cell count (WBCs 12,000 P/cml).
4. Divinorum,
5. Galantamine,
6. Succinylcholine,
7. Gamma-aminobutyric acid

This is considered strange for a human.

It was also discovered that a radioactive isotope was found to have contaminated the sample.

Even though at this point, we have yet to observe the artifact directly, we are becoming aware of its effects.

For the second time, the team witnesses the pagan death rite practiced by the people of the infected town. It is to be understood that the ritual did not conclude as expected this time.
If I am to understand correctly, the raft holding the deceased capsized, and according to the gathered, this is an omen of some sort.

Allegedly, an overturned raft leads to some kind of thinning of the "spectral barrier." Reported one observer of the ritual.

May 12th

The NDF has been contacted, all transports coming and going from the township are being stopped. A slash and burn team is patrolling the woods around the village.

Officials are being consulted. Our team was advised to abandon our current containment efforts. ▮▮ ▮▮▮ has ordered us to disregard this warning, capture, and cantonment of ▮▮▮▮▮ cannot be postponed.

Resources have inhibited, primary communications are suspended. We are switching to short band radio; future contacts will be temporally recorded on portable, and analog devices.

Operative L has contacted the domestic government to inform them of the situation. (Clearance type 1 intel only). Chief constable Jo Kogotana has agreed to act as an operative on behalf of the agency for the duration of this mission. SLAPP order is to be filed after debriefing.

More instances of the butterfly glyph have been observed. Some members of our team imply that they believe that ███ ███████ cult spoken of by our asset may be alive and well. Perhaps we should file these ████████ cultist as ████████████

May 13th

Previously observed alien sickness, to be referenced as ████████████ is becoming noticeably pandemic in the community. It has been noted that dead bodies are starting to pile up on the streets, cleanup efforts have failed.

Strange weather patterns continue.
Contact with off coast satellite relay network has been compromised. The lost ship was quickly found by field agents, run ashore. SCRAM (Security Control, Redirect Assessment, and Mobility) protocol was enacted. All institute software abord the derelict vessel was scrubbed.

May 14th

███ ███████ at the Health and Wellness Center has provided our team with the first hard data on type 3 hostile life form ████ ████████ previously observed.

████████████ Describes.

"...patient skin temperature is at 68.8°f; heart rate is 0 b/pm, brain activity is 2.5zH and sustaining, the room has been scanned for background EM. Interments are expected to function within 1.4 deviations. 0 detectable raspatory activity. Skin and muscle are showing no signs of rigamortis. It would appear the vascular systems are functioning without the need for the heart to be beating...."

"....The body is laterally symmetrical, two harts, six-chambered, in both hemispheres.

Lungs attach to shoulder blades, hidden completely by ribs and heart; it would seem that the bone structure is hollow, and there is segmentation between the shoulders. Stomachs are multichambered. The small intestine, kidneys, and pancreases all seem to be absent...."

"...Liver and sex glands are engorged, a secondary uterus is present, as is an unknown organ that seems to bridge the oval ducts. Muscular fiber is porous. A pocket-like protrusion can be seen within the chest cavity.

"...venom glands bleed into the esophagus. There seem to be a half dozen other organelles lined up along the spine and around the neck..."

"...those that die from the 'infection' ▮▮▮ ▮▮▮ can be manipulated by It ... It is my feeling that the infection has originated in the waterways under the town..."

Agent Zed was announced KIA by his team in a confrontation with ▮▮▮

Jo Kogotana has recovered the body and the research notes in Zed's possession. The institute will recover the intel.

May 16th

NDF has cut power and water to the town; exit is now impossible. CDCI has imposed a maximum-level quarantine. Sterilization is imminent.

One last push will be made to find ██████ ██████ before it is lost permanently. To continue, the mission team needed to act as CDCI investigators.

May 18th

Researchers witnessed significant particle field disruption. Groundwater tables under the Center for Health and Wellness shifted discreetly, resulting in the structure being sucked into the ground. Numerous injuries.

May 21st

Sterilization has begun. Under the orders of the Emperor, NDF has burned the town of Chīsana-Mura, Japan, to ashes. We were fortunate to have had assists in the area. Several Persons of Interest were recovered from the wreckage █ ████████ has been recovered. Research can now begin in earnest. In a stroke of luck, we were also able to capture a live specimen of ▮▮

Statues: **Thaumiel**
Identification: Chromon Artifact

Description:

Approximately egg-shaped, 96 ounces, diameter 319.6 mm.

Object has fused itself to ▮▮ Object would seem to have sentients. But can not live on its own. It must attach itself to a host, dermally, possibly feeding off the endothermic nature of the host.

For 36 hours after contact with object, little to no effects were observable. The subject complained about head pain and hearing a continuous humming or whispering sound.

Object appears to take actions to guide and protect the host. After 'incubation' is complete, ▮▮ generates a zero-point EMF. The size of the field generated is inconsistent. Sometimes as small as three yards, other times stretching to 100 yards. Object coming in contact with zero-point EMF becomes geocentrically locked in space.

Subject after 90 hours in contact with ▓▓▓▓▓▓ pulsates with cosmic radiation. A microwave field entwines the body. The host is losing sense of self. Can speak if spoken to but no longer in any know languages.

Researchers how had close contact with ▓▓▓▓▓▓ within the first hours of it becoming attached to its host suffer dramatic head pain and trouble sleeping. Those that have been in contact with EMF have shown signs of cytopenia, difficulties breathing, and hair loss. These individuals have been quarantined until the nature of their infliction can be better understood.

▓▓▓▓▓▓ has also affected the climate controls of the laboratory. ▓▓▓▓▓▓ cell will not drop bellow 106°f; every 16 hours, it would also trigger the fire alarms until we started 'watering' the cage.

Computers, watches, and phones are not promoted within 300 yards of ▓▓▓▓▓▓ The illness related to the EMF seems to be able to be transferred by contact with these devices. ███████

Containment:

The host life form has been placed into a 100x100 cell. Concert with led backing. And fitted with a tether preventing him from approaching the door to the cell. A buffer hallway has been added 300 yards long in approach to the hoist life form.

Anyone wishing to observe ███████ is to be fitted with a SCUB-suit and will not be allowed more than 3 hours of observation per week. All activity will be documented in hard format before copied onto the network at a later time.

███████████

Statues: Unclad
Identification: Sanguine/Chromon ALF
Name: Sakura Tomoji Takamaki

Description:

At the time in which ███████ arrived, it was entwined in a semi-plastic-leather like substance, a blue-red film covering it. After the first time, ███████ triggered climate controls and raised the temperature in the labs to 107.6°f, the cocoon split.

From out of it stepped a toddler; within hours, she grew to the size of a teen and before sunset, she was a full-grown woman, she discarded her skin and transformed into an exoskeletal thripid. Four arms, two legs, two sets of wings. Her body sprouted white and tan fur, her eyes approximately three times the size of a normal human eye. A hook grows from the center of her face hiding the bladed tongue underneath.

She seems to have a secondary set of fangs that are hidden by a cavity in the side of her head located paralleled to the nasal cavity. Despite the idea that she is only days old, she has a lifetime worth of memories and experiences to call on. She can speak and is oddly accommodating to our desire to perform test on her. She insists on us calling her Sakura.

It has been discovered that there is a sex gland located under ███████████ tongue that has the secondary effect of filling the bloodstream with a Nero-inhibitive substance. Every eighty-sixes hours if acid buildup around the organ is not drained, it forces ███████████ to self-destruct.

It seems if ▮▮▮▮▮ dies in this way, her body returns to an infinitely state, and so long as the conditions in the facility are favorable, she returns to her adult form within 48 hours.

We have found through continued examinations that ▮▮▮▮▮ has many built-in self-defense mechanisms. A swollen olfactory gland, a pheromone gland, and a venom gland. These three units activated in tandem seems to have a powerful effect on anyone caught in the area of effect of the blast.

The pheromone gland alone leaves a trail behind ~~Sakura~~ ▮▮▮▮▮ inspiring people to treat her in a friendly way. Despite her monstrous exterior, she does not inspire fear.

The venom gland, when triggered, releases a toxin that lowers inhabitation. People exposed lose the will to fight when tested under laboratory conditions 1/7th of the people exposed become openly self-destructive. In 1/16th, it inspired uncontrollable cardanol needs. In more copious amounts, this results in cardiac arrest.

The pheromone and venom together have an effect that can only be described 'domination of the mind.'

Test subjects for weeks after exposer to either chemical complain about nightmares and chronic musical fatigue.

Most impressive is the effect of contact with the acid drawn from ~~Sakura's sex gland~~ neurotoxin.

If the acid realized from the tongue is exposed to human blood, the blood gains a level of awareness. It seems to mutate and divide. We are about to commence human testing.

Containment:

~~When containing Sakura it is critical to remember, the air anywhere she has been in 72 hours is potentially toxic and anyone that has been within~~

Upon-farther consideration of Sakura Tomoji's case, it has been concluded by the foundation that there is no possible risk to public safety; Sakura Tomoji is to awarded ownership of ▇▇▇▇▇▇ and is to be released at once.

Also by Dustin Feyder:

08/27/2020

Made in the USA
Monee, IL
20 August 2020